A novel by...

BEATRICE BRADSHAW

TACKLED BY TROUBLE

He's her PR nightmare. She's his only chance.

BRODIE

My career's been built on winning and never backing down.
One gambling scandal later, I'm at the mercy of the one
woman I can't stand: Charlie Harrington.

If I want redemption, I have to let her rebuild my image. And
the more we work together, the harder it gets to remember
why we hate each other.

CHARLIE

The last time I saw Brodie MacRae, I was engaged to the man
who ruined him. Since then, I've launched my own agency.
Now I own Brodie's contract.

He's reckless and magnetic. If I can't keep this professional, I
risk everything I'm building…

Content Note

Tackled by Trouble is written in British English ('recognise' instead of 'recognize'). It also includes a wee hint of a Scottish accent here and there.

Please be aware: this book contains several explicit/smutty open-door sex scenes and a staggering amount of profanity.

It also touches on topics that could trigger certain audiences, such as parental neglect, an unfaithful ex, disability, misogyny, and gambling. It's best to be prepared.

Your mental health matters. <3

To the girls who want more, and the boys who rise to meet them.

Chapter 1

Brodie

I slam my BMW's door hard enough to rattle the windows. Fucking Edinburgh. Fucking rain. Fucking everything.

Puddles pool between the cobbles. Rain slicks the stone. The whole city's dipped in grey. Not even proper rain. Just that misty, sideways shite that soaks you before you realise you're wet.

In August.

The Elite Edge Sports office looms. Some trendy converted old warehouse. A bloody co-working space.

My new agency.

Not by choice. Not by a fucking mile.

Until seven months ago, I was Glasgow's golden boy. Brodie MacRae, twenty-six, star fly-half with the Knights. Then it all went to shite. Poker with the lads, bit of fun. That's how it started. Never thought it'd catch up to me the way it did.

Now I'm trudging through puddles to meet whatever suit inherited my contract when they bought out Henderson Sports Management because apparently, I'm a commodity.

Like a fucking filing cabinet.

I shove through the doors hard enough that some suited

prick has to swerve to stop them from slamming back in his face.

Good. Let him flinch. Let them all fucking flinch.

A blonde behind the reception desk beams like she's never had a bad day in her life.

'Hi. How can I help you?'

'Brodie MacRae.'

Her smile widens like I've just made her week. I used to get that sort of reaction a lot more often – before the head-lines. Not that I give a toss. I'm too busy clawing my way out of the mess that is my life to bury my dick in some stranger. And I've had my share of hook-ups. But I'm not the type to chase it. Rugby always comes first.

'Of course, Mr MacRae. We've been expecting you.'

I almost laugh. Expecting me. The gambler who never actually gambled on rugby but got crucified anyway. Who let Callum Fraser and his conniving publicist fiancée bury him alive.

'Third floor, end of the hall,' the blonde woman adds, still bright as a weather girl. 'The assistant will meet you there.'

The lift is an old freight cage with steel bars and bolted-on mirrors, trapping me with my reflection. Dark circles, unshaven jaw, hair too long. Even my suit feels too tight. Wore it anyway. They're not seeing me in joggers, licking wounds. But it's choking me.

I fucking hate my life.

Every morning, I wake up in that fully furnished terraced house in the tiny town on the arse end of Stirling and wonder how the fuck I got here.

Not true.

I know how.

Callum made sure of it.

We've hated each other since the academy days, always competing, always butting heads. But I never thought he'd stoop that low. Telling the press I've been throwing games.

A voicemail from the Director of Rugby, ten seconds long, ending with, 'You're done.' Graham didn't even say my name. Too dirty for his tongue. A week later, the only messages on my phone were from bookies looking to cash in on the lie. Not one teammate stood up for me. Not one journalist wondered if the story made sense, if I'd really gamble away everything for a few bets.

Callum is behind that, and it's so fucking obvious I can't believe they don't see it.

I hate that cunt more than I hate my life.

And that says something.

The lift doors slide open, an assistant is standing there with bright eyes and breezy energy. Blouse with cherries on it, navy skirt. Bit retro. Way too perky.

'Hello, Mr MacRae. I'm Theo. Welcome to Elite Edge.' Her voice is all sunshine as she extends a hand like we're about to be best pals.

I don't take it. 'Walk.'

She's exactly the kind of woman who'd roll her eyes at a lad like me. Glass-walled offices fade by, people glancing up, pretending not to watch. They know who I am. They remember the headlines.

MACRAE'S GAMBLING PROBLEM: IS SCOTTISH RUGBY'S BAD BOY BETTING ON MATCHES?

KNIGHTS DISTANCE THEMSELVES FROM TROUBLED FLY-HALF.

CALLUM FRASER: 'I'M DISAPPOINTED IN MY FORMER TEAMMATE.'

That last one still makes my vision go red. Sanctimonious prick. Played poker like he had money to burn and somehow came out squeaky clean. Let me take the fall when his own debts piled up, acting like he hadn't spent years trying to undermine me. Like his PR fiancée hadn't whispered those gambling rumours into the right ears to keep his image spotless.

Seven months since the scandal broke mid-season, and it still burns like a fresh wound.

Theo stops at a door and knocks. 'Mr MacRae is here.'

A woman's controlled voice. 'Send him in.'

I frown. My agent had been some faceless middleman, a name on a contract and in my e-mails. But that voice? That voice isn't some suit behind the scenes. It sounds husky and faintly familiar. I step inside, already gearing up to lay into whatever smug piece of work has the misfortune of repping me now—

And my stomach drops through the fucking floor.

Charlotte Harrington.

She sits behind the desk like she owns the place. Which, considering who her daddy is, she probably does. International sports agent George Harrington's posh princess.

The sight of her hits like a blindside tackle. I don't move. Don't breathe. I just stare at her, pulse hammering, brain scrambling to make sense of what the fuck I'm looking at.

I've only met her a bunch of times, after a few games and at events, dangling on Callum's arm. But I'd recognise her anywhere.

The woman who ruined my life. Or stood by while Callum did. Doesn't matter. She had a hand in my destruction. She was his mouthpiece. Of course, she knew. Of course, she helped him bury me.

The woman who is Callum Fraser's publicist. His fiancée.

The woman who is now, by the looks of it, my fucking agent.

How?

'You have got to be joking.' My voice is a snarl, my entire body braced for impact.

She tilts her head, slowly, like she's savouring the moment. Her full lips pull. First a smirk, then a proper smile that says, *I win, MacRae.*

'Theo, please close the door. Thanks.'

The click behind me sounds like a trap snapping shut.

She looks different from when I last saw her at the Knights' Christmas party. Sleeker. Angrier. Like she's carved the last scrap of softness out of herself. Her caramel hair used to be wavy. Now it's straightened and glossy. The charcoal suit clings to her like it was made for her alone. But that silk blouse? The middle buttons pull apart by a fraction to make it obvious – her tits are half a size too big. Not much. Just enough that some poor sod at reception probably walked into a glass wall with a semi.

Her eyes are the same, though. Hazel-gold, sharp as a scalpel. And right now, they're locked on me. Calculating.

I used to think she was too striking for that troll Callum. Not because of her looks. More like she had a self-possession he never had, no matter how many magazine covers he grinned his way onto. I thought she was better than him. More...principled.

Turns out, she's just as ruthless as he is. Maybe more.

This is the woman who helped him burn my career to the ground. And however polished she looks now, I hope she knows I'd still set a match to hers in a heartbeat.

'Sit down, Brodie.'

'Fuck off.'

One perfectly arched brow lifts. 'Always the charmer.' She leans back, fingers lacing together. 'Please, be a good boy and *sit.*'

Her voice is baiting me. She's expecting me to snap, waiting to sink her teeth in when I do.

And normally, I would.

A woman telling me to be a good boy is like a red rag to a raging bull. My vision narrows. I go taut, head to toe.

I'm not a good boy.

I'm not a boy.

And I'm definitely *not good*.

I remain standing, just to be difficult.

She's poking a tender nerve on purpose to make me crack.

I don't.

I plant my hands on her desk and lean in. She wants to play games? She's about to lose.

'Careful, Harrington.' I don't raise my voice. I don't need to. 'You're not the first woman who's tried to put me in my place and failed.'

Her lips curve again, but it's not a smile. It's a challenge. A fucking dare.

'And yet, here you are. In my office. Depending on my goodwill.' She cocks her head again, like she's already won.

A switch flips.

I shove the chair back so hard it grates against the floor with a screech. Drop into it, arms crossed, every cell vibrating with anger.

'If you think for one second I'm letting you anywhere near my career—'

'You don't have much of a choice.' She places her hand on a folder in front of her. 'What I wanted to talk to you about today is this, Brodie,' she lowers her voice, 'I own your arse.'

'The fuck you do!'

She opens the folder and flips to a page with a neat contract, my own signature glaring back at me like a death sentence.

'Your contract was part of my recent acquisition of Henderson's,' she says. 'I represent you now. Your PR, your sponsorships, your contract negotiations. It's all in my hands.'

The room tilts. My breath locks in my chest, fury clawing

at my ribs. I signed with an agency. Not my arch enemy's fiancée. And if I remember it correctly, Charlie is only in her mid-twenties. About my age. How does she get to be the boss of me?

'What *is* your play here, Harrington? Last I heard, you were daddy's little nepo baby, fluffing Callum's career. Thought that was a lifetime appointment.'

Her jaw tightens just a flash. But it's enough. I see it. A tiny crack in the ice. I've hit a nerve.

Good.

'Well, last you heard, I was engaged to a bastard who couldn't keep it in his trousers.'

That throws me for a second.

Was engaged?

Since that whole shite about me being a match-fixing disgrace who'd sold his soul to the bookies hit the fan, I've not read a single headline, tweet, or tabloid. Not wasting my time on lies. And I'm not talking to anyone in Glasgow anymore. So, if Charlie's been through something, I've missed it.

She exhales. 'Callum shagged a TV presenter. And I—' she lifts a shoulder like it's nothing, '—was forced to write the breakup statement for my own relationship. And yeah, maybe I went a bit overboard. My father wasn't thrilled. Bad PR, he said. Reflects poorly on his agency, he said. I should've taken better care of Callum, he said. "Fuck you," I said. And then I left.'

She gestures around the office. 'I started my own small agency. I run this place. I make the calls. And that includes you.' Her voice is steady, but there's an edge to it now. A quiet, blistering fire.

She leans back again, as if this were just another meeting, as if my whole fucking life weren't in her grip.

I death-stare her, blood pumping hot. 'I request a new agent.'

'You think this is some make-a-wish scheme? When I acquired Henderson, I took on all their contracts. Most of the stars jumped ship before it sank – at least the ones who weren't too busy wallowing. I'm left with a handful of clients, and you're the biggest name. A damaged asset, but still valuable if managed correctly.'

An asset. Not a person, not a player. An item on her balance sheet. To be managed correctly.

Fuck you.

The room suddenly feels too small. Too hot. 'And if I refuse? I'll buy myself out.'

'With what? The buyout clause is three times your annual pay. So, unless you've got a spare million lying around – and after what happened, I highly doubt that – you're stuck with me.'

I let out a frustrated growl.

She slides the folder across the desk. 'The numbers are on page three. Feel free to look if you don't believe me.'

I snatch it up, flipping pages until I see the figure. Christ. Money I don't have. Not after the deal with the Stirling Rebels came in lower than I'd hoped. Not after the gambling rumours tanked my sponsorships. And not after racking up six-figure debts. Fuck.

'This is extortion,' I spit out.

She throws her head back and laughs like this is the funniest thing she's ever heard. Then she stands and walks around her desk until she's next to me.

'This is business, not extortion. I control your deals, your public image. And I can do something with it, if you let me.'

For half a second, my muscles clench. Tight. Too tight. Because fuck her. Fuck her smug little doll face. Fuck that fucking smirk.

But I don't move. I won't give her the satisfaction.

'To be fair, Brodie, I didn't know they had your contract. It was a bulk acquisition in a fast-tracked deal. And Henderson's admin was a bin fire. You were…an unexpected gift in the package.'

My heart thunders so loudly I can barely hear over it. 'You and Callum destroyed my career.'

Something glints in her eyes. Anger? Guilt? I can't fucking tell. 'You were his publicist. You fed those gambling stories to the press.'

'I did no such thing.' Ice coats every syllable. 'You did plenty of damage all by yourself. Those poker debts weren't imaginary, were they?'

My fist hits her desk so hard pens jump. 'I *never* bet on rugby. Never.'

'No, you just racked up enough debt that people started to wonder what else you *might* be willing to do for cash.' Her expression doesn't budge. 'And now you're here. And I'm responsible for cleaning up the mess you made.'

'I refuse to work with you. I can find another agency.'

She steps in, right up against the edge of my space, and the expensive scent of her seeps into my lungs like a fucking threat.

'Go ahead, Brodie. Walk out that door. No one is going to take you on, believe me.' A slow, satisfied smile. 'Or…' she drags out the word, toying with me, 'you could let me fix what's left of your career.'

I want to scream. I want to flip her fancy desk. I want to walk out and never look back, but I can't. She knows it. I know it.

I'm trapped.

'You crushed everything I worked for. I was geared up for the national team.'

'No, Brodie. *You* did that when you couldn't stop gambling. And when you punched a reporter. And then again when you told your coach to go fuck himself.'

Each word slices deep. Because she's not wrong, is she? I did all that. I mean, those twats had it coming, but…aye.

She watches me, still waiting for me to crack. When I don't, she exhales and leans back against her desk. 'Here's the deal. You sit down, shut up, and let me save your career. Because like it or not, I'm the only one willing to.'

I glare at her, every molecule screaming with rage. 'I hate you,' I say calmly.

'You do you.' Her smile lights up her entire face. 'Now listen up. We have work to do.'

'Fine. But this doesn't mean I trust you.'

'Trust is earned.' She walks back behind her desk, sits down, and opens another folder. 'Same as respect.'

I'm not an eejit, I catch the implication. She doesn't respect me. Why would she? I'm the cautionary tale. The man who had everything and pissed it away because he couldn't resist the thrill of chasing win after win.

'So, what's your grand plan, then?' I drench my question in as much sarcasm as I can muster.

The Stirling Rebels are new. The Canadian billionaire owner who founded the team thinks money solves everything. But you can't buy chemistry and trust. Or history. Or instinct. And I doubt Charlie Harrington can change any of that.

'First, we address the gambling.' She clicks her pen once. 'You need to be clean. Completely clean. No poker, no betting on anything, not even a friendly wager with teammates. One hint that you're still gambling, and everything we do is worthless.'

'Don't be dramatic. I played a bit of poker, I'm not an addict. And I haven't done that in seven months.'

'Good. Keep it that way. Anything else I need to know or be prepared for? Any illegitimate children with disgruntled baby mommas that could run to the press and make a fuss?'

I would like to shake some fucking sense into her. Instead, I crush the armrest in my grip. 'Not that I know of.'

'I guess that'll have to do. But glove up, understood?'

What the actual fuck? How dare she?

I mean, she's probably been dealing with horny athletes her entire life in her father's fancy London sports management agency. I reckon she knows what money and fame can do to a lad. Or a lass. There's a reason they want us married by twenty-one.

She continues outlining her strategy. Community outreach. Carefully managed interviews. Promo tour. Social media overhaul. Sponsorship meetings with brands that align with a 'redemption narrative.'

Each point is logical, well-thought-out. She knows what she's doing. I hate that she knows what she's doing.

'You also need new headshots.' She eyes me critically. 'And a haircut. You look like you've been living in the woods. Get rid of that mullet.'

'I said it before, and I'll say it again: fuck off, Harrington.'

'Not very eloquent.' She makes a note. 'We'll work on your media training, too.'

For the next ten minutes, she talks, and I listen, seething quietly. I'm tuning her out, looking around her office. Clean and cold. Not a single personal touch, except one framed image on her desk. Can't see who's in there. No posters of athletes. No trophies. Not even a plant to break up the sterile space. Who doesn't have plants? Makes me wonder if she's really like that or if she's just playing the part in an effort to look cool and successful and unbreakable.

This woman holds my future in her manicured hands. And there's not a damn thing I can do about it. Except needle her a bit.

'One question.'

She cocks a brow. 'What?'

'Did you really not know Callum was balls-deep in someone else, or were you too busy managing his image and ruining my career to care?'

Low blow, I know.

I play dirty sometimes.

Her face goes still for half a split second. Then she recovers, too fast for my taste. 'And here I thought you had no interest in my personal life, MacRae.' Her brief smile is all teeth, no warmth. 'But since we're trading blows… How does it feel to go from Scotland's rising rugby star to a toxic PR nightmare?'

My back teeth grind enough to crack enamel.

She leans forward, satisfied. 'That's what I thought. We're done here for now.'

I get up to leave, but I stop at the door. 'You think you know everything, don't you?'

She barely glances up from her screen, already dismissing me. 'Not everything. But I know you'll scramble back to the top where you belong, Brodie MacRae. And when you do…' She clicks her pen again. '…you'll thank me on your knees.'

I stomp out without another word, past the staring people who work here, down the lift, out onto the street.

Charlie fucking Harrington is my agent. The woman who helped destroy me is the only one who can save me. She *does* own my arse, and I'm going to have to play by her rules.

At least until I find a way to break them.

Chapter 2

Charlie

'Did you really not know Callum was balls-deep in someone else,' Brodie snarls, 'or were you too busy managing his image and ruining my career to care?'

I don't flinch. Not outwardly. Inside? That one lands hard.

But I smile as coldly as possible. 'And here I thought you had no interest in my personal life, MacRae.'

He's seething. Every muscle pulled tight like he's one insult away from snapping his chair in half.

Fine. Let's go.

'But since we're trading blows… How does it feel to go from Scotland's rising rugby star to a toxic PR nightmare?'

I've reached the edge of what I can fake. My pulse is rioting, my skin's too hot, and rage is braided so tightly with shame I can't tell where one ends and the other begins. I hate him right now. I want to scream at him. I want to throw something.

He feels the same. I can practically *hear* his teeth cracking.

'That's what I thought,' I declare calmly. 'We're done here, for now.' Another second and I might say something I can't claw back from.

He stops at the door. 'You think you know everything, don't you?'

I don't even look up. My voice is cold, controlled, and practised. 'Not everything. But I know you'll scramble back to the top where you belong, Brodie MacRae.' I click my pen. 'And when you do… you'll thank me on your knees.'

He doesn't respond. Just turns and walks out. No shouting, no slammed door, no parting shot. The quiet, furious click as it closes behind him hits harder than a bang ever could.

And something in me buckles.

I slump back in my chair like my strings just went slack. The armrests are the only thing keeping me from sliding to the floor.

Brodie MacRae. In my office. Eyes locked on me like he wanted to rip my throat out with his teeth.

My chest rises and falls too fast, adrenaline still racing through my veins. I press my palms flat against the cool glass of my desk, trying to ground myself. But the memory lingers – that barely-contained power simmering under his skin.

The sheer force of him. The primal heat.

And the fury.

Jesus, the fury.

I knew he'd be pissed off. I *prepared* for him to be pissed. But nothing could have braced me for the weight of that rage. It practically shimmered around him, thick as smoke, as if he'd combust any moment. And in the space between inhale and reason, my body reacted – before my brain could pull rank, before I reminded myself that Brodie MacRae might be volatile, but he wouldn't touch me.

Yeah, it's clear as day: Brodie MacRae hates my guts.

I squeeze my eyes shut.

Focus, Charlie. You handled it. Stayed cool, stayed in control. Didn't let him see how much he rattled you.

I pull up the spreadsheet for my next meeting. The

numbers blur, but I read through them anyway. Just to be sure. Even though I know them by heart.

My mobile buzzes, and my pulse jumps.

What does my dad want?

He hasn't been in touch since I left Harrington Sports Management at the end of March.

What is he up to now?

He's not the type to chase, and he sure as hell isn't calling for a chat.

I glare at the screen, pressure clamping around my ribs. Four months since I walked out of Harrington Sports, and he still can't accept that his eldest offspring chose her self-worth over his empire. That I dare to exist outside of his shadow.

He never calls anyone unless he wants something. He most certainly never apologises. I could pick up to find out what my price is this time. But I don't. I turn the phone face down until it silences itself. He lost that privilege four months ago.

I can still hear his clipped voice, exactly as he said it then. *You're being emotional, Charlotte. Boys will be boys. You're tainting everything I built because Cal slept with another woman. So? Move on.*

He still doesn't get it.

Edinburgh summer rain lashes against the window. A steady drumming that matches the riot running through my bloodstream. The sky is slate grey, heavy, pressing in like it wants to crush the city. Feels appropriate.

I stare at my reflection. Tense shoulders, jaw set like I'm holding back a war cry.

This is what I wanted. What I chose.

To be the boss.

I glance around, corralling my thoughts into line. The office is small and practical. Nothing flashy. Glass, brick, and simple furniture. A single step up from a glorified start-up, but it's mine. I'd scrounged together enough to rent this space for a year – my office and the two adjacent ones.

Theo's in the smallest one right now, pacing like she always does when she's planning a social media campaign. The other is shared between Alex and Mac, legal consultant and junior agent-slash-publicist, respectively. Frosted glass walls separate us, muting voices but never fully shutting them out. I can hear Alex murmuring into their headset and Mac clicking away at his laptop.

It's not much. But it's real. And I'm building it with my own damn hands.

On my desk, the only personal touch: a framed photo of Mum with my little sister Hannah. They're laughing, heads thrown back, Hannah's face lit up from some joke Mum cracked right before I took the picture. I know, London's only a day away and the move to Edinburgh was the change I needed. But I miss them.

I've sunk everything into this agency. Leveraged my future on the gamble that I could make it without George Harrington's safety net. Charmed investors. Hired three fabulous people whose ability to pay the rent depends on me.

And now I'm shackled to a ticking time bomb with a temper.

Shit.

I drag my fingers through my hair, pressing hard against my temples.

Shit, shit, shit.

Brodie fucking MacRae.

The man who's been Callum Fraser's nemesis since they were teenagers. The loose cannon. The walking PR disaster whose behaviour could single-handedly sink my fledgling agency before it gets off the ground.

A soft knock. Theo pokes her head in. 'Charlie? Your ten o'clock is here.'

My spine straightens so fast it aches. I exhale through my

nose. Damage control. Regroup. Fix things. That's what I do. No time for panic. No time to fall apart. If I slip now, even for a second, it's over.

I smooth my suit and force a cool smile. 'Send him up. And then let him wait two minutes outside my door.'

I know how to play power games. Daddy taught his daughter well. Or did he? I've never beaten him before. Never even went up against him. Until now.

Theo hesitates, eyeing me. 'You okay? You look...' She gestures vaguely and lifts her shoulders.

I meet her gaze, expression bulletproof. 'Like a woman about to close another contract with an up-and-coming golfer? Thanks, Theo. I appreciate the confidence.'

She doesn't seem convinced, but she disappears.

I exhale slowly as I reach for the next folder—

And put it back down when I realise my hands are still trembling.

My gaze flicks to the chair Brodie just vacated. It's too small for him. Everything is. He's not a giant, not like a forward. His body is made for movement as well as confrontation. Hardly contained in that suit, broad shoulders straining against the fabric. He's burned onto the back of my eyelids. The set of his jaw, how his nostrils flared when I told him to sit. That constant fidget in his hands, the way his throat worked when he swallowed back the instinct to throw my desk across the room.

He wanted to. I felt it. Hell, I dared him to.

My office still smells like him. Like rain and a hint of sweat and whatever aftershave he douses himself in. It lingers on my skin, in my lungs, like it's marking me.

I close my eyes. This is becoming a problem.

Not the bare-knuckled temper. Not the straining suit. Not even the steel-threaded quiet in his voice when he told me to be careful.

No, the key problem is that I kind of own the most

talented, uncontrollable player in Scottish rugby, and I don't have the luxury of fucking this up. This agency, this office – it's my one shot. I left London and moved to Edinburgh to be as far away as possible from my father and his cronies without actually having to leave the country. And if I let Brodie MacRae blow it up, I lose the only thing that's mine.

He's just a client.

Except…

Except I remember watching him play. Before everything. Before the scandal. Some players are a joy to watch, and Brodie is one of them. Because you don't know what he's doing next. He's unpredictable in the best way. How he moves, like gravity is optional. Like he could shape the game around him with skill, instinct, and sheer, brute will.

That same energy was in my office today. But this time, it was focused *on me*.

My phone buzzes again. Not Dad.

Callum?

Cold pressure grips my insides. I don't want to look. Shouldn't. But I do.

(DICKHEAD 10:02) Heard you have MacRae. News travels fast in rugby circles. Desperate much?

Naturally, the gossip mill is already turning. Word gets around when Scottish rugby's biggest fuck-up du jour shows up somewhere.

Fuck right off, Fraser.

Five months since I caught Callum shagging a sports presenter in his house in Glasgow. I was making a surprise visit to celebrate a new sponsorship I got for him. Guess how surprised I was when I saw him pumping a woman on the kitchen counter?

And Cal is still trying to twist the narrative, still playing the jilted victim, still sneering at my choices.

The laugh that leaves me is hollow and mean. Five months ago, I'd have called him just to hear him lie to me. Five months ago, I'd have let him spin it, let him make me feel like I was overreacting.

But I'm done being gaslit. Done playing his PR girl, starry-eyed ego-booster, and trad wife-to-be. I type back:

> (ME 10:04) Jealous much? Leave me alone and go crack your skull.

Then I block his number. For good. The pressure in my jaw could make a diamond.

When the knot under my sternum doesn't ease, I open the top drawer and pull out a compact mirror. My lipstick's still intact, but there's a smudge of mascara at the corner of one eye. I swipe it away, fix my hair, and tell myself to look the part. Confident and untouchable.

Four more meetings, two contract reviews, and a sponsorship crisis to handle.

Welcome to being the boss, Charlie.

This is what I signed up for, isn't it? To prove them all wrong. To show Dad I'm more than his backup plan and mini me. To prove that walking away from Callum and our relationship wasn't personal and professional suicide.

To build something that's mine.

Even if it means handling Scottish rugby's most competitive and combustible player and most gifted fly-half. Even if it means facing that ferocious stare and devastating scowl every day. Even if it means refusing to notice how devilishly hand-some he looked wrapped in sleek black wool and attitude.

Which is irrelevant. The only reason my body had the audacity to react in the first place is because I haven't had sex since Callum. Apparently, my vagina has developed an unfor-tunate soft spot for rough men with too much swagger and thighs like tree trunks.

I dig my nails into my palms to centre myself. It's nothing. A physiological glitch. A side effect of prolonged abstinence. Because I refuse to be *that* woman. The one who gets weak-kneed over rugby players built like brick shithouses. Did that before. Look how brilliantly *that* turned out.

I nudge the framed picture of Hannah and Mum back into place. Centre it just so. Better.

I am Charlotte fucking Harrington. I don't do attraction. I don't do men with gambling problems and anger issues and enough baggage to sink a ship. Not anymore.

I do *results*.

A top-tier asset, that's all he is. A chance to prove that I can turn water into wine. Even if he hates me for it. And step one? Figure out what Brodie MacRae wants more than he wants to fight me.

I grab my coffee, drain it, and put the empty cup on my desk. Before my next client walks in, I shove Brodie into a mental box and slam the lid. Time to get to work.

And time to figure out how to outplay the man who could destroy everything.

Chapter 3

Brodie

The ball spirals through the air, a perfect arc that should hit Scottie Kerr right in the chest. *Should* being the key word. It smacks off his fingertips. Hits the ground. Again.

'For fuck's sake, man!' I rake my fingers through my sweat-soaked hair. 'That's three times. Are your hands made of butter today?'

Scottie huffs out a breath. 'Maybe if you didn't throw like you're trying to take my head off.'

Scottie's usually decent, but today he's got the hands of a wean on a sugar crash. He looks…disheartened.

I don't have time for that.

'Maybe if you weren't moving like you've got concrete in your boots.' I spread my arms. 'If your feelings are hurt, you can fuck off. I'm here to win. Let's go again. This time, catch it with your hands, not your face.'

Coach Cameron Wallace's moustache twitches, lips pressing into a thin line. He's been breathing down my neck all day, probably wondering if I've finally lost it. But I haven't. I'm just done carrying dead weight.

'MacRae.' Coach's voice is a warning. 'Ease up.'

I ignore him. We're five weeks from season start, and half

these lads still can't consistently execute an advanced passing drill. We're all new here, thrown together. A mix of transfers, academy kids, and cast-outs like yours truly. Starting a new URC team from scratch isn't easy, I know. But someone needs to light a fire under their arses.

And that job falls to me.

Rare August sun bakes the training ground. We've been at it for hours, running the same play over and over because nobody can get their shite together. My shirt sticks to my back, muscles burning from the endless repetition.

I exhale hard and roll my shoulders, trying for patience I don't have. 'Five weeks till the season starts,' I say. 'You want to play in a real league, or should I start booking tickets for the kiddie touch tournament?'

'Aye, right.' Finn Lennox shouts from his position on the wing. 'It's always our fault, never the great MacRae's.'

My knuckles crack as my hands ball into fists. 'You like to say that to my face, Lennox?'

Finn stretches, lazy as a cat. 'Already did, mate.'

The rest of the lads shift, watching. They've seen this dance before – Finn pushing buttons, me rising to the bait. A few of them chuckle. James MacKenna mutters something to his mate. The rest avoid my gaze, like I'm the one weighing us down. But I'm their captain. The Stirling Rebels' best player. Even if none of them actually want me here.

Even if *I* don't really want to be here.

Coach Wallace's whistle splits the air. 'MacRae. A word.'

I head over, cleats catching on brittle patches of dry turf. Wallace stands with his arms crossed, clipboard tucked under one elbow. Everything about him – his stance, his stare, the bark in his voice – screams ex-military. A man used to discipline, control, and others following orders. His expression says I'm about to get my arse handed to me.

'What's the problem, MacRae?'

I wipe sweat from my forehead. 'No problem. Just trying to get the basics right.'

'By tearing strips off your teammates?'

'They need to step up.'

'They need a leader, not a dictator.' He taps his clipboard. 'You're the fly-half. The conductor and the captain. Your job's not to bark orders. It's to make everyone around you better. Am I clear?'

A muscle jumps in my forearm. 'That's what I'm trying to do. But I'm not here to hold their hands.'

Briefly, I wonder if Wallace is right. If I'm just lashing out to prove I'm still worth something. But I can't afford to think like that. Not when everyone's already waiting for me to cock up.

'No, you're trying to prove you're better than them.' He levels me with a look. 'And that's not leadership, son. That's ego.'

It shouldn't sting. But it does. Yet, I can't show weakness. Not here, not now.

'Run it again,' Wallace calls to the team. 'And MacRae? Try working with them instead of against them.'

I don't answer. Just turn back to the pitch, the weight of his words digging in like studs to my ribs. Fury simmers under my skin. Finn smacks Scottie on the back, a shared silent commentary, as if I'm the one who fucked up. As if I'm the punchline. James catches my eye and shakes his head, distancing himself from whatever potential explosion might happen. Smart lad. The rest of them tense, waiting for the storm.

I bite down on the twords knifing through my throat and will my shoulders to drop, not petrify.

We're having another go, and this time, it fucking works.

Pure magic.

The ball moves cleanly through the hands like it's supposed to. No fumbles, no hesitations, no confusion. Scottie takes the pass and straightens his run, dragging the inside defender with him. Finn reads it, steps off his left, and carves through before the defence can adjust. For the first time today, it flows.

Ball to James – pop to Scottie – straight back to me. I fire it wide to Finn, who glides through the space like he's been greased, legs devouring the metres. He makes it look easy, because when it works, when everyone's switched on, it *is* easy.

I don't celebrate. Just stand there, hands on my hips, breath heavy, sweat dripping down my nose. That's all I fucking wanted. Exactly that.

Wallace blows his whistle. 'That's it, boys. We got work to do. But let's end on a high.'

Finn lopes past me, barely winded. 'Aye, rare sight. MacRae actually *ending* something on a high.'

My neck tightens. 'Wanna repeat that, Lennox?'

He grins, all lazy confidence. 'Just saying, mate. Must be exhausting up there on that high horse, carrying that ego around at altitude.'

But before I can open my mouth to scold that cheeky wee fucker, a low engine growl drowns out the banter, and pulls my attention to the sleek black Maserati rolling up to the fence.

Of course, she'd arrive in a car that screams 'fuck you' without even needing to honk.

Next thing I know, a visceral shock punches through me – part impact, part instinct.

Because Charlie Harrington steps out of that car like she's walking onto a runway. The sun catches her hair, turning it to gold. Her oversized white linen shirt – practically see-through in this light – barely skims the top of her denim shorts, leaving far too much leg on display. Long, toned, lightly tanned. Smooth, too. I know, because my fucking brain decides to clock that detail like a goddamn traitor. My mouth goes dry. I'm a man with eyes. Any guy would be looking. Doesn't mean I have to like it.

Eventually, my brain catches up with my dick – and reminds me that I hate her guts.

'MacRae.' Her voice carries across the pitch. 'A minute of your precious time?'

Finn whistles low. 'Who's that snack?'

'My agent,' I growl. 'And she's leaving.'

The heels of her ankle boots sink into the grass as she stalks towards us. 'Actually, I'm not. Since you've been dodging my calls all week, we're doing this here. Right now.'

'We're training,' I declare.

'You're finishing, by the looks of it.' She glances at Wallace. 'Right, Coach?'

'Aye,' Wallace says, 'we're done for the day.'

The boys start filing off, but not before Finn shoots me a dirty smirk. I'll deal with him later. I've got bigger problems. About five foot five, but with an attitude from here to the moon.

Charlie plants herself between me and the pitch, close enough that I catch the scent of her perfume. Citrus and honey, smoothed out by something darker. Sandalwood? Spite? Hard to tell. But it sticks, just like her.

'You're being difficult,' she states sternly.

'I'm being a professional athlete. I have to train. It's what I do.'

'Professional?' She barks out a laugh. 'Is that what we're calling ignoring your agent's calls?'

'I've been busy.'

'Busy being a pain in my arse.' She pulls out her phone. 'You've missed a handpicked PR opportunity, declined a photoshoot, and told the *Daily Record* to, and I quote, "get fucked" when they asked for an interview.'

I cross my arms, which I know shows off my biceps. Not

sure if I want to intimidate or impress her. Probably both. 'And?'

'And you're doing Ailsa's Kitchen on Monday.' She's scrolling through what looks like a calendar on her phone.

'I'm doing what now?'

'A cooking show. Local channel and YouTube, good publicity, great way to show your softer side. Perfect for your image rehabilitation.'

The laugh that rips out of me is harsh. 'Not a chance in hell. I'm not doing a fucking cooking show.'

'It wasn't a request.'

'I don't cook.'

'You'll learn.'

'I don't do publicity stunts.'

'You'll adapt. Gordon signed off on this. So, unless you care to explain to the club manager why you're refusing to do the parts of your job that don't involve beating others up for a living, you're doing it and that's final.'

'I'm not your puppet, Harrington.'

'No. You're my client.' She steps in close, voice dropping to a whisper that slides down my spine. 'And right now, you're also being a nightmare.'

The thrum from her body reaches across the space between us. My pulse kicks hard against my ribs. 'Find someone else to dance for the cameras.'

'There's no one else who needs to dance as hard as you. You want to rebuild your reputation? This is how we do it. One appearance at a time. One cooking show at a time.'

'Fuck. Off.'

'You're repeating yourself. It's boring.'

But she doesn't look bored to me. Guess she's not used to being told no. That'd explain the pink climbing up her cheeks.

A rush of heat surges through me – not just anger, but something sharper. I hate that she has this effect on me. Like she's carved out a space in my head just to fuck with me. And for a moment, my eyes drop to her mouth.

She notices. Of course she notices.

'You done staring, MacRae?'

'You done trying to control my life?'

'When you stop being a liability? Perhaps.'

I lean in, sweat-soaked shirt clinging to my back, and use my height to loom over her. 'You *really* want to push me, Harrington?'

She doesn't back down an inch. 'I don't push, MacRae. I manage.'

I jut my chin out. 'That what you think you're doing?'

'That's what I know.' She presses a finger to my chest. 'You're doing the show. You're doing the photoshoot. And you're going to smile and play nice. It's in your contract. And believe me, you don't want to get on my bad side.'

My blood boils. 'That's blackmail.'

'That's business.' She steps back, smoothing her shirt. 'I'm picking you up Monday at nine. Wear something that isn't black. And for god's sake, get a haircut.'

'This a fetish of yours, Harrington? Bossing men around?'

Charlie holds the line, unbothered. 'You're the only one who needs this much bossing. Which makes me wonder whether or not you *are* a man.'

Some of the players whistle and chuckle.

Low blow. Meant to cut. I don't give any of them the satisfaction of seeing if it landed. Which it did.

She spins on her heel and stalks back to her car – full hips swaying in those painted-on shorts – and leaves me with a pitch full of gawking teammates. I watch her go, fury and something else churning in my gut. My whole team is staring at me like I've just been neutered. My head throbs, as if I just took a boot to the skull.

'Oi, MacRae!' Finn grins like it's Christmas. 'Bit fucked there, eh?'

'Shut your mouth. Or I'll do it for you.'

He laughs. 'I've not seen anyone handle you like that. It was beautiful, man. Scottie, did you see that?'

Scottie appears from nowhere, still in his training kit. 'Saw it. Filmed it. Sent it to the group chat.'

I'm going to murder them both in their sleep.

'The great Brodie MacRae,' Finn continues, 'taken down a notch by a gal in heels. Poetry, that is.'

I let out a grunt. Recently, my signature sound.

'What's wrong, Captain?' Finn wiggles his eyebrows. 'Can't decide if she handed you your arse or gift-wrapped it?'

Scottie laughs. 'Both.'

The tips of my ears are burning. 'You're running suicides next practice.'

'Worth it.' Finn claps my shoulder as he passes. First time he's ever done that. 'Have fun on your cooking or baking show, Captain. Perhaps you can teach me how to make a Victoria sponge?'

'I can teach you how to eat dirt.'

Finn sighs, mock wistful. 'Just think, MacRae. A year ago, you were taking down the All Blacks. Now? You're rolling pastry for daytime telly. Oh, how the mighty have fallen.'

I flip him the bird without looking. If I make eye contact, I'll end up doing time for assault.

They laugh and I watch them go, the taste of defeat bitter on my tongue. Charlie Harrington played me in front of my entire team. Undermined me, humiliated me, and made my dick stir in the process.

Have I mentioned how much I fucking hate her?

Chapter 4

Charlie

The engine purrs like a panther as I gun it down the M9. My Maserati Grecale Trofeo – the only thing I kept from my old life in London. I love that car. Makes me feel safe and powerful, in control, no matter where I'm headed.

The morning light gleams over the Kelpies, two colossal steel horse heads rising out of the ground. I've been awake since five, drafting contracts and rescheduling meetings because a certain rugby player can't manage basic time-keeping and is as reliable as the Scottish weather.

Let's face it: I'm a babysitter. I'm babysitting a six-foot-two, sixteen-stone toddler with stubble and a grudge the size of Scotland.

Fuck my life.

Half an hour later, I'm rolling past Duncraig's houses, their blonde sandstone frowning in the morning chill. Brodie's address gleams on my phone screen. Willowbank Crescent. Cosy and quaint.

As if.

The morning fog hasn't fully lifted here yet, wreathing the street in milky shadows. Perfect weather for murder. And if he's not ready for this cooking show appearance, murder is precisely what's going to happen.

I shove the gear stick into park outside Brodie's terraced house. Twenty minutes early because I don't trust him as far as I could throw his irritatingly muscled body.

My phone buzzes. Theo.

'Studio's ready. Hair and makeup waiting. Please tell me he's awake.'

'We'll find out.' I check my lipstick in the rear-view. 'If not, I'm dragging him there in his Spider-Man panties or SpongeBob jammies. I don't care.'

'I have no doubt,' she says. 'Good luck with broody Brodie, boss.'

I hang up and march up his front path, heels clicking against stone. His BMW M4 Competition xDrive gleams in the driveway.

Tight ride, MacRae. I'll give you that.

The house is decent enough. Red sandstone, black door, tidy garden. Came with the Rebels contract, furnished and all. Perks of being captain. Most of the team is stuck flat-sharing in Duncraig — Knox Everett Montgomery's experiment. Five years ago, the Canadian billionaire showed up, looking for his Scottish roots. He took one glance at the struggling former mining town and threw his money at it. New jobs, new tourism, and the Stirling Rebels, complete with a 5,000-seater stadium. Better than building a rocket, I guess.

One sharp knock. Two. The sound of heavy footsteps approaching.

The lock clicks. The door swings inward.

My lungs collapse.

Brodie leans against the frame. Shirtless and sleep-mussed. Morning light gilds the ridges of his abs. A trail of dark hair arrows down, disappearing beneath the waistband that sits indecently low on his hips. And–

Oh.

Those briefs hide exactly nothing.

My throat closes up. This is inappropriate. This is out of line. This is…

A big problem. Literally.

'You're early, Harrington.' That lazy Scottish drawl, all rough edges and sleep-thick heat, could probably charm the knickers off someone who wasn't me.

I drag my gaze up, slow and deliberate, taking in way too much before I get to his face. My throat goes sandpaper-dry. Jesus.

'And you're still naked,' I say.

The corner of his mouth pulls up with the hint of an arrogant smile. 'If I *were* naked, you wouldn't still be standing here.'

Heat surges up my neck, swift and humiliating. I want to slap that self-satisfied look clean off his stubbled face. Maybe then I'd stop thinking about what's in those briefs.

I grasp for composure. The flex of his biceps as he scrubs a hand through freshly trimmed hair. *My* directive. He actually listened. Shorter on the sides, long enough on top to run your fingers through.

'At least you followed one instruction.' I push past him into the house, refusing to let my arm touch his bare torso. 'Now put some clothes on. We're leaving in ten.'

'Fifteen.'

I spin to face him and immediately regret it. Because sweet Jesus, he's all lean muscle and sculpted strength, built to take a hit and keep moving. Tall enough to make me feel small even in heels.

Callum was fit, sure. But this? This is different.

I grew up around athletes. I've seen them dressed, half-dressed, in gear, in ice baths. Brodie MacRae is something else. It's not just the body, it's the restless energy thrumming beneath his skin. The reality-bending willpower. His whole presence.

I steady my breath, chin lifting like that'll help. 'Ten, MacRae.'

'Fourteen.'

'Nine, now.'

He stretches, muscles shifting like it's all for show. 'Coffee first,' he grumbles.

'No time.'

'Then I'm not going.'

I grit my teeth. 'Eight minutes. Tick-tock.'

He disappears upstairs, muttering curses that would make a sailor blush. I lean against his wall, pressing my forehead to the cool plaster.

Get it together, Charlie.

The lounge is a bombsite. Rugby kits strewn across a battered sofa, PlayStation, a massive flatscreen paused on *Match of the Day*. I nudge a stray boot. This room tells me nothing. Blank walls, generic furniture, the kind that screams 'furnished rental property'. A bushy basil plant on the windowsill, an extraordinarily green rubber plant, and a Benjamin Fig that looks like it's never shed a single leaf in its life. No other personal touches except…

Wait.

A cluster of frames on the mantel catches my eye. Brodie, younger, grinning with two other lads who share his dark hair and sharp features. Brothers, clearly. In another photo, a stern-faced man with Brodie's build stands beside a petite woman whose smile could light up Glasgow. His dad looks like the type who'd push his sons to excel. To compete. To prove themselves.

Explains a lot.

More photos. Rugby matches. Trophies. Medals. The visual timeline of a career built on innate talent and relentless drive. Even with the Knights, Brodie was notorious for staying late, pushing harder, and demanding more. From himself, from everyone. Natural ability wasn't enough, he had to dominate.

Footsteps thunder down the stairs. I turn away from the photos. Brodie emerges in dark jeans and a grey Henley that stretches across his chest, sleeves rolled to reveal corded forearms.

Keep focusing, Charlie.

'Finally.' I dangle my keys. 'My car.'

'Not a fat chance.' He grabs his BMW fob. 'I don't need a chauffeur.'

'And I don't trust you not to conveniently get lost on the way to the studio,' I say.

A breath grates out through his gritted teeth. 'I said I'd do it.'

'You also said you'd answer my calls.' I edge forward. 'Get in the car, MacRae.'

'On one condition.' For a beat, he glowers at me. Unyielding. I stare back. Then he snatches the keys from my hand.

'I'm driving,' he declares. 'Need to see if that Maserati's all show or if there's something real under the hood.'

I fold my arms, squaring off with him. 'You're not prepared for what she can do.'

'Bet I am.'

'Ah, I wouldn't use that particular word if I were you.' I smile intentionally sweetly, but there's a sting in my words.

He slants a look in my direction, and I hesitate, weighing the pros and cons.

'Okay, fine,' I give in. 'This once.'

Honestly, the things I do for my clients.

The Maserati purrs to life under his touch and he seems… pleased. The leather seat cradles me as he adjusts everything – mirrors, seat position, temperature. His scent fills the car. Clean, sharp, maddeningly masculine. My body lights up like it's been flipped on at the mains.

I cross my legs and press my thighs together. This is ridiculous.

'Stop touching everything,' I snap.

'Stop being a control freak.'

He says it like it's a character flaw. And yeah, perhaps I am too controlling. But with guys like him, it's the only way to survive. If I let him get away with even one thing, he'll bulldoze right over me. He's too used to being the biggest, baddest guy in the room. I can't afford to be steamrolled, not with so much riding on this.

The success of my entire agency.

And now he's changing the radio settings.

'Grubby fingers off my radio! What's next? You gonna mark your territory?'

'I could, if that's what you're into.'

I grab my knees, suppressing the urge to wrap my hands around his thick neck. 'Just drive my car like a normal human, instead of acting like it's your dick on wheels.'

'Maybe if you weren't riding my arse every minute, I wouldn't have to mark my space.'

The way he says it makes something tingle low in my belly, and I hate him a little bit more for it.

'Serious case of small dick energy. Classic.'

'You keep talking to me like that, and we're gonna have a problem, Harrington,' he grumbles under his breath.

He pulls out onto the street with unnecessary aggression, the engine growling. My nipples stiffen in response, and I hate how my body doesn't give a damn that he's a stubborn prick. I hate how his thigh shifts every time he changes gear, the way his shoulders fill out that shirt like it's painted on.

I'm supposed to be in charge here, not getting hot over Brodie fucking MacRae.

He tightens his knuckles around the steering wheel, tendons flexing under his skin, but he says nothing. Keeps his eyes on the road, tension welded into every line of his frame. Like he's holding something back.

We're possibly going to kill each other before we reach the studio.

If my hormones don't kill me first.

The studio hunkers in an old warehouse on the outskirts of Stirling, sandwiched between a craft brewery and what looks like an artisan cheese shop. Very hipster. Very YouTube-friendly. The building's facade has been painted with murals. Inside, fairy lights are strung across exposed beams, and the 'kitchen' set is barely bigger than my first flat's cooking space. Cream cabinets, wooden worktops, copper pots hanging from hooks. It's meant to feel homely, intimate.

I shoot Brodie a sidelong glance. 'The woman's basically the local Mary Berry but with more sass. Her show started out locally on Central Scotland TV, but it's been blowing up online. 800k views on her last episode.'

A production assistant appears at my side, headset in place. 'Hair and makeup first, Brodie. A quick touch-up.'

I turn to look at her. So does Brodie. Only my expression is apologetic, and his could strip paint.

'Not happening,' he says.

The assistant falters. 'It's just some powder—'

'Not. Happening.'

'You're on camera—'

'I'm not a Kardashian,' he states grimly.

She looks at me. I look at Brodie. Brodie looks like a man about to walk straight out of the building and into a pub.

'Jesus Christ, would you stop being such a diva? Studio lights make you look like a deep-fried Mars bar,' I explain.

He doesn't move, and my patience is fraying like a worn-out bootlace.

The assistant shifts nervously. 'It's literally two minutes.'

'So is getting knocked out,' Brodie mutters, loud enough that half the room hears it. 'Doesn't mean I'll volunteer for it.'

I dig my nails into my palm to keep from snapping back. Arrogant, stubborn, insufferable piece of work.

I'm done playing nice. I close the distance, keeping my voice low and lethal. 'I don't give a shit if you think you're too good for this, but if you blow this, it's my arse on the line. So, pull your head out of it for five fucking minutes.'

Tense silence hums between us. Then a deep, suffering exhale. 'Fine.'

He stomps off toward the makeup station, drops into the chair, and sits there radiating raging misery while a makeup artist pats his face with a brush like she's defusing a bomb.

'This is a joke.' Brodie's voice could cut glass. 'A fucking joke.'

'Shut up and smile,' I hiss.

Ailsa emerges from behind the counter, beaming as she wipes her hands on a gingham apron. 'Brodie MacRae! Welcome to Ailsa's Kitchen. So thrilled to have you. Thank you for coming.'

Brodie stares at her like she handed him a live grenade. 'Right. Thrilled.'

Undeterred, Ailsa clasps her hands together. 'We're making spaghetti with meatballs today. Your gran's recipe, actually.'

His entire body goes still. 'What?'

'Well, a vegetarian twist on it,' she clarifies and nods in the direction of the prep station where neat bowls of ingredients wait. 'We thought it'd be fun. Bit of nostalgia, bit of a challenge. Sound good?'

Brodie's gaze flicks to the recipe card. A muscle ticks beneath his eye as he picks it up, reading the measurements.

That's when he turns to me. 'Was this your idea? Where the fuck did you get this?'

I bristle, irritation needling under my skin. Typical. Immediately assuming I'm out to sabotage him.

'Research,' I say. 'You mentioned it in a Knights interview three years ago. Not exactly state secrets, MacRae.'

The lights catch the sharp planes of his face as he reads, and something shifts in his expression. Something boyish that makes my chest tight. He doesn't get to look vulnerable when he's been nothing but a man-child with a mood problem since he walked in.

'You contacted my mother?' He asks.

'Theo did. Your mother told her about your nonna's recipe. How you'd help make the meatballs every Sunday.'

He turns away, but not before I glimpse that crack in his armour. I try not to feel guilty – or anything at all. I'm not out to torment him, no matter what his paranoid brain seems to think.

His fingers trace the measurements and the instructions. For the length of a breath, he's somewhere else entirely.

Ailsa bounces over, all sunshine and curls. 'Ready to start? The ingredients are all prepped.'

'Aye.' Grit in his voice. 'Let's do this.'

Ailsa hands him the first bowl of ingredients. He blanks for a second, like he's forgotten how hands work, before he takes it with a muttered *'cheers'* and sets it down with unnecessary force.

He's expectedly monosyllabic, but Ailsa is a bundle of charm. And Brodie's transformation is subtle but unmistakable. His stance relaxes by degrees, movements losing that wound-spring tension. When Ailsa asks about the recipe's origins, his answers flow more easily.

'Nonna came from Naples in the sixties, met Grandda, and opened a café in Edinburgh.' His hands work the meatballs with practised ease.

'And your mum learned from them?'

'Aye. Every recipe, every trick.' A ghost of a smile touches his lips. 'She'd let me help, even when I made a mess of everything.'

Something hot and disobedient unfurls deep behind my navel. This gentle version of Brodie sends warning signals firing through my brain and body.

The studio lights paint his forearms in gold as he works. Those hands that can send a rugby ball spiralling sixty metres now shape meat with surprising delicacy. The sauce bubbles, rich and red, filling the air with garlic and herbs.

'Smells amazing.' Ailsa stirs the pot. 'You clearly know your way around a kitchen.'

'Only with this.' He shrugs. 'Everything else is beans on toast.'

My lips tug upward, but I force them flat.

'So.' Ailsa's tone remains light, but her eyes sharpen. 'While we wait for the sauce, can we talk about what happened at the beginning of this year?'

We'd briefly discussed this possibility in prep, and he'd agreed. Still, the wooden spoon in Brodie's hand stills. Heat prickles across the back of my neck.

'The gambling,' Ailsa clarifies.

The word drops like a stone. Ripples of tension spread through the studio. I straighten, ready to intervene, but…

'Aye,' he says. 'We can talk about it.'

What? Is he really going…there?

'It's simple.' He keeps stirring, eyes on the sauce. 'I'm competitive. Always have been. Three boys, strict dad – everything was a competition. Who could run fastest, study hardest, win biggest. So I guess you could say I don't have a gambling problem. I have a competition problem.'

'Makes sense to me.' Ailsa smiles and nods, encouraging.

'Poker seemed perfect. Strategy, skill, that rush when you win.' His jaw grinds. 'I got caught up in it. Lost more than I should've. But I never…' His eyes cut to me, sharp as glass,

'…bet on rugby. Never. That was bullsh—…lies someone fed to the media.'

Warmth spreads its way upward all the way to my ears. Because he's right, isn't he? Someone leaked those rumours to the press. Someone made sure they stuck.

But that someone wasn't me, even though Brodie seems to believe otherwise. I had no reason to do that. I was busy trying to build up Callum's sponsorship deals and…

'The headlines must have hurt.' Ailsa says gently. 'Your reputation—'

'Got torched.' His laugh holds no humour. 'Amazing how quick people turn on you, isn't it? One rumour, and suddenly you're toxic.'

Guilt sits like lead in my gut. Was it Callum? Logically, it makes sense. Brodie left the Knights, and now Callum's their starting fly-half. His market value has doubled, and he's up for the national team. Something Brodie had his eye on, too. If Brodie had stayed, Callum would still be in his shadow. But with him gone, suddenly Callum's not just a contender. He's *the* contender.

Would he have been that calculated? I never thought he was the strategic type. But then again, I also never thought he'd pound another woman while I was working my butt off to make him a star. Perhaps I wasn't just blind to Callum's lies. Perhaps I was blind to what he was willing to do to get what he wanted.

Brodie thinks I was in on it, helped ruin his career.

And maybe I was. By staying with the man who did.

The realisation burns. I didn't swing the axe, but I stood by while someone else did. Oblivious. Naïve. Complicit.

'But you're still here.' Ailsa touches his arm. 'Still fighting and starting over with the Stirling Rebels, right?'

'Rugby is everything.' He tests the sauce, adds a pinch of salt. 'Has been since I was five. My whole life, that's been the one constant. The one thing that never let me down.' His eyes find mine again. 'I'd never risk that. Not for anyone or anything.'

I can tell he's not lying. This man, this proud, stubborn, annoying man – he'd cut his balls off and eat them before he'd compromise the game.

'The pasta's ready. I bet it's the best sauce you've ever had.' The words are barely out of his mouth before he catches himself. His face turns crimson.

There's that cursed word again: bet.

A heartbeat of silence. 'I mean…'

Ailsa, bless her, keeps stirring like nothing happened. 'You do seem rather confident in your sauce.'

'Because it's good. And to be clear: it wasn't a *bet*. It was a *statement*.'

Ailsa's eyes twinkle. 'Of course. Just like how I don't bet this will be the best episode we've ever filmed…I simply know it.'

Brodie exhales, some of the tension easing from his posture. 'Exactly. Want to do the honours?'

Ailsa perks up. 'Yes, please.'

He lifts the pot with those strong hands, movements precise and controlled. Steam rises as Ailsa pours spaghetti into the sauce, the scent of basil and garlic wrapping around us. In the quiet pause that follows, Brodie's face softens into something approaching peace.

My heart stumbles.

Ailsa giggles, shooting the camera a knowing wink before grabbing a spoon. 'See, folks? This is what we call a high-stakes dish.'

The moment is defused. And Brodie actually looks like he might survive this after all.

Five minutes later, the cameras stop rolling, and the tightness bleeds out of me.

He did it. He actually did it.

Brodie MacRae, the man who punched a reporter a few

months ago, charmed his way through thirty minutes of cooking television without a single death threat or f-bomb. Not only that, he also…shone. That's the only word for it. When he talked about his grandmother's recipes, his whole face changed.

Wish I could ignore that.

Only temporary, though. He approaches with a scowl deep enough to curdle milk, rubbing his palms dry with a tea towel. 'Happy now?'

'Ecstatic.' I push off the wall. 'You were almost human.'

'Miracles happen.'

'Clearly.' I lean into his space, straightening his collar. 'Who knew the big bad rugby player was actually a softie who makes his nonna's meatballs?'

His grip on the tea towel tightens as if he imagines strangling me with it. 'You're pushing it again, Harrington.'

One second, he's all soft over his nonna's cooking. The next he's back to being a sulk factory.

'And you're not finished.' I grab his wrist, ignoring the static shock that zips through my fingertips. 'Come on. Time for your glamour shots.'

'What?'

I drag him around the corner to where Mac waits with his camera. The warehouse's exposed brick will make a perfect backdrop. Industrial, masculine. Since I already have him here, I have to make the most of it. Is it a trap? Not really. But sort of.

'No.' Brodie plants his feet. 'I did your cooking show. I'm done.'

'New headshots. Now.' I position him against the wall. 'Stand still. I don't think your face muscles are capable of smiling, but try not to look murderous.'

He glowers at the camera.

'I said *not* murderous.'

'What do you want from me? This is my fucking face.'

'Then make a better one.' I reach to fix his hair without thinking. My fingers ghost over his forehead, and he stills. My pulse jumps, nerves flaring as I realise how close we are. His eyes lock on mine.

I snatch my hand back. 'Your hair's a mess.'

Mac clears his throat. 'Ready when you are.'

I step back, head spinning.

What the fuck was that?

'Right.' It comes out steadier than I feel. 'Five shots. Make them count.'

The camera clicks. Again. Again. Each shot capturing that rare curve of his mouth, that knowing glint in his eyes. He's not looking at the lens – he's looking through it. Straight at me.

I need to leave. Now.

But I can't leave without him. Brodie still has my car keys.

Fuck.

Chapter 5

Brodie

I can't believe she's making me do this.

I can't believe I fucking *let* her.

It's been ten days since the cooking show, and I'm still getting tagged in videos of me talking about Nonna's sauce like a cheap Gordon Ramsay.

And now this.

Weans.

The children's section of the Stirling library looks like a Crayola factory exploded. Shelves crammed with picture books, bean bags in shades that should be classified as visual assault, and walls plastered with cartoon frogs and worms with glasses perched on their non-existent noses.

A fucking nightmare.

And in the middle of it all? A plastic chair designed for someone a quarter of my size. Just waiting to collapse under me and humiliate me in front of twenty tiny humans.

'This another sick joke?' I level another of my death stares at Charlie, who leans against the wall looking far too pleased with herself.

Her black turtleneck hugs curves that have no business being that distracting in a children's library. She's always been classy – stunning, actually – and somehow that pisses me off more than the fact that I have to actively force myself to look anywhere else. I hate that I'm this easy to wind up.

'Problem, MacRae?' Her lips curl into that grin I want to wipe off her face. Preferably with my mouth. Which is a thought I need to delete from existence.

'I'm not sitting on that.' I gesture at the plastic chair. 'It'll snap like a twig.'

'There's a bean bag,' Charlie says.

'I'm not sitting on a fucking bean bag, either.'

A librarian wiggles a reproachful finger at me. Her glittery nails catch the light with every movement. 'Language, please. The children will be here any minute.'

Charlie's grin widens. 'Yes, Brodie. Language.'

I scrub a hand over my face, half-heartedly scanning the room for escape routes. There is no escape. Not with Charlie watching over me. I'm doomed. Twenty tiny chairs arranged in a semicircle. A box of puppets. A stack of books.

'I'm a rugby player, not a clown.'

'You're whatever I need you to be today.' Charlie pushes off the wall and saunters over. 'The Rebels' community outreach program needs this. *You* need this. Your image needs this.'

She pats my chest, her touch burning through my shirt. 'Now be a good sportsman and read about *Hoppy the Hungry Rabbit*.'

The librarian offers a thin smile. 'We've actually selected *Gordon the Grumpy Goalie* today. We thought it would be…appropriate.'

Charlie bursts out laughing, the sound rich and warm and infuriating.

'Fuck me sideways,' I mutter.

'Language!' The librarian and Charlie retort in perfect stereo.

The door bursts open, and a stampede of small children

floods in, chattering and pointing and staring. They're five, six, seven. I guess. I know fuck all about wee ones. Twenty pairs of eyes fixate on me like I'm some exotic zoo animal.

'Is that him?' One small boy tugs his friend's sleeve. 'The man from the telly?'

Charlie leans in close, her breath tickling my ear. 'Smile, MacRae. They can smell fear.'

I glare at the chaos like I can intimidate it into order.

The kids are one thing, at least they're honest in their curiosity. But the mums? They cluster by the bookshelves pretending to browse, whispering behind paperbacks, and shooting glances that could melt steel. One adjusts her neck-line, tugging it lower when she catches my eye. Another acts riveted by her toddler's attempt to eat a cardboard book while sneaking peeks at my legs. The worst offender doesn't even try to hide it. Just stands there with her phone, angling for the perfect shot.

I grab Charlie's elbow and yank her closer. '*This* was the "safest option"?'

'Scared of being mobbed by mums? Maybe you should stop treating every female in sight like she's out to mount you.' Her eyes dance with unholy delight. 'No one here to yell insults at you, so yes. Or would you rather do a training video for the detection of testicular cancer? Because that *was* an option, too.'

A jolt of tension roots me to the spot. 'You wouldn't.'

'The script had specific instructions about demonstrating proper examination technique.'

'You're evil,' I hiss. 'Actually evil.'

'On the contrary.' Charlie beams at me. 'I'm your lord and saviour who's rehabilitating you. Now go read about that grumpy goalie before I sign you up for prostate cancer aware-ness month.'

The librarian clears her throat. 'We're ready when you are, Mr MacRae.'

I trudge toward the bean bag, wondering if getting tackled by the entire Glasgow Knights defence might have been less painful.

Aye.

I grip the ridiculous picture book. 'Okay then,' I clear my throat. 'The Grumpy Goalie.'

My voice booms in the small space. Three children in the front row physically recoil.

'Maybe a bit softer,' Charlie stage-whispers from behind me.

I lower my voice. 'The Grumpy Goalie by…who the fuck writes these things?'

The librarian makes a strangled noise. A mother gasps.

'Sam McIntyre,' Charlie supplies smoothly. 'And that's another pound in the swear jar.'

'There's a swear jar?' I glance around.

A tiny girl with pigtails points to an actual glass jar on the librarian's desk. It's empty now. Won't be by the time I'm done.

'Carry on, Mr MacRae,' the librarian says tightly.

I open the book. The illustrations are bright and garish – a cartoon goat wearing goalkeeper gloves and scowling at everyone.

'Once upon a time, there was a goalie named Gordon.' I pause, staring at the picture. 'Gordon, the goat, was the best goalkeeper in the league. He even thought he was the G.O.A.T. – the greatest of all time.'

Seriously, who writes this stuff? That's insulting even for a six-year-old.

A small boy shuffles forward on his bum. 'Like you?'

'I'm not a goalkeeper in football, mate. I'm a rugby fly-half.'

His face scrunches in confusion.

'I'm the one who tells everyone on my team what to do on the pitch,' I explain.

'My maw says you're the one who shouts a lot,' he replies.

A ripple of adult suppressed laughter circles the room. I glance back to see Charlie biting her lip, shoulders shaking.

'Gordon, the goat, was very good at stopping goals,' I continue, ignoring them all. 'But he wasn't very good at sharing and making friends.'

Christ, this is brutal. I shift on the bean bag, which makes a loud farting noise. The children erupt in giggles.

Let them have their fun.

'Gordon liked to win,' I read, 'but he didn't like it when others scored goals against him. He would stamp his hooves and kick the ball away and say mean things.'

I look up at the children. 'Oi, don't be like Gordon, awright? Nobody likes a sore loser.'

Some of them nod.

Charlie coughs into her hand. I swear I hear her mutter 'ironic' under her breath.

'Or a smug winner,' I add pointedly in her direction.

The story drags like a muddy scrum. A small girl with rainbow hair clips clambers onto my leg without warning, her tiny hands gripping my jeans for stability. Before I can react, another one – this one with missing front teeth and glitter smeared across her cheeks – scales my other thigh like I'm Mount Everest.

'You're bigger than my da,' Rainbow Clips announces, bouncing slightly on my quadriceps.

'And louder,' adds Glitter Face, settling in like she's found her new favourite chair.

I go statue-still. What the fuck am I supposed to do with them? Push them off? Pat their heads like puppies?

'Story,' Rainbow Clips demands, jabbing a sticky finger at the page.

Why do they always have fucking sticky fingers?

The librarian watches with barely concealed amusement.

'Right. Where were we?' I balance the book between their heads. 'Gordon learns to…something.'

'Share!' they shout in unison, directly into my eardrums. And they called *me* loud.

Then a boy hauls himself onto what's left of my lap. Then another.

What am I? A fucking climbing frame?

Fine. Might as well give them the best story time they've ever had.

Gordon learns to share. Gordon makes friends. Gordon realises winning isn't everything.

Load of pish, if you ask me.

Of course, winning is everything.

I'm almost through Gordon's redemption arc when I realise I'm doing voices. Not just reading – actually performing this shite. The goat gets a gruff Glaswegian accent, the bunny sounds like my Scottish gran after too many gin and tonics, and I've somehow given the fox an Edinburgh drawl. Makes the kids howl with laughter.

What the hell am I doing? This is getting dangerously close to effort. But I can't stop now, so I keep going.

'And then Gordon said…' I drop my voice to a dramatic rumble, '…"I'm sorry for being such a grumpy goalie. Next time I'll remember that friendship matters more than winning."'

The children clutching my legs gasp like I've revealed the secrets of the universe. One boy's mouth hangs open, a string of drool connecting his lip to my jeans.

A mum in the back fans herself with a library brochure.

I half-turn and look at Charlie, expecting her trademark smirk. But she's not smirking. She's watching me, bottom lip caught between her teeth. Her phone's up, capturing the whole disaster, but her eyes aren't mocking.

For a split second, I catch something else there. Something

that digs in low in a way that has nothing to do with fifteen stone of children using me as furniture.

She's working hard. For me. Like she actually means it.

Is she overcompensating? Is it guilt for how things went down with that bastard Callum? Maybe she's just determined to fix the mess she helped make. Maybe it's something else. Whatever. Doesn't matter.

I close the book with a decisive clap. 'The end.'

There's a small silence. The kind that makes you wonder if you've messed it up completely.

Then a tiny voice pipes up from somewhere near my armpit. 'You should read to us again.'

That catches me off guard. A wee lad with missing teeth stares up at me, and something pulls tight behind my ribs.

The mums lean forward, a chorus of hopeful faces. *Say yes, say yes*, their expressions beg. Christ, you'd think I was offering them a raunchy night out instead of butchering a children's book.

'Please, Mr Fly,' Rainbow Clips tugs on my sleeve. 'You do good voices.'

'Aye, well.' I shrug, like it doesn't matter either way. 'I suppose I could come back one day.'

The room erupts in cheers. The kids bounce on my legs like I've promised them Disney World. The mums exchange knowing glances.

I gently extract myself from the pile of children and hand the book back to the librarian. The swear jar sits on her desk, a single pound coin alone on the bottom. I dig into my wallet, fish out a fifty, and drop it in. The librarian's eyebrows nearly hit the ceiling.

Charlie eyes the bill. 'Fifty? You only swore twice.'

I shrug. 'Paying it forward.'

We say goodbye to the kids, the mums, and the staff. As we walk towards the exit, Charlie sidles up beside me. 'That wasn't so bad now, was it?'

'It absolutely was. And charity's not meant to be a damn PR stunt.'

'It is if you want to keep doing it and not end up needing one.' She taps her phone screen. 'This material is gold, Brodie. You, reading to kids. You, smiling. You, not breaking someone's nose. This is what we needed.'

'I doubt that.' I stop next to our cars parked side by side.

She tucks her phone away. 'Think about it. We'll push this out on socials. Your accounts and the Rebels'. People love a redemption arc. And a man with thunder thighs covered in happy children.'

I side-eye her. 'You think the internet's gonna forget everything because I read a bloody picture book?'

'No. But they'll see something else. A different headline. *Brodie MacRae: Rugby's Loose Cannon*, or *Brodie MacRae: Secret Softie Who Reads to Kids*? What looks better to a potential sponsor?'

I frown because she's right. 'You really think this'll make a difference?'

'It's a start. Keep this up, and we can get you something good. And I don't mean Ladbroke's.' She laughs.

'You're not funny. And still evil.'

'But effective.' Her shoulder bumps mine. 'Admit it.'

I stare straight ahead, refusing to give her the satisfaction. But something tugs at the corner of my mouth.

'Never.'

Shocking truth: having Charlie Harrington as my agent might not be the worst thing that's ever happened to me. Doesn't mean I have to say it to her face. She'll take that victory and lord it over me until the end of time.

Besides, admitting it means letting her win – and I'm not wired to lose.

Chapter 6

Charlie

Oh God. My ovaries. Betraying me with some primal, deeply unprofessional reaction to a hard-bodied grump with kids draped all over him. No, more than betraying. They're screaming like the front row at a boy band concert.

The Maserati's leather steering wheel creaks under my grip as I navigate through Stirling's narrow streets back to Edinburgh. I force my fingers to unclench, nails leaving half-moons in the hide. Rain spits against the windscreen.

Focus on the PR win. Not the way his tone softened when he did the voices. He read a children's book. He didn't save orphans from a burning building.

To let myself get blindsided by charisma and good intentions once was bad enough. Doing it again – especially with a client and another rugby player – isn't an option.

I jab the radio off as I get on the M9. Silence amplifies the memory as I drive. Corded forearms flexing as he held a picture book that looked like a postage stamp in his hands. How steel-cut quads strained against denim. How helpless he looked when those kids clambered onto him like he was a jungle gym.

And he let them.

Not only let them, but encouraged them. With those voices.

The children were entranced.

I was entranced.

'Stop it,' I hiss, swerving around a delivery van. 'He's a client. A reluctant, pain-in-the-arse client who loathes you.'

The light turns green, and I accelerate, fighting to recalibrate. This was meant to be straightforward. Drag the rugby grouch to a community event. Grab a few photos for damage control. Tick another box in Operation: *Make Brodie MacRae Seem Like Less of an Angry Dick.*

How his expression melted when that girl with the rainbow clips climbed onto his leg. The genuine laugh – not a media-trained chuckle, but an actual laugh – when one of the boys asked if he could lift the librarian over his head.

I hit the brakes at a red light, and a horn blares behind me.

'Sorry,' I mutter to no one, heart jerking. 'Shit.'

My phone rings in the cup holder. Theo's name lights up.

'Tell me you got the footage, boss.'

I thumb the speaker button. 'In your inbox.'

'Brilliant. I'll post the reel before the lunch crowd hits. I'll tag the library, use #RugbyDads or something.'

A lorry overtakes, spraying my windscreen with gutter water. I flick the wipers up.

'You alright?' Theo asks. 'Sounds like you're rowing across the Firth of Forth.'

'Peachy. Just plotting how to spin MacRae's sudden aptitude for children's literature.'

'Pfft. Mums will lap it up. Did he really do voices?'

'Like a panto actor.'

A Tesla swerves in front of me and noses in without warning. I slam the horn, swerving into the next lane. My whole ribcage jolts like it's trying to eject me.

Theo clicks her tongue. 'Drive carefully. I just started

working for you, I haven't had enough time to begin despising you in order to rejoice at your funeral. See you in a jiffy!'

The traffic light ahead turns amber. I floor it, engine snarling through the intersection. I crank the AC, so the cold air bites my collarbones. That doesn't help. Memory ambushes me: Brodie's calloused thumb touching mine when I handed him the book. Static shock, or some biological glitch.

Roundabout ahead. I take the third exit too fast, tyres screeching.

The rest of the drive takes me forty minutes, which I spend mostly on calls.

And thinking about him in the library.

'PR win,' I remind myself, pulling into the car park behind the café where I'm meeting Theo for lunch. 'This is a PR win.'

It wasn't supposed to make me question my professional detachment. But as I grab my purse and step out of the car, I can't shake the image of Brodie MacRae gently telling wide-eyed kids not to be like Gordon the goat.

Who even *is* this man?

And why, for the love of god, can't I stop thinking about his thighs and hands and arms?

The café hums with midday chatter and Edinburgh's lunch crowd. Theo waves from a corner table, her dark ponytail swinging.

'You're late. But better late than dead,' she says and slides a flat white toward me. 'I ordered for you. You look like you've had a morning. Sit. Caffeinate.'

I drop into the chair and dump my handbag on the floor.

Her blue eyes glint over her cup. 'MacRae's reel is already at ten thousand views.' She spins her phone toward me, showing Brodie with children clinging_to him like baby monkeys. 'Comments are ninety per cent thirst, ten per cent mums asking if he does birthday parties. The rest is filtered by keywords.'

I snatch up my coffee. 'Perfect. Exactly what we wanted.'

'What's perfect is your face right now.' Theo's freckled nose crinkles as she smiles. 'You look like you just saw a big surly bear cuddling a baby bunny.'

I rake my fork through a kale Caesar salad. 'Stop grinning.'

Theo licks hollandaise off her thumb. 'You're the one who sent me that video. A man built like a Norse god of war doing puppet voices. I nearly spat oat milk all over my laptop.'

'Children respond to animated storytelling. It's basic psychology.'

'And their mums respond to biceps the size of their babies' heads. Did you see the one in the lilac cardigan? Looked ready to climb him like a—'

'Stop it right there.' My phone clatters onto the reclaimed wood table. 'This is about damage control.'

Theo's straw slurps loudly through her iced matcha. 'You're blushing.'

'I'm overheating. They crank the radiators in here like we're in Greenland. It's August. What kind of arsehole needs a radiator in August?'

'It was a bit nippy this morning. Tell me again how he did the bunny voice.'

I shred a piece of chicken. 'It's irrelevant. What matters is the result.'

She leans in. 'You're rattled.'

'Drop it, Theo.'

The clatter of cutlery sharpens. My earlobe throbs where I tugged it during the drive.

Theo sighs, relenting. 'This new collaborative Brodie's almost likeable.'

'Please don't use that tone. He's not a rescue dog. He's a client.'

'Who you stare at like he's a leaking dam you're hell-bent on fixing.'

My knife scrapes across the plate. 'I fix things. It's part of my job. *Our* job.'

Theo's smile fades. After a moment, she says, 'From what I can tell, Callum would've rather gargled bleach than read to kids.'

The name drops between us like a lead weight. Theo presses further, gentle in a way that doesn't send me running. 'He'd probably have called it beneath him, am I right?'

'Callum only did charity events if there was a TV camera in his face. No big cameras, no big show, no Callum. Brodie's…a different breed.'

'Better breed? How do they compare?'

'One's a difficult client. One's a cheating bastard. There's no comparison.'

Theo's foot hooks around my ankle beneath the table. 'You chose Brodie as a client for a reason.'

'I didn't *choose* him. His contract got absorbed when I bought—'

'Yes, but you fought for him. Upgraded his PR package, redesigned his—'

'Because his potential has been squandered!' I realise I'm almost shouting, so I lower my voice. 'Callum is good, but Brodie? He's a once-in-a-generation athlete. Gifted. Obsessive. Hungry. The way he dissects game footage, you'd think he's prepping for—'

Theo's grin cuts me off. 'You're really behind him. No, you're *impressed*.'

'It's professional appreciation for our biggest asset.'

'Keep telling yourself that.'

I kick her under the table. 'Are you my assistant or my tormentor?'

'Can't I be both?'

I grunt noncommittally.

'Was it always that bad? With Callum?' she asks.

I set down my fork. 'Not at first. In the beginning, he was...' I search for the right word. 'Nice? Perhaps even dazzling?'

'They usually are.' Theo's mouth twists, and a shadow crosses her face. 'The worst ones shine brightest at the start. Then they crash and burn.'

'I met Callum when my dad took him on and I had finished uni, working at Harrington's as a junior publicist. Callum wooed me for over a year before I gave in. He'd fly down to London just to take me to dinner. Send flowers to the office.' I trace condensation on my water glass. 'Made me feel like the centre of his universe.'

'When did it change?'

The café's exposed bulbs cast shadows across the table. Outside, rain streaks the windows in silver rivulets.

'That's the thing. It never really did in our two years together. Until I walked in on him with his trousers round his ankles and his dick inside another woman.'

Theo reaches across, squeezing my wrist. A pulse jumps in my throat. Too much. I shake her off, reaching for my coffee.

'What a narcissistic tosser,' she declares.

'A tosser my father still represents.' The bitterness tastes metallic. 'Dad called it "a personal indiscretion that shouldn't affect our business or your future".'

'Your dad said that? After Callum *cheated* on you?'

'Which he did multiple times, as it turned out. With multiple women.' My voice stays flat. 'One was a sponsor's daughter. Another was a waitress at his favourite pub. The last one – the one I caught him with – was a TV presenter.'

Theo lets out a long exhale. 'That's low. Even for a guy like Callum.'

'And the worst part? When I confronted him, he wasn't even sorry. He said... '"What did you expect? You're never here. I felt neglected. Your job's more important to you than I am." The irony being that *he was* my job, and I had just secured a new sponsor for him. I was devastated.'

Theo's eyes widen. 'Bastard indeed. I hate that he made you feel like that.'

'Dad said I should've been more understanding of the "pressures" Callum was under.' The memory still burns. 'That's when I quit. Moved here and started Elite Edge.'

'And now you represent Callum's biggest rival.' Theo grins. 'That's some delicious karma.'

'I didn't do it on purpose, but yes. Brodie despises Callum even more than I do.' My lips quirk. 'Might be the only thing I really like about him.'

'The only thing?' She arches an eyebrow. 'You sure about that?'

'Don't start.'

'I'm just saying…' She finishes the last of her iced drink with an ear-splitting noise. 'The way you described his arms in your voice message—'

'Shut up, Theo.'

She smiles, and my chest goes soft around it. 'You're not used to having friends who call you on your shite, are you?'

The word 'friends' catches me off guard. It doesn't quite fit. Not with me. When was the last time I made an actual friend? Not a colleague, not a client, not someone who wanted something from me? Never. For a second, something tightens behind my ribs, like a muscle cramp I can't stretch out.

'I don't have time for friends,' I mutter.

'Too late.' She taps my hand with her fork. 'You're stuck with me. At work and otherwise.'

'Lucky me.' But I know she's right, and I'm smiling, and we both know I mean it.

'So.' Theo leans forward, eyes dancing. 'About those forearms…'

I throw a napkin at her face.

My phone vibrates against the café table, and Hannah's grinning face lights up the screen.

'Hey Button! You're early.'

'Charlie! Hello! Hi!' Hannah's words tumble out in a breathless rush, consonants softened by the gap in her front teeth. 'Miss Lorna says I'm ready for the big casting! I'm singing Beyoncé. The one with the…the…'

'*Halo?*' But I'm teasing her. Of course, I know the song my baby sister's going to perform at her school's Christmas show. Three and a half months away, and I'm almost as excited as her.

'No! The cowboy one. About Texas.'

'*Texas Hold 'Em.*' I bring the phone closer, drowning out the café clatter. Hannah's been a Beyoncé fan since she was a toddler. 'You'll slay, Button.'

'But Daddy says it's too hard. I should pick easier songs.' Her voice dips, and I see her twisting the hem of her sequinned jumper. 'He says don't get your hopes up.'

Theo's watching me, fork suspended over her eggs benny.

I turn my back to the room. 'Daddy's a pillock. Remember what we practised?'

A giggle bursts through the speaker. 'Harringtons don't do easy. We win! Daddy is being silly.'

She handles Dad's mood swings better than I ever could. Makes him laugh when I'd just argue.

'Damn right, Button. Now send me the track.'

Through the phone speakers, Hannah's voice wobbles on the first verse but gains strength by the chorus. A sting lodges just below my collarbone, so sharp it makes me swallow twice. She's improved since January, vowels rounding, pitch steadier than my heartbeat.

Theo mouths '*holy shit*' behind her napkin.

'You're smashing it, Han. Just ease off the vibrato a little.'

'The what?'

'The wobbly bits.'

'Oh! The shaky-shakes. Miss Lorna says that's my style.'

'Your style's brilliant.'

She hums, considering. 'Okay. But Charlie?'

'Yeah, Button?'

'Will you come? Even if I'm not perfect.'

Rain blurs the café windows. I still see Dad's face when the doctor placed Hannah in his arms. *She'll need extra help. She's never going to live her own life. Best to adjust expectations early.*

I was ten when she was born, but I remember it so vividly. And I remember how it hurt me hearing him speak about his own daughter like that. My beautiful little sister with so much fire and sass, a great sense of humour, ambition, kindness, and also an extra chromosome.

There's so, so much more to her than that.

Maybe he thought he was being pragmatic, attempting to shield himself from disappointment. Maybe he thought if he braced himself for the worst, it wouldn't hurt so much. Or maybe it was just his way of taking charge, like everything else in his life – putting plans in place, risk management. He's still like that, talks about 'sensible options' for Hannah's future. By which he means care homes and residential support. And I know it comes from a place of love – but of fear, too. He wants her to be safe. To have someone to look after her when he's gone. But his love is a cage, built from good intentions and low expectations for her. And far too high ones for me.

Pillock, as I said.

'Button. Look at me.'

A beat. 'I'm looking.'

'You're already perfect to me. Everything else is just...sparkles.'

'I love sparkles!' Hannah's breath hitches. 'So, you're coming?'

'Yes! Of course. Front row.'

'And when I sing it on TV one day, you'll be watching, right?'

'Every damn minute. Now go drill that bridge. You're a star, baby sis. Love you so much.'

'Love you infinity-squillion.'

The line dies. I stare at my reflection in the dark screen – smudged mascara, cheeks blotchy.

Theo clears her throat. 'She's quite good.'

'Of course. She's a Harrington.' I check myself in my phone camera, swiping under my eyes. 'We're made to excel.'

Theo's smile falters. 'Your dad really said that to her? About the song?'

I stab a rogue crouton. 'He's an arsehole with a spreadsheet where his soul should be.'

I'm gripping the fork like a battle axe. Theo nods, wise enough to let it drop. Outside, the rain slows to a drizzle. I text Hannah's music teacher three times before the bill comes.

The café door jingles shut behind us as Theo and I make our way back to the office. Edinburgh's grey damp wets my cheeks. I check the time, flicking through emails on my phone.

Work. Focus. Excel. That's what I'm here for.

Brodie MacRae is a job. My ovaries are not allowed to weigh in.

The Rebels' fixture list burns behind my eyelids. Three weeks until their first game. Three weeks until Brodie either becomes Stirling's star or confirms every critic's sneer that he's washed up.

Three weeks for me to step up my game and put him in everyone's good graces. And perhaps a smidge out of mine.

Chapter 7

Brodie

We just fucked that session. Turned it into a shite fart. No class to it at all. Yesterday was grand, but we're inconsistent. And we can't afford that.

Finn – Scotland's most annoying flanker – shoves his kit bag into his cubby hard enough to rattle the bench. James stares at the floor, silent as a corpse. My kit reeks of sweat, mud, and failure, clinging to my skin like a second layer of shame.

Finn pulls his shirt off and leans back against the wall. His pink hair sticks up in damp tufts, sweat turning the tips neon. Tattoos crawl down his arms and over his ribs. Mismatched ink and bad decisions. He tears into a protein bar with his teeth. 'Well, that was a clusterfuck.'

'Aye,' Scottie mutters beside him, throwing his boots into his bag with the heavy sigh of a man who knows he's too strong for his own good. Built like a monster. Thick shoulders. Wide chest. I've seen him squatting 240, two times his weight. Sweat drips from his furrowed brow onto the bench. But even now he looks too nice for this shamble of a team. 'Under-twelves could've skinned us.'

'Aye, but whose fault's that?' Finn's stare burns into my shoulder.

I shuck my shirt off, the fabric catching on my ears. 'I know there's lots of pressure, but we must be more precise. You lot are playing like you've never held a ball. How's that my fault?'

Finn steps closer. His breath smells like cheap energy gels. 'Maybe if you didn't hold the ball like it's your baby, we'd get somewhere.'

The room freezes. Scottie stops packing. James lifts his head. My knuckles ache, tendons tight as bowstrings.

'Pass earlier?' I grunt. 'You couldn't even catch a cold in February, Lennox. How did you learn to play rugby – by wrestling sheep?'

'Enough!' James slams his hand against the side of the cubbies. The sharp thud silences everything. 'Stop acting like twats. We're bad because we're not a team. Grow up.' He snatches his towel, turns around, and walks out. The door slams behind him.

His outburst leaves the room tense and quiet.

Finn spits in the sink. 'Now that's an exit. Who knew stoic Jamie had so much drama in him?'

Scottie zips his bag and laughs. Even I feel it tug at my mouth.

It's getting closer to game day. The pressure's on. People are losing their shite with each other. Rugby requires an aggressive mindset. It's primal, bone to bone. Of course, it boils over sometimes.

I'm doing everything I can, grafting my arse off to find my best form, to get us going. It's frustrating. I'm getting pissed off with myself. Before that scandal, I had an edge to me. I need to get that back to win the physical battle. Otherwise, what the hell am I doing here?

I wipe sweat from my face. 'James is not wrong. We have to get it together.'

Scottie's face drops like I've just sprouted wings. 'Stop the press. MacRae admits fault? That's a first.'

'Shut up.'

'No, seriously.' Scottie slaps a hand to his chest. 'Have to mark this day on my calendar and print it on a T-shirt.'

'The apocalypse is coming,' Finn agrees.

I try ignoring them. They're both twenty-three, little more than boys. But Scottie keeps staring at me, his head tilted like a confused puppy.

'What?' I bite out.

'You almost smiled, pal.' Scottie points at my face. 'Right there. I saw it.'

'I did *not*. You're delusional.'

'You did! For a second, you weren't scowling like an angry troll.'

Finn barks out a laugh. 'Careful, Scottie. You'll scare it away.'

'Piss off, both of you.'

Finn tugs off his boots, grinning as he tosses one into his kit bag. 'You know, I've been thinking about this new softer side of our captain. First, that cooking show—'

'We are not talking about that.'

'Oh, but we are.' Finn's grin widens. 'Ailsa's Kitchen! With special guest Brodie MacRae, who's going to show us how to make…what was it again? Beans on toast?'

'Spaghetti,' Scottie supplies helpfully.

Shame pricks the back of my neck like a swarm of midges. 'My agent made me do it.'

'Aye, that blonde one's got you leashed good.' Finn winks. 'How she waltzed onto the pitch and put you in your place. Fucking beautiful, big man.'

I chuck my sweaty shirt at his head. He catches it one-handed, still smirking, and tosses it into the laundry bin. 'You try to act like a block of ice, MacRae, but even I can see it.'

'See what?' I ask. 'My fist coming towards your face?'

Scottie snorts. 'You ever thought of not looking at her like you wanna fight her or shag her?'

The words hit like a boot to the ribs. I scrub my towel over my face to hide whatever the fuck my expression's doing. 'Leave it, or I'll rearrange your pretty features.'

Finn slaps my shoulder, laughing. 'Aye, you're done for, mate. It's only a matter of time.'

'Hear that suspicious silence?' Scottie's voice drips with mock awe. 'He's not denying it.'

Finn sprawls on the bench, legs stretched out. There's something else in his tone this time. 'Naw, but for real, pal. You're different. Less of a raging cunt. It's a bit unsettling, to be honest.'

I flip them both off, knuckles white around the fabric. 'Fuck. Off.'

Finn mimics a swoon, clutching his chest. 'Careful, lads. Our captain's got feelings.'

I shove past him towards the showers. 'I'll show you feelings when I boot your arse into next week.'

Their guffaws follow me.

The shower spray pounds against my shoulders, hot enough to scald. Steam rises thick, clouding my vision until the world narrows to just water and white tile and the thoughts I can't outrun.

The usual post-training ritual – scrub away the sweat, the mistakes, the fucking noise. But today? It's not working.

Muscles strain. Not from the drills. From the itch. That clawing need to prove, to dominate, to make every fucker in a ten-mile radius bend.

Memories surface through the steam. My dad drilling passes in the back garden. My brothers tackling me into mud. Always competing. Always fighting to prove myself worthy. Dad's voice rattles through me, clear as yesterday. *'If you're not first, you're last.'*

The shower can't wash away over two decades of that

mindset. I tilt my head back, let water fill my mouth, spit it down the drain. Tastes like rust and regret. It's not healthy, going 'round being angry at everyone. I know that. Knowing doesn't make it easier to change. But something's shifting. The fury that used to consume me is dulling to a throbbing ache. I press my palms against the tile, letting hot water sluice down my spine.

Finn's laughter still rings in my ears. Scottie's shite-eating grin. James's outburst. All of it burrows under my skin. The lads were taking the piss, sure. But they weren't wrong about everything being inconsistent. We're all new here. All finding our feet. That granite-faced arse James had a point. We're not a proper team yet. Just individual players colliding, trying to out-muscle each other, waiting for someone else to make the first move towards trust. Admitting it feels like chewing on glass.

The team's struggling, but we're learning. You have to go through pain sometimes to get where you want to be.

Rugby is a team game.

It's gonna take shiteloads of effort, edge, and physicality. And even more shiteloads of trust.

Whatever our potential is, we can keep stretching that.

The water pressure drops as someone else starts their shower. Finn's voice carries over the hiss, singing some awful pop song. Scottie joins in, deliberately off-key. Their laughter bounces off the walls.

A month ago, I'd have told them to shut it. Now? The corner of my mouth tugs upward.

Their words echo in my skull. Not their teasing. The other bit.

About Charlie.

Her face flashes behind my closed eyes. The way she marched onto that pitch. She's fierce. Doesn't take my shite, just flips it back at me with interest.

We've worked together for almost a month now. And one

thing I've learned: she's not some annoying PR lady pushing her agenda, holding my hand through image rehabilitation. If I didn't know any better, I'd even say she's seriously invested in my career.

Still have to figure out how she was involved in the whole leaking lies to the press thing, though. Makes less sense every day.

I rake my hands through wet hair, steam rising around me. My back hurts, but not just from training. Carrying anger around this long has worn me down to the bone.

I don't think I hate her guts anymore. Not as much.

Water runs cold. I stay under it, letting the chill shock my system. But it doesn't clear my head the way it usually does. And it doesn't stop me picturing the way her eyes gleam when she's challenging me. How her voice dips low when she's proving a point. The curve of her mouth when she's about to demolish my defences. Worst of all, the sway of her hips when she walks away. Like she knows I'd watch. Knows I'd want to. Knows I have, every single time.

'Oi!' Finn's voice punches through my thoughts, and thank fuck for that. Last thing I need is a raging boner in the team shower. 'You drowning in there, Cap?'

I slam the tap off. 'Mind your own business, Lennox.' But there's no bite to it. And that's new too.

I drip onto the tiles. That's the thing, isn't it? No one wins alone. Not in this sport. Not in this team. We have to bleed together.

I haven't felt this…awake since before the scandal. Since before I started with the Rebels. Since before I forgot what it's like to want something beyond the next win. Despite the crap session, despite everything, I feel…almost hopeful.

I put on fresh clothes. Joggers, black tee, trainers. Same as always. Then I fish my phone out of my bag. Two missed calls and one text from Charlie.

(CHARLIE 18:12) Giddy up, cowboy. We're going on a road trip.

Jesus. Suffering. Fuck.

Chapter 8

Charlie

The ferry engine thrums through my soles as I grip the rust-speckled railing. A fine drizzle mists the deck and seeps through my Burberry trench. The sea churns slate-grey, same as the sky. Early September and Scotland is already showing its autumn colours.

Brodie leans against the starboard side, arms crossed over his Rebels training jacket. Rain clings to his ridiculously long lashes.

'You must be aware this is pure shite.' His voice carries over the wind.

I shrug, watching a cormorant dive into the foam. 'Management wants you playing nice with whisky folks and rich tossers. Consider it an extension of your captaincy duties.'

'Captaincy duties don't include prancing around with crystal glasses while my team drills set pieces without me.'

God, the drama. He's missing a strength block, a skills drill, one tactical, and a match sim. Survivable. Otherwise, Wallace wouldn't have let him go.

The ferry lurches, and my hip bumps into the railing. His hand shoots out, palm catching my elbow. I jolt away, but the heat lingers.

'They'll manage three and a half days without your divine guidance,' I say. 'Might even enjoy the break from your charming leadership.'

He steps closer, rainwater tracing the scar bisecting his left eyebrow. 'And you? Are you enjoying this?'

'Watching you sulk like a toddler denied a biscuit? Immensely.'

His harsh laugh is swallowed by the wind. 'You're shitting yourself that I'll tank your precious PR circus tonight.'

'Maybe,' I admit and turn into the gale, letting it whip salt spray against my burning cheeks.

The ferry slices through the Sound of Islay, the island's pelt of heather and pine emerging through the mist. It's a bit savage here. Beautiful in a way that claws at your ribs.

The ferry dips, and our shoulders brush. Neither of us moves away.

'I'll behave.' He turns those peat-dark browns on me. 'But only because you asked so nicely.'

'I didn't ask,' I say.

'Exactly.'

'Dal Riata's master distiller is a former Scotland prop player. Show him respect and schmooze a little, and he'll have every whisky connoisseur in Argyll funding your comeback.'

'And if I don't?' The challenge in his voice skims down the nape of my neck.

'Then I'll have to find creative ways to motivate you.'

'Like what? Threaten to leak another false betting story?' His mouth edges upward. Not a real smile. More like he's baiting me to deny it.

He knows I can take it. That I'll hit right back and he'll love every second of it.

Something about the rough, stubbled line of his jaw catching the light just enough to highlight how chiselled it is, about the stubborn tilt of his angular chin, makes my belly pull tight, heat curling between my legs.

For one reckless second, I want to lick the rain from his throat.

'You're paranoid, MacRae. Not everything's a conspiracy.'

The ferry horn blares, signalling Port Askaig. I shift back, pulse rabbiting against my collarbone. The deck judders as we dock.

Brodie shoulders his duffel, nodding toward the waiting cars. 'Coming, agent?'

His broad shoulders part the misty drizzle as he walks ahead. I press my fingers to my lips, tasting salt and dangerous, dangerous wanting. Impossible, out-of-the-question, vagina-flooding, career-killing wanting.

His BMW's heated seats are a luxury. I sink into leather, knees skimming the gearstick as Brodie takes a corner a smidge too fast. My Maserati would've handled this single-track road like a queen.

But he insisted on driving and taking his car, so…

For once, he's not filling the silence with complaints. I should be grateful, but it makes me wonder what's eating at him.

Peat bogs streak past, rain sluicing over windscreen wipers stuck on intermittent. The hotel appears ahead – a whitewashed inn with slate roofs and squat dormer windows.

Brodie parallel parks with maddening precision, tyres kissing the kerb. Not that I'd ever tell him that he out-parks me. He kills the engine as I step out into the Hebridean air, crisp despite the last trace of summer warmth in the September grey.

'It's atmospheric.' I grab my Rimowa suitcase from the boot, wheels sticking in gravel. 'Authentic.'

He swings his duffel over one shoulder. 'Authentically mouldy.'

'You're hopeless. Okay, bags, then venue. Unless you have to style your hair for an hour first, MacRae.'

'Unlike some, I can dress in under ten minutes. I'm not high maintenance.'

'Because you're no maintenance.'

The reception smells of wet Labrador. My heels sink into thick carpet as I walk in behind him. A large antique mirror reflects us side by side – him towering and broad-shouldered, me compact but commanding in grey and navy.

I catch the way he looks at me in the glass. And for one breath – one charged, electric second – it's there. A glint of something raw, something dark, something that *burns*. Hunger caged behind smouldering brown eyes, teeth bared against its leash. As if he didn't expect to want. As if it hit him low, fast, and mean – right in the gut – and he'd rather bleed than admit it.

And I'd rather choke on my own damn pride than admit that I feel it too.

The receptionist glances up from her computer and smiles. 'Evening and welcome to Islay. I hope the crossing wasn't too rough. You're in rooms 204 and 207.'

The key jingles on a tartan fob. Brodie hefts his bag and my suitcase with insulting ease.

Show-off.

There's no lift, so we have to squeeze through a tiny, narrow, and steep Victorian staircase to the second floor.

'Still think authenticity's worth it?' he asks.

'Still think complaining's a personality? Now shut up, get ready, and let's go save your career.'

The amber glow of Dal Riata's copper stills bathes the tasting room in liquid warmth. A hint of peat smoke and yeast hangs in the air, settling into wool jackets and polished wood panelling. Outside, rain lashes against leaded windows, but inside it's all crackling hearths and the velvet burn of single malt.

I perch on a leather armchair at the edge of the small semicircle, watching Brodie handle himself with surprising calm and grace. He slouches comfortably in the central armchair, one ankle hooked over his knee, tumbler balanced on his broad thigh. He looks almost relaxed in dark jeans and a white shirt that stretches across his shoulders.

Because there's simply no other way for a shirt to be on this body than stretched.

I cross my legs, silk stockings whispering. Brodie's forearm rests against the chair's wing, veins mapping tension down to his fist.

'The transition from Glasgow to Stirling wasn't what I expected,' he admits. His voice carries through the intimate space where thirty or so whisky enthusiasts and potential sponsors lean forward in their seats. 'But sometimes the path you didn't choose turns out to be exactly where you have to be.'

The master distiller – a burly ex-prop with hands like shovels – nods. 'Second chances are like good whisky,' he says. 'Takes time, patience, and the right conditions to mature.'

A ripple of knowing chortles flows through the room. These are wealthy, cultured snobs who love nothing more than a redemption story they can attach their brand to. And Brodie's giving them what they want. Humility wrapped in quiet confidence, vulnerability without weakness.

I take a sip of the eighteen-year single malt, letting it scorch a path down my tongue. Pride blooms in my chest. He's nailing this. Absolutely fucking nailing it.

'What about discipline?' The question cuts through the comfortable atmosphere. My gaze cuts to a middle-aged man in the third row. Expensive watch, cheaper suit, old school notebook in hand. 'Do you think your…extracurricular activities showed a lack of discipline that might affect your captaincy?'

I recognise him. Oliver Pembroke. *The Scottish Sentinel*'s sports columnist with a hard-on for taking down athletes he deems 'unworthy'. I've tangled with him before. Never ends well for anyone.

Brodie's shoulders lift almost imperceptibly, but his voice remains steady. 'Fair question. I've always been disciplined on the pitch. Off it, I made a few choices I regret.'

'Choices?' Pembroke's smile is a shark's. 'Gambling debts exceeding a hundred thousand pounds isn't a choice, it's a pathology. Wouldn't you agree?'

The room temperature drops ten degrees. I straighten and tighten my fingers around my glass.

Brodie's jaw works. 'I played poker. Competitively. But as I've said many times before, I never bet on rugby.'

'But surely, you understand how it *looks*?' Pembroke leans forward, eyes gleaming with predatory interest. 'A professional athlete with a gambling problem—'

'I don't have a gambling problem.' The first crack in Brodie's composure. A hairline fracture in the careful veneer.

'Six figures suggests otherwise. Were you addicted, Mr MacRae? Are you still?'

The master distiller shifts uncomfortably. A sponsor from Edinburgh whispers to his companion. This is spiralling.

'No bets.' Brodie says, voice tight.

I taste copper and realise I've bitten through my lip.

'And your temper? The incident with the reporter in Glasgow – was that also a lapse in discipline?'

Brodie scratches his nose. 'The reporter in question made comments about my family that—'

'So, provocation justifies violence? Interesting philosophy for a team captain.'

That's it. I rise, glass clinking as I set it on the side table.

'Mr Pembroke, fascinating line of questioning. Reminds

me of your piece on women's football last month. Equally nuanced and not at all full of ill-informed contempt.'

Pembroke's head swivels toward me. 'Miss Harrington. Didn't realise you were moderating tonight. Does your father know you're here?'

'Does your wife?' I smile. 'I'm sure she worries. It can't be easy, you attending a whisky event after you've spoken so openly about your recovery.'

His face drains of colour.

See, that's the perk of preparing yourself. I'm a Harrington. I was bred to excel, to win. But I'm also a young woman and older guys never take me seriously, so of course I do my fucking homework. Research. Basic due diligence.

When they go low, I'm not going high. I'm already down there, waiting for them with my fists out.

I step into the circle, positioning myself between Brodie and the journalist. 'Since we're discussing integrity, let's talk about yours. Your editor might be interested in how you're pursuing a vendetta against a player who refused to give you an exclusive last year.'

His face flushes. 'That's absurd.'

'Is it?' I smile again. 'Because I've read the email chain, and it's petty.'

A murmur ripples through the audience. Pembroke's mouth opens, then closes. Brodie pins me with that dark, shuttered stare. I can't tell if he's about to thank me or rip me a new one for stepping in. I'd take either.

I'm doing it because it's my job. Or because I can't stand watching vultures pick him apart like he's too broken to be worth anything.

That's far from the truth.

I turn to the room, voice warming again. 'Now, I believe we were discussing resilience and second chances? Mr Campbell, as someone who's rebuilt after injury, what advice would you give to athletes facing setbacks?'

The master distiller seizes the lifeline gratefully, launching into a story about his career-ending knee injury. I catch Brodie's eye, and the corner of his mouth lifts. Not quite a smile, but close.

Pembroke slumps back, defeated. I remain standing, a guard in stilettos, letting him know I'm ready for round two if he so much as coughs in the wrong direction.

The conversation flows back to safer waters. Ten minutes later, when the formal portion ends and guests mingle with glasses refilled, I feel Brodie's hand on my lower back.

'You didn't need to do that,' he says, his breath warm and private against my ear.

I turn, finding his face closer than expected. 'Yes, I did. He was being a prick.'

'I could've handled it.'

'By knocking his teeth out? Because your right hand was locked into a fist so tight I thought you'd crush that poor tumbler.' I keep my voice light, but my heartbeat pounds loud enough to feel it in my teeth.

He narrows his eyes. 'You researched that twat?'

'I research everyone who might be a threat to my clients.'

'Including me?' There's no distance in the way he looks at me. No armour.

'Especially to you.'

'What you said back there,' he continues after a moment. 'About Pembroke. Was it true?'

'Every word. He's had it out for you since you told him to piss off last season.'

'I'd forgotten about that,' Brodie says.

'Well, he hadn't. I keep files on problematic journalists.'

'Ruthless.' His breath gusts hot against my nape.

'Prepared. My job is protecting you, even from yourself.'

The pause after is heavy. When he speaks again, it lands lower, tighter. I look up. His eyes are darker than I've ever seen them, almost black.

'Is that what you were doing in there? Protecting me?'

'Yes,' I say simply.

'Why?'

'Because you're my client.'

His nostrils pinch, and I see it. The second he realises he's let too much slip.

'If you say so.' He's deflecting. But his short laugh rolls right through me. 'You're terrifying.'

'You're welcome. Now let's make our excuses and get out of here. I'm famished.'

Brodie follows me as I navigate through the crowd, making polite farewells. The master distiller presses a bottle into Brodie's hands. 'For standing your ground, lad.'

And then we slip out into the rain-soaked night.

The hotel pub's low ceiling presses down like a sodden cloud, peat smoke clinging to my silk blouse. I root through my purse for lip balm, fingers touching something cold. Dad's platinum Amex winks beneath a tampon wrapper. Forgotten relic from a life I torched.

Brodie slouches in the corner booth, long legs invading my space. His knee bumps mine, and he doesn't move it. 'Pub grub's on me. No need to flash your plastic.'

'Don't flatter yourself.' The card's embossed edges bite my palm. Not so much a safety net as a reminder, a fuck-you to a father who never expected me to make it on my own.

I spin it between my fingers. 'Let's use it for liquid therapy. And you're paying me back in humility.'

'Season starts in two weeks,' he says. 'Not getting pished now.'

I ignore him and flag down the waiter. 'Two of your most inventive cocktails. Local ingredients only. Surprise us.'

Brodie's eyebrow arcs. 'Inventive?'

'Competitive inventive. Loser covers breakfast.'

He leans forward, elbows denting beer-stained coasters. 'Define lose.'

'Whoever taps out first, can't finish their drink, or pukes, loses.'

'Christ, you're mental.' But he's smiling now, that rare crinkle-eyed grin that has my pulse stuttering like it's deciding whether to speed up or stop altogether.

'Shitting your knickers, MacRae?'

'Never. But first, tell me why'd you really keep that Amex?'

Air evacuates my lungs. The truth claws its way up. 'To prove I don't need it.'

He just nods. I know he gets it.

The first round arrives in clay mugs frothing with sea buckthorn foam.

Brodie sniffs his. 'Smells like my Scottish gran's cough syrup.' He watches me, fingers drumming against his glass. He hasn't tried it yet. 'You really want this, don't you?' His voice is quiet and a bit rougher than before.

I shrug. 'I want to win.'

'Aye, but—' He exhales hard through his nose, shakes his head. 'Och, fuck it.'

He clocks my grip on the drink, then meets my eyes. That look. The one that makes my stomach tighten, like the moment before you dive into deep water.

Then he lifts his drink, never breaking eye contact, and knocks it back in a few gulps.

'That's what I thought.' I sit back and sip mine.

Heat slides down my spine. Because now he's watching me like a problem he *wants* to have.

'You're a bad, bad influence, Harrington,' he murmurs, voice sandpapered at the edges.

'You say that like it's a bad thing.' I clink my mug against his, brine and citrus bursting on my tongue. 'The taste of victory.'

He takes another swig and swallows hard. 'Tastes like arse.'

And I laugh so hard that the liquid spurts out of my nose.

Round two: heather-infused gin with pickled elderflower garnish. Brodie licks salt from his wrist before shooting it. A droplet escapes, gliding down his stubbled neck. My fingertips burn with the treasonous urge to chase it.

'Not bad. I've had worse at stag dos.'

'Liar.' My own words slur ever so slightly. 'You're two drinks from singing karaoke.'

'Three.' He corrects, stealing my lemon twist. 'Minimum.'

By round three – a peat-smoked old fashioned – the room tilts pleasantly. Brodie's laugh sounds deeper, hand accidentally-on-purpose grazing mine when reaching for napkins.

'Cheating.' I stab a cherry with a cocktail stick. 'Distracting me with...' My gesture encompasses his shoulders, his mouth, the way his shirt strains at the biceps.

'With what?' He pops his cherry in his mouth, tongue swiping syrup from his lower lip. 'My natural charm?'

'With your inability to follow rules.' The card slaps the table. 'Barkeep! Your most lethal concoction. Extra fire.'

Brodie grabs my wrist. His hand is as rough as the island's coastline, and his thumb presses my pulse point. 'You're gonna regret this.'

'Already do.'

The final round arrives flaming. Literally. Blue fire licks the brims of twin copper mugs.

Brodie eyes his like it's a live grenade. 'What's in this? Jet fuel?'

'Drink or forfeit.' I blow out my flame, liquid scorching a trail to my stomach.

He hesitates. Swears under his breath. Tips the mug back. Firelight dances across his throat as he swallows. Slams the mug down. Grins, wild and unchained. 'Still in the game, Harrington.'

So am I. Barely.

'You're lucky your beard isn't on fire, MacRae.'

He's looking at me like I'm an opponent he's trying to figure out, unable to decide whether to let me win or drag me down with him. But that wild grin stays in place. He's not letting up.

And hell, I'm just getting started.

Chapter 9

Brodie

Charlie Harrington sings like she does everything else. As if she's got nothing to lose and a world full of bastards to prove wrong.

She's up on that tiny, sticky-floored stage of the hotel pub, gripping the mic like she's daring it to break. Her eyes are half-lidded as she sings *Livin' on a Prayer*.

And fuck me, but I can't stop looking at her.

I lean back in the booth, head tipped against cracked leather, empty glass in my hand. Tipsy but lucid. Loose, but locked in.

Because something is happening here, and there's no stopping it.

The small crowd is eating her up. Of course they are. Charlie's got that thing. That thing that makes people lean in without meaning to, makes them watch. It's not about being pretty or the best. It's about being impossible to ignore. And Charlie Harrington? Always impossible to ignore.

But *especially* when she's belting out Bon Jovi.

Barefoot, tights torn at the knee, blazer long gone, she's a fucking sight for the gods. The simple grey dress clings in all the right places, riding higher every time she jumps, the hem threatening absolute chaos. Her hair – caramel and whisky in the stage lights – has won the battle against the straightener, waves bouncing as she moves, defiant and unruly.

And then she throws her head back and pours her whole ambitious, untamed self into one note.

She's not just drop-dead gorgeous. She's everything at once. Pure temptation with boardroom fangs, a high-maintenance hurricane with a heart of gold, a brilliant menace wrapped in cashmere.

I clutch my glass.

There's something free and unguarded in her, the way she loses herself to the song. She points straight at me when the chorus hits, mischief and intent. The whole pub is screaming the words, but her voice rises over the noise. For a split second, it's just us. And I swear to god, my dick twitches like it's applauding her.

Something sharp braces between my lungs as it sinks in.

I *might* be fucked.

Charlie Harrington. Aye.

It hits me in pieces.

Starts with how she had my back tonight. No hesitation, no question. When that dickhead journalist tried to dig his claws in, she eviscerated him.

Not for PR. Not for herself.

For me.

She always challenges me. Pushes and pokes, calls me on my nonsense, stands her ground when most people fold. I don't intimidate her. I fuel her. How's that even possible?

And it's the way I feel when she's around. Comfortable and at ease. I can let my guard down without someone waiting to twist the knife.

But the worst part? The part that knots my stomach and makes my pulse hammer?

I find myself wanting to be near her, let her light chase away my clouds.

Yep, probably fucked.

Charlie hits the last note, winking at some poor sod in the front row, then stumbles off stage and laughs as someone claps her on the back. A blink later she's in front of me, flushed and high on chaos, hair messy, eyes bright.

She needs this tonight. That's why I agreed to join her.

Not for me. For her.

Charlie's dad's a cunt. Callum's always been one. Pembroke? Just the latest recruit to the cuntery club.

And because Charlie's so professional, so sharp, so fierce, it's easy to forget that she's only twenty-six. Same as me. After being screwed over by the men in her life, after weeks of dealing with my antics, and after fighting a battle that shouldn't be hers at the distillery, she deserves to let loose. To be loud, to be careless, to feel good for no other reason than that she fucking can.

'What?' she asks as she slides onto the bench opposite me, heels in hands and voice still hoarse from singing.

I tip my empty glass at her. 'Wasn't aware you had pipes.'

'I have layers, MacRae. *Layers.*'

'You did good tonight,' I say, voice low. 'You did good… with me.'

She stills, caught off guard. As if she didn't expect me to say it. Hell, maybe I didn't either. But something shifts in the air between us. That current. That charge. That buzz under my anger. The part I've been ignoring for weeks, acting like it isn't real.

She pulls back, clears her throat. 'Another round?'

'You trying to keep up with me, Harrington?'

She grins, a bit wobbly but full of fire. 'No. I'm trying to win.'

For a second, I almost let it slide. Almost let the moment stretch out without bringing up the thing that's been gnawing at the back of my mind. But she's got that look. Wide open and real. And that makes it impossible.

I can't keep acting like it doesn't matter.

If I don't ask now, it'll make it harder and harder to separate what I thought I knew from what I'm starting to see. To…like.

Aye, I need to know once and for all.

'Was it *really* not you? Leaking the gambling rumours to the media?'

Charlie doesn't freeze or yield. She just goes quiet in a way that cuts and looks at me. Flat and blank and direct.

'You *know* it wasn't me.' Her voice isn't sharp or cold. It isn't anything, and that's what hits hardest.

She runs a thumb over the condensation on her glass, watching it smear.

'I never leaked a damn thing, Brodie,' she says in that way that tells me she's beyond tired of this conversation. 'Wasn't even *aware* that you had poker debts. And yes, I'm loyal. But I don't do anyone's cheap dirty work. And certainly not Callum's. Never have, never will.'

The space between us stretches, too tight, too thin.

She inhales slowly, weighing up if it's even worth continuing. I'm glad she does.

'But you *had* to blame someone, right? And I was convenient. PR girl. Callum's fiancée, in his thrall. Easy target.'

Something tightens painfully behind my ribs.

'Me and Callum—' she huffs a laugh that isn't really a laugh, '—we made a neat package deal, didn't we?'

I swallow. They did.

'Not saying it was definitely him.' She shrugs. 'But I wouldn't be shocked. And he *was* shagging that presenter from the station that first broke the "story". Could've been a coincidence. But I doubt it. Well, I'll guess we'll never find out.'

I'm an absolute eejit. I let this sit in my chest for months. Let it fester. Let it turn into something that coloured the way I saw her. Part of me still doesn't want to accept it – because if I do, I have to admit I've been wrong this entire time. But the more I look at her, the better I get to know her, the harder it is to hold on to my version of events.

She says she never even knew about the fucking poker debts. I want to believe her. More than I should. And if she's lying, she's doing a damn good job of it.

So no, I don't think she was involved.

I misjudged her. I put her in the same box as Callum, and I should have known. Should have seen her the way I'm seeing her now. Exhausted from having to defend herself, fight for herself, looking at me like she's tired of caring whether I believe her or not.

And that makes me feel worse than anything. I'm not exactly generous with apologies. But even I know when one's due.

'I'm sorry, Charlie. Truly. You've always been better than Fraser. Always been too good for him.'

Her shoulders drop, and the tension that's been locked in her spine unwinds. She watches me for a beat. Then she knocks twice on the table, like we've settled a deal.

'Now that's out of the way,' she says. 'Go get us another round. I'm in the lead!'

I push up from the booth, rolling my shoulders. 'Aye, Your Highness.'

The barman's wiping down the counter, and I catch his eye. 'One gin and tonic. Heavy on the tonic. Or do you have that non-alcoholic stuff?'

He clocks the request, nods, and reaches for the zero-proof bottle tucked behind the proper stuff.

When I set the drink in front of her, Charlie barely glances at it before taking a sip, and another.

She smacks her lips and frowns. 'Ugh. That's weak.'

I lean back. 'Barman's slacking.'

She scoffs and downs the rest in one go, none the wiser. 'You're at least two drinks behind, MacRae.'

That's not true. But I let her think she's winning. And I keep her upright.

Because Charlie Harrington deserves to have someone looking out for her for a change.

Charlie stumbles, and I catch her. She's light in my arms, laughter bubbling up like it's got nowhere else to go, warm and careless. Her forehead knocks against my shoulder as she tries to straighten up.

'Woah! Steady, agent.' My palm finds the small of her back, right where the curve begins.

'Steady's boring,' she mumbles and presses her face into my shirt for half a second before peeling away, blinking up at me.

I don't think she realises how close we are. How easy it would be to dip my head, let my mouth skim the top of her ear, pull her flush against me. I fight the urge to grab her properly. Not just a hand at her elbow, a palm on her back.

I can't. I'm not an arsehole.

The dim hallway buzzes around us. The walls are damp with age, the air thick with the smell of old carpet, but all I can focus on is her. The way her body moves and leans against me, as if she trusts me not to let her fall.

I wouldn't.

She giggles again, high on whatever the fuck it is – alcohol, relief, winning, exhaustion, something else or all of it – and fumbles for her key card in her purse. It clatters to the carpet. I stoop to grab it. She sways forward, knees bumping mine.

'You're not as much of a dickhead as I thought, MacRae.' It tumbles out with a laugh, unfiltered and a touch too honest.

And hell, it hits me right in the ribs before I've got a chance to shove the feeling down.

I lean against the doorframe as she swipes the card the

wrong way up. 'That sounded like a compliment, Harrington. Don't tell me you're going soft on me.'

She half-turns and looks up at me.

Really looks.

And something in her heavy-lidded gaze slams right through me, blood rushing south so fast I'm dizzy.

I should step back.

I *should*.

But her face is right there. So close that I see where her lipstick has worn off at the edges, the ghost of it still clinging to her plush bottom lip. There's a flare of something untamed in her eyes. Fierce and fevered. Her breath stutters. Mine stalls. The air between us crackles, swollen with whatever the hell this is turning into.

And I know – I fucking *know* – what's about to happen before she even moves.

I don't stop her.

Charlie fists the front of my shirt and kisses me.

Not tentative. Not testing. Full fucking tilt.

I make a sound I don't recognise, something raw. Because Christ… She's on me like she's been dying to do this as badly as I have.

And I have it bad for her.

She twists her fingers in the fabric and yanks me closer. Not bossy – needy. Her mouth is hot, parted, eager, and when her tongue brushes mine, something inside me breaks. Another low, guttural sound rips out. Me or her? Don't know. Don't care.

I dig my fingers into her hips, and I feel it. Her gasp, the way her body tenses and yields in the same sharp second. I'm already so hard it's painful. My balls are drawn up tight, heavy with that aching build of pressure that's only got one way out.

She tastes like salt and gin, but it's the fire of her that's got me fucking gone. Her mouth's soft and open, head angling just right. She's rising onto her toes, pressing in hard, closing every last inch between us. Like she knows exactly how hard I am for her.

Like she *needs* to feel it.

I drag my hands down from her waist, greedy for the shape of her thighs, the burn where her dress has hitched up. My grip tightens as I haul her into me, back bumping the door with a muffled thud – and that sigh… That fucking sigh. It strikes down my spine like a match.

I need more. More Charlie. I deepen the kiss and swallow the sounds she makes when I take what she's giving.

Goddammit.

I've kissed a lot of women.

But never like this.

Never like her.

Blood pounds thick and insistent. If I don't stop this, if I don't stop her, I'll end up dry-humping her like some desperate fucker who can't control himself. Could already be happening – because she tilts her hips against mine and a white-hot rush lances straight through me.

'Yes, Brodie. Yes, yes!' she hitches out between kisses.

I groan into her mouth. Because it's not enough. The friction of her core against mine isn't enough. The grip I have on her isn't enough. Not when she's clinging to me like that, tugging my shirt, dragging me closer.

It's all fucking not enough.

I could come from this, clothes on and all. From her mouth on mine, from the way she grinds as if she owns every pulse in my cock. As if she already knows I'd let her have it. All of it. Everything.

She lets her fingers slip from my shirt and trails them down. 'Brodie. Touch me. Here…right here…'

And before I can think, before I can fucking *breathe*, she grabs my wrist and tugs my hand between her thighs.

My brain flatlines. Static. White noise.

Heat. Heat so scalding it punches the air from my lungs. My fingers skim the soft stretch of… Not tights. A lace band. Bare skin above it. Nothing underneath. And my cock jerks so hard it hurts.

'Stockings, Charlie? My fucking god.'

She shifts, pushes my palm harder against her, and fuck, fuck, fuck – she's so soaked it's insane. The damp lace has turned to nothing. Does fuck all to hide how badly she wants me. I feel everything. The frantic throb under my fingertips. The lush swell of her sex, and I can't help it, my fingers slip past the seam, once, enough to feel how…

I press. Just a little. Just to see.

A tremor pulses against my fingers. And the sound she makes? I'm a dead man.

It's not a moan, not yet. A whimper, a sharp little inhale. As if she wasn't ready for how good it felt.

And I wasn't ready for what it does to me.

No.

Fuck.

Stop.

She's still kissing me. Messy now. Open and panting. Her tongue slides against mine, nails digging into my shoulders. I'm hanging on by a thread, and if she moves – if she so much as rocks forward – I'm going to lose my fucking mind.

Every inch of me is screaming not to stop. To keep going. To push her inside, kick the door shut, bury my face in that delicious, drenched pussy and not come up for air until the sun's burning through the curtains.

But I can't. And not because she's my agent and a twisted part of me still tries to hold a grudge against her for some reason.

God help me, that woman pisses me off as much as she turns me on.

It's not just the way she tastes, the way she moves against me like she was made to fit right here.

It's her.

All of her. How she makes me mad, pulls me in. How she laughs. Fights. The fact that she's got every reason not to trust me, and yet – right now – she does.

And fuck, I want to deserve it.

I let out a shuddering exhale and rest my forehead against hers, lungs burning, chest heaving, sucking in the scent of her.

'Not like this.'

Charlie squints up at me, dazed, lips kiss-bruised.

'What?' Her voice is small. Confused. As if I told her the sky isn't blue. As if she can't wrap her head around the fact that I'm not already hauling her inside fucking her raw.

Which, by the way, I most definitely want.

'You're tipsy. I'm a bit pished.' I cup her jaw and trace her cheek with my thumb. 'And when I finally fuck you, Charlie, I want you to remember every damn second.'

The look she gives me – as if she doesn't know if she wants to kiss me again or kill me right here in the hallway – makes my stomach bottom out. My balls feel like they might rupture. I've never done this before. Never stopped when I didn't have to. Never stopped when she didn't want me to. Never put someone else before me like this.

But Charlie's not just someone, is she?

I force myself to step back, fighting for an inhale that does absolutely fuck all to contain what's breaking loose in my chest.

God, I'm dying.

'Sleep tight, agent. I'll see you tomorrow.'

I kiss the tip of her nose, and then I turn and move to my door next to hers. What the hell did we just do? My throat is burning. Not from holding back what I wanted to do, but from everything I didn't say.

I can't. Not tonight.

Because, what I didn't realise until just now: I want her too much to fuck this up.

Chapter 10

Charlie

O uch. I wake up face down, feeling like someone took a jackhammer to my skull. My mouth tastes like something died in it. My eyeballs hurt. Still fully dressed. I groan and peel my face off the pillow, barely cracking one eye open to squint at my watch. 5:45. In the morning. Jesus. Why am I awake?

And then—

Oh god.

The drinks. The karaoke.

The *kiss*.

I fucking kissed Brodie MacRae.

Not just kissed him. I *grabbed* him. Pulled his massive hand between my legs like some sex-starved lunatic. And I knew what I was doing. No doubts, no hesitation. I wanted it. Wanted *him*. The way he felt against me... Hot, solid, overwhelming. The way he touched me. As if he couldn't help himself. As if he wanted me as badly. As if he was seconds from sinking his thick fingers inside me right there against the door, from giving me exactly what I was begging for.

But he... What did he say again? My brain stutters, wading through the alcohol still sloshing around my system.

Something about me being drunk. Him being drunk. And how when he finally fucks me, he wants me to remember it.

Oh, mighty Jesus.

I roll onto my back and slap both hands over my face. My mouth feels like I've been chewing on a wool sock. Tongue is too dry, too thick. Full-body ache. I prop myself up, and everything shifts in a sickening lurch. My insides revolt. The booze, yeah – but it's not the only thing making me churn.

It's everything else.

Unprofessional. Completely, unforgivably unprofessional.

This isn't me. I'm tough, controlled, clever. I'm in charge. I don't do this. I don't make impulsive, irresponsible decisions. I don't get off my face and throw myself at clients like I'm starring in some low-budget office porn. I don't go off the rails.

Except I did.

All the above.

And if I'm really honest with myself, it was bound to happen. I had it coming. Of course, the instant I let myself loosen – just a little, just for one night – all the shit I'd been holding back came pouring out at once.

For almost five months, I've been charging through at full speed. No breaks. No processing. No time to feel anything because the minute I slowed down, it would all crash in.

As it just did.

I never took a moment to grieve the cheating. The humiliation of ending my engagement in the public eye. The betrayal by my father, who should have supported me. The sheer panic of leaving the nest. Walking away from my old life, Harrington Sports, the legacy I was meant to take over. Selling my London flat, scraping together my savings, begging and convincing investors to take a chance on me. Relocating to Edinburgh. Buying out Henderson's. Building Elite Edge from the ground up, working sixteen hours a day, seven days a week, barely sleeping, barely eating, barely functioning…

And last night, my body and brain finally called it.

So maybe I shouldn't be so shocked. This was inevitable. It doesn't make last night any less mortifying, though.

I groan again, swing my legs over the edge of the bed, and—

Trip over my own fucking shoes.

A table lamp hits the carpet with a loud thud. My ankle smacks into something hard, my arms windmilling as I try and fail not to face-plant onto the floor.

I push up onto my knees, wincing as the spike drills through my temple and pulses right in time with the pounding behind my forehead. My dress is twisted, riding up my hips, and the sheer effort of wearing it feels like too much. I mumble some half-formed curse and yank the thing off. I fumble for anything on the chair beside the bed. First thing my fingers grab is soft. I haul it on and barely register the faint, clean smell still hanging in the fabric.

All I care about is water.

I stagger to the bathroom, muttering profanities as I go. Turn the tap on. Drink straight from the faucet, swallowing down mouthful after mouthful.

And then—

Knock, knock.

'Hey. You okay?'

No. No, no, no, no.

Brodie. Right outside my room. I clamp my lids shut. If I'm very, very quiet, he might go away.

Another knock, firmer this time. 'I know you're in there, Charlie. I heard a bang. Are you okay?'

I croak and shuffle to the door, yanking it open with a miserable scowl before he can wake up the entire hotel with his baritone.

He stands there, rumpled and disgustingly well-rested, in

a plain white tee and grey joggers that shouldn't look that good. But of course, they do. Everything on him looks fabulous.

His pupils widen when he sees me. 'You know what they say?'

'Hngh?' That's all I've got. I have no words. No thoughts. No brain function.

He lifts his chin, eyes dark and amused. 'Wear the shirt, try the player.'

I blink. Slow. Wait. What?

I glance down, and a jolt fires through my chest.

Big. Loose. Hem at mid-thigh. Crisp scent clinging to it.

Oh shit.

I'm indeed wearing a rugby shirt. *His* rugby shirt.

His fucking shirt. Yeah, makes sense. I packed a bunch of signed #10 shirts for photo ops and giveaways.

'Try the player how?' I sound squeaky and scratchy.

His mouth kicks up at the corner. 'Do I *really* have to ex—'

And then I stumble back and dive for the toilet, about to vomit up my entire goddamn soul.

The second my knees hit the cold tiles, there's a sick pull behind my ribs. I gag once, and barely get the lid up before I'm retching. The room tilts and spins like a washing machine on high, and somewhere far, far away, I hear the bathroom door open.

Sweat beads along my hairline, cold and slick against my skin. I wave a weak, pathetic hand in the general direction of the door. 'Go away.'

But instead of obeying like a decent person, he crouches beside me. A wall of muscle and quiet warmth, right there. A large hand sweeps my hair back, gathering the tangled mess and holding it firm, fingers settling against the nape of my neck.

His voice – low, calm, far too gentle – lands somewhere behind my ear. 'Easy, Champ. I've got you.'

Kill me now.

I press my forehead against the rim as another wave heaves through me, acid burning my gullet. There is no lower point in my entire career – hell, my entire life – than this moment. And that includes the break-up. A public relations professional, CEO of an agency…throwing up into a hotel toilet with my highest-profile client rubbing soothing circles into my back.

I should be utterly humiliated.

But weirdly… I'm not. At least not as much. He's steady, sure of himself, like looking after me is his calling. It shouldn't be. I'm his bloody agent, not his responsibility.

'You're a menace, you know that?' Brodie murmurs, his breath grazing my temple.

I mutter something unintelligible and spit into the bowl. Probably the last of my credibility and authority.

His huge thigh braces against my side, steadying me. 'I've never met someone who could drink a rugby player almost one-and-a-half times their size under the table.'

My stomach keeps twisting. But again, not from the alcohol.

I know that at some point last night, he made sure I wasn't drinking anything with actual alcohol in it. Far too late, obviously, but still.

He *let* me win.

The most competitive man who's ever graced the earth – well, except *maybe* Michael Jordan – wants me to believe that I won a silly drinking contest when we both know I didn't.

Why?

Brodie pulls his hand away, leaving behind a warmth that settles in and stays. The tap runs. Then a damp flannel appears in my periphery, chilled but not cold.

'Here. Forehead or neck?'

'Neck.'

Another convulsion racks me. Jesus. I grip the porcelain,

burning up from the inside out, but Brodie simply adjusts his hold. Unshakable.

'Why…are you…'

The next heave brings up nothing but bitterness. I sag against the cistern, temples throbbing.

'Because you'd do the same for me,' he answers my half-asked question. 'Because you're not the only one who needed to cut loose. And because someone should remind you it's allowed.'

Silence stretches, broken only by the drip of the shower head. He cradles my skull – one broad palm cupping my crown, the other pressing the cool cloth to my nape.

'Breathe.' He kneads gentle pressure into my scalp with his thumbs. 'In through the nose. Out through the mouth.'

I want to bite him. But I'm too weak. So, I obey.

His breath matches mine, steady as a metronome. The rhythm unravels the knots between my shoulders. My eyelids droop.

'Aye, that's it.' His lips almost brush my ear, sending a traitorous shiver through me.

Slowly, gradually, I give in. My body eases against his. The warmth of him seeps into my skin. His touch is hypnotic and grounding, undoing me in ways I don't even have words for. I let my cheek rest against his arm. Let his hands smooth over my hair. Let him hold me.

Too easy, that letting.

He threads his fingers through the strands, stroking absently. 'Think you're done here, Champ?'

I'm heavy. Utterly fucked. Bone-deep tired. 'Yeah.'

Brodie shifts and rises, joints cracking. Before I can protest, before I can even think, he scoops me up and tucks me against his chest. My muscles stiffen with instinctive resistance. I don't get carried. I've been holding myself up for months, gritting my teeth through every blow, hauling my own body forward step after step.

But his arms settle around me, and my pulse trips.

It doesn't feel like being handled. It doesn't feel like being rescued.

It feels like being supported.

Instead of telling me to push through, he lifts the weight for a little while. The fight slips out of me, and I curl my fingers into the cotton of his T-shirt.

Then I let him carry me straight to bed.

I probably should say something. About yesterday. About what we did. What *I* did. About how my body still remembers the feel of his mouth, the scrape of his stubble against my jaw, the weight of his hands…

But I can't.

He tucks me in as if he's done this a hundred times before. No hesitation as he pulls the duvet over my shoulders, pressing out the air between me and the rest of the world.

I should be resisting. Asserting control. But my muscles don't get the memo. My body sinks, lids already shut.

So what if I let this happen? For a few hours. Until my body stops screaming at me.

Brodie doesn't move. He sits there, arms on his thighs, watching me like I might spook if he so much as sneezes. 'We should talk about last night.'

I meet his gaze. 'We should.'

'But not now. You've got enough to deal with as it is.' A pause. 'But don't think I'll let it slide.'

A breath leaves me, too shallow to be relief. 'Didn't think you would.'

'Good. I'll handle your schedule.'

'No.' I sigh. 'I need to get up in a bit.'

'No, you fucking don't.'

I salvage what little dignity I have left. 'Yes. I do. We have an event later. Rugby kids—'

'—at a local community club,' he finishes. 'Nothing that

can't happen without you. No reporters, no worries. I'll be fine.'

'It's work,' I argue and shove a hand over my eyes.

'And this...' he gestures at me, a shell of a human being bundled under the covers, '...is what happens when you don't let yourself rest.'

His voice is calm, but something in it sticks. Something that lands deep in my ribs and lingers. I force my eyes open. 'I don't have time to rest.'

'How long have you been running at this speed?'

I don't reply.

'I mean it, Harrington. How long?'

A muscle in my jaw tenses.

He nods, like that's answer enough. 'So what, you finally slamming the brakes last night is just a coincidence?'

'I was drunk.'

'You're exhausted. And since you've clearly forgotten how to pace yourself, I'm stepping in.'

I glare at him. 'That's not how this works, MacRae. You don't get to decide what I do with my day simply because I had one rough night. You're not the boss of me. I'm the boss of you!'

His brows lift, unimpressed. 'Not today. Charlie, you didn't have one rough night. You've been running on fumes for ages. Pretending it's fine, pretending you can keep going. Last night was the final crack.'

He leans in, forearms braced on his knees. Rugby scars. A silver slash along his thumb I've never noticed.

'You wouldn't let an athlete train without recovery time, would you? You'd call it reckless and unsustainable. But that's exactly what you're doing to yourself.'

The words sink in before I can block them. A nerve hit dead-on.

'I'm not an athlete,' I mutter weakly.

'No,' he agrees. 'You're the whole damn team.'

I look away, but it doesn't stop his words from finding their mark.

'And since you're my agent,' he continues, that impossible, steady conviction rolling through every syllable, 'and I literally can't afford to lose you, you're going to take the day off.'

I swallow hard and don't say anything. But I don't exactly fight it, either.

'Good. I'm going to make sure you get rest.'

Brodie's phone is already in his hand. He dials.

'Theo. It's Brodie. Aye, could you shift whatever's in Charlie's calendar for today? Reschedule. She's fine, she's just been a stubborn pain in my arse and run herself into the ground. Aye, I'll tell her. You're a star. Cheers, love.' He hangs up and tosses the phone onto the nightstand like it's nothing. Like he didn't just pull me out of my entire day with a single phone call.

'You—'

'Handled it. Theo thinks a break's overdue and said to keep you in bed.' He stands, stretching like the conversation is already over. 'Now, you sleep. I'll be back with Irn Bru, paracetamol, and food.'

I should argue. Tell him I'm perfectly capable of taking care of myself. But I merely watch as he heads for the door, pausing only to glance over his shoulder.

'This,' he declares, 'is Charlie Harrington's day off.'

I swallow sourness and what's left of my pride. 'Aye, aye, Capt'n.'

The door closes, and silence floods in from all sides.

I stare at the ceiling. I should feel better. Lighter. Grateful. But instead, something quiet curls in the hollow space he left behind. And I don't know if it's shame, the hangover, exhaustion, or something much, much worse.

Chapter 11

Brodie

I take the coastal road back to the hotel. The Isle of Islay doesn't care who you are. Famous, minted, stacked with medals... She'll still sucker-punch you with an incredible view, just to prove she can. I crack the window, let the salty air slap my face.

The event went smoothly. The weans today – nine-year-olds with as much grit as half my old Glasgow squad. Taught them the chip-and-chase, and their wee faces lit up like I'd handed them the Six-Nations-Cup. One lad kept calling me *'Mr MacRae Sir'* until I told him to knock it off and call me Brodie.

Luckily, the parents hung back. I signed some shirts, took some pictures, and made sure the sponsor's media guy had everything they needed.

Should've felt good. And it did, mostly. But the whole time, my neck itched like someone was watching. Kept checking behind me, half-hoping she'd be there. Arms crossed, wearing that crooked smirk that says *you're not a complete dick, MacRae.*

Wish she could've been there.

I sent Theo the sponsor photos myself. Weans hoisted on

my shoulders, mud-streaked grins, the lot. The road curves, cliffs dropping away to reveal Beinn Bheigeir looming in the distance.

My phone vibrates in the holder. Theo's name flashes.

'Is she awake yet?'

'Dunno. Left her snoring. On my way back now.'

'You're a saint, MacRae. Tell her to call me when she feels ready.'

'Will do.'

I chuck the phone onto the passenger seat and it slides into the Co-op-bag stuffed with a can of Irn Bru, a pack of Paracetamol, and a squashed sausage roll in its wee paper bag.

Saint my arse. Saints don't think about the give of soft skin under their hand, or how her breath snagged when the flannel touched her neck. Saints don't get hard over memories.

I inhale through my nose, tension pulling tight through my ribs as this morning replays in full HD. Charlie Harrington, curled up in a hotel bed, wrapped in my rugby shirt. Not weak, never weak. But soft, like a sheathed blade. And she let me stay. Let me take care of her. Let me see.

She could've pushed me away. Told me to piss off with her cutting tongue and steel-spined glare. But she didn't.

She let me in.

And now I don't know where the hell I stand. She's in my bloodstream. Under my tongue. Living rent-free in every fucking thought I've got.

The car eats up another mile of damp road. The sea glints through the rocks, grey and moody under the leaden sky. The clouds break open, and a shard of sunlight slices through, turning the water to silver.

I should've pushed her on it earlier, but she was barely holding herself together. Aye, I needed to make sure she rested. To stop her running on empty. But also...

I didn't want to hear her say last night was nothing.

I bite back my frustration and give the accelerator a nudge.

This is fucking ridiculous. She's my agent. We've been at each other's throats for months. She's just got under my skin, that's all. All this time together and my brain's fucking up what's real.

The hotel appears ahead, perched by the shoreline. I park and turn off the engine, sitting there, hands braced at ten-and-two. The key card burns a hole in my pocket. I'm not some deluded romantic pining for something impossible. Fuck, but maybe I want to be the one who gets to see all of her – the fierce and the fragile.

And that terrifies me.

I can cope with pressure. A stadium screaming my name. A match-winning kick in the final seconds. A six-foot-four, twenty-stone forward with a grudge barrelling towards me. National media tearing me to shreds.

But the chance she doesn't want the same thing? That I could want her and she'd walk away like none of it mattered?

Fucking kills me.

She needs time. And I need an answer I can live with.

I slam the car door harder than needed.

The hotel hallway is empty, carpet swallowing my steps. The key card clicks. I nudge the door open with my shoulder, quietly as I can, balancing the Co-op bag in one arm. The air smells of her. I force my breath steady, grip the bag tighter, and try to ignore how much I fucking like it.

Inside, the room's dim, curtains still drawn. The only light is the sliver of daylight sneaking through the edges.

Charlie's still out cold. Sprawled across the bed in a tangle of sheets, cheek mashed into the pillow, one bare leg kicked free.

And she's still wearing my shirt.

My gut tilts, like the ground's shifted half an inch.

It's not just the sight of her in it – it's the feeling. Like I left something of mine on her, and she didn't shake it off. She kept it on her skin, as close as possible.

The rugby shirt's bunched up her thighs, hem riding high enough to show the sweet curve of her arse in those lace knickers. My brain goes places. Forbidden places. Straight into the gutter without brakes. Charlie in that shirt, under me. Her in that shirt, over me. The fabric bunched up around her waist, me gripping her hips. Her in that shirt, snuggled up against me on the sofa, one of those terrible crime dramas playing in the background while she rants about police procedure.

The second thought should kill the first. It doesn't. Just makes it worse.

Fuck.

I cross the room, as quietly as possible, and set the bag down. Pull out the Irn Bru and the paracetamol, place them on the nightstand. Her lashes flutter and she stirs, shifting onto her side, arm flopping over her face with a groggy groan.

'MacRae?' Her voice cracks. She rolls onto her back and stretches like a cat. Fabric pulls tight across her chest.

'Alive then,' I grunt.

She squints at me. 'Tell me you got coffee.'

I rub the back of my neck. 'Irn Bru, painkillers, water, and a roll.'

'Didn't peg you for a nursemaid.'

'Didn't peg you for a lightweight.' I sit down on the edge of the bed. Springs dip. 'Got your cure here. Hydrate, Harrington.'

She snags the can of Irn Bru, cracks it one-handed. The juice glugs down, and I track the way her neck moves.

'Better?' I ask.

'Still want to die.' She wipes her mouth. 'But a bit less.'

Sunlight cuts through a slim gap between the curtains, striping her legs. I want to nibble the inside of her knee. Want to drag this rugby shirt over her head slow, watch her squirm.

Want to order room service pancakes and argue about syrup brands until she snort-laughs again.

'How was the event?' she asks.

'Good. Kids were class. Made sure they got all the photos they needed for the sponsor.'

'Did you do my job for me, MacRae?'

I shrug. 'Somebody had to.'

'You're staring. Do I have something on my face?'

I swipe my tongue over my teeth. 'No. Just getting used to you looking this…' I tip my head, searching for the word. '…less terrifying.'

She grins. 'Enjoy it while it lasts.'

'Theo says hi. You're to call her when you're up for it, not a minute earlier. Her words.'

'Yeah, I really should check in with her.' She reaches for her phone. 'Look at you. Not a single tantrum today. Proud of you, MacRae.'

Before I can reply, her phone trills. She sits up fast, the rugby shirt sliding off one shoulder. Her whole face shifts, softening in an instant when she sees the screen.

'Button! How are you?' Her voice wraps around the nickname like melted honey. I pull my legs onto the bed and lean against the headboard next to her, watching. How her thumb worries the edge of my Rebels shirt. How the crease between her brows dissolves.

'That's amazing! I knew you could do it!'

Charlie tucks her knees up, drowning in my rugby shirt. Her voice warms, brightens, and I feel it like sunlight through glass.

'Daddy's being silly. Ignore him. Remember what Nana said? Harringtons thrive on challenges.'

A pause. Her throat bobs. 'No, Han. You're right. It's okay to be upset. And perfect's boring. You're volcanic.' She shoots me a glare when I grunt. 'Yeah. Like Beyoncé.'

Charlie's got this glow about her. Protective, proud. Like there's nothing in the world she wouldn't do for this girl.

'Mum's right, you got this. And I know you. I know you can do this. If you want it, you go for it. You hear me?'

They chat a bit more – school, friends, some true crime show that Hannah's obsessed with, a rabbit named Blorbo – before Charlie sighs. 'Alright, superstar. I'll call you soon, okay? Love you to the moon and back.'

The call ends. Charlie stares at the screen, thumb hovering for a second longer than necessary. She sets the phone down, but doesn't let go. Her fingers curl around the edges like she's holding on.

Her jaw shifts. Not a frown. Not a smile. Something caught between the two.

I say nothing and simply observe. Letting her have the space. Letting her decide if she wants to share whatever it is.

After a long breath, she picks at the hem of my shirt. 'That was my little sister.'

'She sounds grand.'

'She is. God, she's brilliant. Wilful as hell. Drives me mad sometimes, typical teenager stuff. Hannah's also got Down's syndrome, and she'll be the first to tell you that's the least interesting thing about her.' Charlie exhales and leans back into the pillows beside me, her shoulder leaning against mine. 'Mum got pregnant with her when I was ten. Risky pregnancy and a total accident. But the best kind. Hannah grew up into the most determined kid I've ever met. And now she's sixteen.'

'Aye, teenagers can be knobs sometimes.' I grin. 'But she's got your fight, then.'

'Very. And Dad loves her. I know he does. But he…sees her as something he has to protect at all costs. Not a liability, more a responsibility. He thinks her best chance is in a special care home. Somewhere she'll be "looked after." My mum and I disagree vehemently.' She straightens. 'Hannah doesn't need constant "looking after". She needs people who support her, believe in her. Like all of us.'

I don't hesitate. 'And you do.'

'Always have, always will.'

I take that in. 'Hannah's lucky to have you.'

'No. I'm lucky to have her.'

Man, my heart's full-on breaking right now. It feels like she trusts me with the softest part of her. I bump her foot with mine. 'Your sister's got Harrington steel. She'll outshine the lot of you.'

Her laugh cracks. 'You've never even met her.'

'You're her sister. That's enough.'

She looks at me then. Eyes glinting wet. 'Callum met her once. At a charity gala last Christmas. Asked Dad why we brought "the slow kid".'

My gut twists, and I want to smash his face in. Again. 'Fucking prick.'

'I know. God, I know.' A tear slips and she swipes it away angrily. 'Hannah asked if he was my Prince Charming. I told her princes are overrated. Dragons steal more treasure.'

I don't think. Just reach for her. Haul her in. She stiffens – instinct, pride, that iron-willed Harrington armour – then melts, face buried in my neck. Her tears scald my skin. Her shoulders shake a little.

I hold her tighter.

Something's happening, and I'm too far in to tell myself it's just a passing thing. But fuck me if I know what to do with it.

'She'd like you,' she mumbles into my collarbone.

I trace my hand up her spine. 'Doubt it. I'm shite at karaoke. But I'd love to meet her.'

Charlie pulls back, eyes red-rimmed and blazing. 'You mean that?'

'Aye. Can't wait to be levelled by the two volcanic Harrington girls.'

She sniffles and giggles at the same time, then sits up. The moment breaks, just a fraction, and she's already shifting gears, pulling herself back together.

But something in me doesn't reset.

I brush my thumb over her cheekbone to catch the last trace of salt. She has no clue how close I am to slipping. How much of me she's already taken without trying.

She stretches, shaking it off. 'Right. We should get ready. It's a long drive to Skye.'

Charlie's back on her feet. Walls up again. But I've seen what's underneath. Fine. She can pretend I didn't get in. I won't.

Chapter 12

Charlie

The bridge to Skye rises ahead, a sleek arc over the steel-blue sea leading toward mist-dusted mountains. The road narrows as we climb, the guardrails disappearing into open sky. A good place to clear my head.

Not that it's working.

Brodie's driving, one hand on the steering wheel, the other resting on the gearstick. He's humming to the radio, utterly at ease. Every so often, he flicks me a glance, checking in without saying a word.

And I don't know how to deal with it.

I don't know how to deal with *him*.

Somewhere between him holding my hair back while I puked out my dignity, going to that event alone, then coming straight back to take care of me – something seriously changed.

His hand grazes my knee every time he shifts gears, and I leave it right where it is, so he doesn't miss it.

I thought I knew what I was getting with Brodie MacRae. Brutally ambitious. Obnoxiously cocky. Hot temper. Impossible to control.

But this? The patience. The quiet steadiness beneath all

that bluster. The way he lets me be imperfect – not just allows it, but accepts it – like it's not something I have to apologise for?

I've never had that.

Callum was nice. Or so I thought. I also thought I loved him. But with him, I think I was always performing to an extent. Always shaping myself into the right kind of girl-friend. Callum never… Callum preferred me polished. And for my father, I had to be the right kind of daughter, the right kind of businesswoman, the right kind of heir to his sports management empire.

Fucking exhausting is what it was.

Brodie doesn't want a performance, and that's a lot for a girl like me.

The real gut punch, though?

He said he wants to meet Hannah.

No hesitation. No polite nod and change of subject. Just straight-up wanting to know her, be part of that side of my life. It's cracking through a place I've kept bolted shut.

Tyres hum. My pulse skitters in my wrists. I stare out at the road as we descend the bridge onto the island. Past Kyleakin, the land unfolds in dramatic sweeps. In the distance, Cuillin peaks pierce low clouds. They move fast here, chasing shadows across the hills.

Beside me, Brodie reaches into the centre console and grabs a roll of Polos. He pops one in his mouth and holds them out.

I shake my head.

'Suit yourself.' He crunches down. 'Still bitter about the song game?'

'You had an unfair advantage. Most of those songs were from the nineties, and you grew up with two older brothers.'

'Excuses.' He drums against the steering wheel, smirking. 'But you won Yellow Car.'

'Damn right, I did. Your reaction speed is tragic for a professional athlete.'

'Maybe I was going easy on you.'

The laugh that comes out of me isn't pretty, but it's real. Unguarded. This *is* easy. Being with him is insanely easy.

We stopped for food in Glencoe earlier. One of those places with wooden beams, mounted stag heads, and an open fire. He stole chips off my plate, told me about his ambition to be the best fly-half of the decade. His dream of leading Scotland to a Six Nations victory, but also building something real with the Rebels. Something lasting.

I loved listening to him talk like that. Loved how his face lit up when he wasn't playing it cool.

I love—

I slam the brakes on that thought.

I can't fall for Brodie MacRae.

He's my biggest client. The entire future of Elite Edge depends on getting his career off the ground again. If I let myself slip, if I let myself want him the way I do, it endangers everything we've built so far.

Everything I want to prove.

One night, one moment of weakness, and I was face-down in a hotel bed instead of at that event.

It mustn't happen again.

But it's not only that.

It's also what would happen after.

It starts with a spark. Then a rush. Promises that feel real. And eventually, it turns. Like a tide pulling back. It wouldn't even be his fault. Rugby comes first. It always does. It's in his bones, the same way it was in Callum's. Probably even more. And when the season ramps up, when the stakes get higher, when the demands of the game start pressing in…

I know how this ends. Slowly, inevitably, I become a footnote in someone else's ambition. And if I let that happen again – if I let it be Brodie – I won't recover.

I can't. No more athletes. No more rugby players. My agency comes first.

I set my shoulders, eyes on the road ahead. We've got one more event tomorrow morning – a promo gig at another Dal Riata distillery – before we head back to Stirling. I have to keep my distance until then.

No lingering glances. No offhand smiles. No thinking about how his hands felt under my dress. Not remembering the low warmth in his voice when he said he wanted to meet my sister.

Not only can I do this, I *have* to.

But I don't have to like it.

Portree is packed. Skye is a tourist magnet, which means the B&B is buzzing with the sort of people who wear waterproof trousers and maps. It's half eight, but the reception's still open. I step up to the desk, stifling a yawn. Brodie leans against the counter beside me, all broad shoulders and wind-ruffled hair, thumbing lazily at his screen like he isn't about to collapse from exhaustion after hours of driving.

The receptionist squints at the computer in front of her. 'Ah, yes. Harrington and MacRae. Booked under Elite Edge.'

Relief unfurls in my chest. Thank god for Theo.

But then the woman hesitates with a scrunched-up face, and my relief dies a sudden death. That's never a good sign.

She clicks around, pressing her lips together. 'Looks like there was a mix-up with the rooms.'

I stiffen. 'What kind of mix-up?'

The typing stops. She glances up and winces. 'We had you down for two rooms, but I'm afraid all that's left is a queen-sized double on the top floor.'

I inhale sharply.

Next to me, Brodie swears under his breath. Half grunt, half muttered curse.

'Excuse me, but how's this possible?'

'If it was booked through a travel platform, sometimes the room inventory isn't updated in real-time. I'm so, so sorry.' The receptionist shrugs, clearly frazzled. 'We've been over-booked all week. I just checked every other hotel in the area. Nothing left. Skye in early September, what can you do? If you want, I can get you a couple of extra blankets and drinks on the house?'

I pinch the bridge of my nose. Brilliant.

Brodie exhales. Not a sigh, exactly. Just this stoic release of a man who isn't going to make this easier for me.

'Not the end of the world,' he says.

I glare at him. 'You're six foot two.' I turn back to the receptionist. 'Are you a thousand per cent sure there's nothing else?'

She shakes her head. 'Not unless you fancy sleeping in the drawing room.'

I hiss a breath out through my teeth and don't look at him. It's past nine, I'm knackered.

'We'll take it.'

The receptionist hands us the key. I snatch it before Brodie can, grab my suitcase, and head for the stairs.

The second I push open the door to our room, I stop dead. So does Brodie. It's nice enough. Cosy, small window, little desk. The air smells like lavender and old books. Cute.

But the bed?

A queen-sized vintage metal frame bed sits in the middle of the room. Looks as though it belongs in a gran's spare, right down to the white throw and patterned pillows. Delicate and decorative, guaranteed to squeak if you so much as cough on it.

Brodie drops his bag onto the floor with a heavy thud. 'Christ.' His voice is far too amused for my liking. 'This'll be fun.'

I cut him a dry look. He lifts one shoulder, eyes flicking to the bed, then to me, then back to the bed. Like he's weighing something up.

Okay, yeah. We've already snogged like horny teenagers. Which was ill-judged enough. But sharing a bed means something else. Something I'm not ready to name, let alone risk.

I fold my arms. 'I'll take the floor.'

Brodie scoffs. 'Don't be daft. I'll take it.'

'You've got a match in two weeks.'

'You're the one who's still crawling out of the hangover hole.'

We stare each other down, silent, the air between us brimming. He's standing too close. I can smell him. Salt, the faintest trace of whatever soap he took from the hotel, and underneath it all…Brodie.

My stomach tenses, and I pull my arms in tight. I am not making the same mistake twice.

He rubs the back of his neck. 'We'll both fit. It's only a few hours of sleep, Harrington.'

Oh, sure. Just sleep. As if that's all it would be. As if I wouldn't be hyper-aware of every carved inch of him. As if my body wouldn't remember the feel of his calloused hands, the scratch of his stubble.

'Yeah, fine.'

But it's not fine. Not even close. And we both know it.

I yank open my suitcase and dig through it with far too much intensity for someone who is getting ready for bed. I only have a strap-top and matching shorts. Far too sexy, far too dangerous. So, I grab his rugby shirt. That'll do.

I grip the fabric, turn…and immediately regret everything.

Because Brodie – entirely too much man for this tiny room – has yanked off his hoodie, and his T-shirt with it. No undershirt or any other barrier. Bare golden skin, cut from years of tackles and scrums, stretching over thick shoulders and a chest that looks like it was forged in a blacksmith's daydream.

I don't stare.

I absolutely don't stare.

Except for the moment his abs shift, going tight as he shoves a hand through his hair like it's no big deal, and – Jesus, Mary, and all the saints – his biceps. They flex, and suddenly the temperature in the room spikes to hellfire.

I snap my gaze back to my suitcase, grab something, spin on my heel, bolt into the bathroom, and lock the door.

I take longer than usual. Brush my teeth, wash my face, do the entire nighttime routine I usually skip when travelling.

I'm not walking back into that room until I've composed myself and he's dressed.

Brodie MacRae looks too fucking good without a T-shirt.

And now I have to share a tiny metal-frame bed with him.

Eventually, I can't delay any longer. I take a deep breath, steel myself, and step out.

He's already sprawled out on one side of the bed, propped up against the rail frame, in boxers and a worn Nirvana tee that's holding on by sheer loyalty at this point, scrolling on his phone without a care in the world.

He lifts his eyes. 'Took you long enough.'

'Didn't realise I was on a timer.'

'Didn't think you'd need hours to put on jammies and brush your teeth.' He tosses his phone onto the bedside cabinet.

I march over, grab two extra pillows, and plonk them right between us in the middle of the bed. A line in the sand.

Brodie watches me, expression unreadable, but his gaze falters for a second. A hesitation. He grinds his jaw once. Biting something back. His fingers drum once against his quad before he stills them. Like he's making a decision. He reaches for his phone and deliberately turns it off. No scrolling. No distractions. Just silence.

I don't know why that makes my stomach flip. I don't know why it feels like some kind of restraint, as if he's holding himself back as much as I am.

He brushes his teeth and comes back within three minutes. I crawl into the squeaky bed and lie down, yank the duvet over me, and stare daggers at the ceiling. It's not the bed or the warmth radiating off his body. It's the fact that every nerve in me is screaming to roll over, sink my teeth into his shoulder, and let him fuck me apart until I forget why I swore I'd never touch another rugby player again.

'Night, MacRae.'

'Night, Harrington.'

I wake to heat.

To the slow push and pull of his breath against my hair. To the weight of his arm slung low over my waist, his palm resting flat over my navel. And for a long, frozen moment, I don't move.

At some point in the night, the two pillows I'd barricaded between us gave up and wandered to the foot of the bed.

This quiet intimacy is more dangerous than anything that could've happened when we were awake.

I should ease away. Should break the contact, should remind us both that this is not what we do. Instead, I lie there and stare into the dark. Only until my heart stops clawing at my ribs. It's safe here. In the hush before morning, before words and choices and regret. Before I have to remember what's at stake.

His fingers curl slightly, just enough that I feel it. His chest is moulded to my back, broad and warm, his muscled thigh slotted between mine in a way that should make me bolt. Should make me shove him off, retreat, stop whatever the hell this is before it starts.

But it's already too late, isn't it?

Brodie MacRae isn't careful. Not with his words, not with his temper, not with anything. But here, in sleep, he is.

And that does something awful to me.

His fingertips dig into my belly for a split second, and I know he's waking up. This is my chance to move. My chance to salvage what's left of my control before—

He makes a sound. An almost pained exhale against the back of my neck. Like he's trying not to pull me closer.

And that's what has my throat closing up, my chest twisting in on itself.

I know what that sound means.

It means this isn't just me.

It means I'm not the only one barely holding it together.

I close my eyes, but it's pointless. There's no escaping the way my pulse flares beneath his hand, the way I can feel him forcing himself still. He's trying to be good.

I stay. Just for another moment. Just until morning comes and I can put it back in the box and lock the lid.

But deep down, I know. Morning won't change a damn thing.

I already feel myself losing.

I am so gone for Brodie.

His palm is hot, branding me through the fabric. His fingers spread, enough to send a warning – he could grip. He could hold. He could lower and… Jesus. Need pulses where I'm already aching, because I remember how it felt when he eased that same hand under my dress, got me whimpering into his mouth like I had no shame.

His breath is speeding up, each exhale hotter against my neck. My nipples pebble, yearning for his mouth, his hands. A broken sigh lodges in my throat. It would take nothing – nothing – for him to move those fingers lower. To find me wet. Waiting for him.

And I think he knows it.

I don't mean to move.

But his thigh is right there. Powerful, sculpted, heat-etched muscle wedged flush between my legs, and when I shift – the tiniest bit – a jagged shock rolls through me. My breath catches and breaks. I tense around him instinctively, seeking more.

And then I do it again. Testing. A tiny rock forward, enough pressure to feel the heavy drag against my clit. Enough to make a flush of tension knot deep in my belly and my pulse jerk.

I seal my mouth on a gasp that would give me away, drowning in the way it feels. The way *he* feels.

His chest presses harder against my back, breath fraying at the edges, fingers twitching below my navel.

He's awake.

Waiting to see if I'll do it again.

And I do. I can't help it.

It feels so good.

So good I can't stop.

A groan rips from him, straight from the chest. 'You really gonna do this to me, Charlie?' He presses his hand against my stomach. 'Gonna ride my fucking thigh, all wet and needy, and expect me to just lie here? Expect me to be good? To not flip you over, spread you out, and bury my tongue in you till you're begging for my cock?'

He exhales hard, forehead resting against the crown of my head. 'Tell me right now if this is just you getting yourself off. If you need to use me – fuck, baby, I'll let you. I'll take it, if that's what you want.' A pause, a sharp, shaky inhale. 'But if this is you giving in – if this is you wanting me the way I want you… Then say the word. Say it, and I'll make you come so hard you forget every single reason you tried to resist me.'

I don't breathe. Can't.

Because my body isn't my own anymore.

Brodie's words settle low in my stomach. They curl hot into the apex of my thighs, creep up my spine, wrap tight around my lungs until I'm shaking.

I've never – *never* – had a man say something like that. Offer himself up like a prayer.

He wants this.

Wants me.

He's been thinking about me. Wanting me.

And my brain can't handle it. Can't process the way his voice cracked. I should shove him away, tell him this can't happen, remind myself that I have rules, boundaries.

But his leg is dense and hard and right fucking there.

And his voice is still ringing in my ears.

And my body is already betraying me.

Because I rock against him harder. A strangled noise punches out of me, too hot, too desperate. Because fuck, riding his thigh feels forbidden and good. Too damn good.

And then…

He moves his palm lower.

And I know what's going to happen. This will break me later. I know that. But right now? I need this. Him.

So, fuck it.

'Yes… Please.' I bite my lip.

And I do it again.

Chapter 13

Brodie

S he's fucking killing me.

Grinding against my leg as if it was made for her. Like she was meant to fall apart right here, rubbing herself raw.

And she's wearing the shirt with my name and number.

Holy mother of God.

Her breath snags, fingers fisting in the sheets, body strung tight with want. For me. I can feel it. Feel *her*. The wet heat of her pussy gliding over my quad. I tighten the muscle under her, pressing her clit harder into me.

She lets out a deep sigh. Fuck. That sigh. It carves straight through me.

And I should be revelling in it, making her do it again, and again, and again. But all I can think is… This isn't enough.

I want more. To hold her when she breaks. Be inside her when she does. I want to fucking keep her.

But I don't say it.

I just touch her.

I skim one hand up and cup her tit. Plush and full, heavy enough to make my palm ache. Her nipple's already hard, begging for my touch. I roll it slowly between my fingers.

Then tug, rougher than I should, like I'm teasing out a scream she's too proud to give me.

'I hate how good this feels. I hate you for knowing it.' She lets her head drop back, offering her throat to me.

'Hate me all you want, baby. Your body loves it.'

I bite her. Can't help it. Sink my teeth into the nape of her neck, feel her pulse jump against my lips. I suck, let my tongue graze over the mark before pulling away.

Her hips buck, begging for more.

And who the fuck am I to deny her that?

I slide one hand to her jaw, pull her mouth to mine, and swallow the ragged, starving sound that slips free when my tongue brushes against hers.

She tastes so fucking good.

I roll my hips up, shoving my quad against her pussy hard, and she chokes on a moan.

I need to hear her say it.

Need to fucking hear it.

I break the kiss, press my forehead against her temple, still gripping her jaw tightly in one hand.

'Say it, Charlie. Tell me you want it.'

She's shaking. Her body is pleading for me. 'Brodie…'

'Say it, baby.'

She exhales sharply. 'I-I want… I want you.'

The growl that tears from me is pure fucking ruin. I crash my mouth to hers. Branding her, owning her, telling her without words that she's mine.

She fumbles behind her, grabs my cock through the cotton. And…fuck.

Her breath catches – stunned – like she just clocked what she's holding. She squeezes, and my vision fractures. Her grip shifts, tentative at first, then firmer. Exploring. Mapping me. Trying to figure out what she's dealing with. A shaky breath spills from her, half awe, half hunger, and I bite down on a curse, because… Fuck, she likes what she's holding.

Then she moves. A twist of her body, a press of small hands against my chest, and suddenly, I'm on my back, sinking into the mattress, breath fucking gone. She's on top of me, knees bracketing my hips.

She strips my shirt off with a growl, flinging it to the floor like it's burning her skin. And suddenly she's bare to me. Glorious. Her tits are fucking art. Round and heavy with that pretty slope. Nipples set low but tipped up, waiting for my mouth. They sway when she moves, and all I can think about is how I want one in my mouth and the other in my hand while I fuck her slow enough to make her cry.

Her throat bobs. Something shadows across her face. But before I can name it, she sinks lower, grazing the trail where my pulse hammers.

She wants to take control? Wants to take me apart? She can have every goddamn inch. I won't even pretend I haven't imagined those lips stretched around me. I have. Her mouth. Her spit. Her throat. All mine.

She hooks her fingers into my waistband. I lift my hips, let her peel my briefs down. She goes quiet when she sees what she's dealing with. Heavy. Flushed. Leaking. Desperate for her.

'Christ, Brodie. Think you could've warned me?'

I let out a hoarse laugh. 'What, so you could run?'

She bites her lip, eyes sparking. 'So, I could brace myself.'

'Too late for that.' My voice is all gravel now. Hunger spilling over. Need eating me alive.

She wraps her fingers around me, strokes once, twice – too light, too teasing. I push up on one elbow, grab her jaw and trace my knuckle along her lower lip until her teeth let go. 'Think you can take it, or is it too much for you?'

There's a gleam below her lashes. That smug, 'challenge accepted' look. Like I've dared her. And I know she fucking *loves* a dare.

'Oh, you'll see.'

Then she goes down.

Holy. Fucking. Hell.

Heat. Tight, slick, suffocating heat wrapping around the head. Her mouth… Fuck, her mouth. Full lips stretching and sealing as she takes me to the base. Pressure builds. Buried low. It claws higher, behind my ribs. I feel it everywhere. In my balls, my gut, my goddamn soul.

'Fucking knew you'd be good at this.' I fist the sheets, legs drawn tight – because fuck – now her tongue is swirling, teasing. My hips jolt, instinct taking over. She hollows her cheeks, and I almost black out. Fire licks up my lower back. My pulse rages in my skull and my heart thrashes like a motherfucker.

Because this isn't just pleasure.

It's her.

Her.

Charlie on her knees for me. Taking me. Giving me this.

Her mouth is a revelation. Hot and greedy and fucking lush.

And she's so damn eager.

But something's…off.

At first, I don't see it. Too lost in heat-drenched suction, the way she gags for it like she's got something to prove.

Until I realise she has.

She's putting on a show.

And that's a problem.

A cold rush cuts through the blaze, clearing my head enough to notice what I should have caught from the start. She's doing it perfectly. Too perfectly. Both hands stroking me, her mouth moving in some fast porn rhythm. Like she thinks she has to get me off asap.

It guts me.

Because Charlie doesn't know how to let go, how to be in the moment. Doesn't know there's a way to make giving head about her, too. To let herself sink into the power of it, instead of working so hard to impress me.

I push my fingers into her scalp, but not to guide. To stop. To pull her off me.

She looks up, lips wet, brows drawn in a question, confusion in her eyes.

My heart cracks open.

Charlie Harrington doesn't know how to fucking *feel*.

She's been taught how to perform, to please, to be the best. How to give, give, give.

But who the fuck taught her how to *take* and revel?

My voice is rough. 'You don't have to, baby.'

Her forehead creases. 'I want to.'

And maybe she does. Maybe she wants to make me come in her mouth. But there's a difference between wanting something and knowing how to let yourself enjoy it.

I tip her face up with one finger under her chin. 'You have no idea how to lean back and be taken care of, do you?'

Charlie blinks and shrugs, followed by a half-smirk. She's ready to dodge.

Not this time, Champ.

I sit up and move fast, flip the script before she can get away. Before she knows it, I'm seizing her hips, pulling her up my chest.

She stills, tension sparking off her in waves. 'What... Brodie, I—'

'I want you to sit on my face, Charlie. Ride my fucking face.'

I see her pulse kicking in her throat. That heartbeat where she wrestles with want.

'I've never...'

I move back down underneath her, and grab her harder, pull her higher, force her right where I want her.

Right where she needs to be.

'Let me show you how to fucking *take*.'

She resists. Of course she does. Strained muscles under my hands, breath hitching.

'Come here, baby.' I stroke up the sensitive skin of her inner thighs, spreading her wider as I tug her closer. 'Don't make me wait for that pussy.'

She shakes her head, breathless. 'Brodie, I…'

'Shhh.' I soothe her with my hands, with my lips trailing open-mouthed kisses along the crease of her hip. 'Let me take care of you, aye?'

She's balanced above my face now.

With my thumb, I push the lace aside. Her muscles stay taut, she tries to stay poised, in control. Still fighting it. Still trying to decide if she can let herself have this.

Well, I can't fucking have *that*.

So, I squeeze her flesh, hard, let her feel my strength, my control. Let her know what's about to happen.

'Don't hover. Sit.'

'Won't I…smother you?'

'No. Now be a good girl and fucking *sit*.'

A helpless gasp. One hand claws into my hair, and then she finally sinks down onto my mouth.

Goddammit.

Lush, silky heat coats my tongue the second I lick up into her. Hotter than I imagined. Wetter than I fucking deserve.

A little mewl escapes her. Bit shocked. Bit desperate. Like she didn't expect this. Like it never felt this good before.

I bet it never has.

Not to me, anyway.

I lick slowly over the spot that makes her seize, body arching, holding on to the metal frame above my head for dear life.

'Oh my god,' she whispers. 'This is… Fuck!'

I hum against her, tasting everything. She melts. Rocks against me.

'That's it.' I'm muffled against her soaked, fucking delicious cunt, but I know she hears me. I *feel* her hear me. 'Take what you need.'

She's not in control anymore. She's learning how to enjoy being eaten out. And I let her ride my tongue like I was built for it.

Because maybe I fucking was.

Her hips roll. Faster. Feral. Chasing it.

'Ah! Oh god! Brodie...' Breathless. Raw. 'I...I can't—'

I haul her against my mouth, devour her, flick my tongue in that way that makes her legs shake.

Then I come up for air. 'You're gonna lose it for me now, Charlie. Right on my face.'

I yank her back down, mouth open, hungry, and suck her swollen clit like I've got a goddamn death wish. Lick fast, hard, deep. Until she jerks like she's been lit from inside.

And she breaks.

A long whimper rips from her chest as she comes apart right in my mouth.

It's the best fucking thing that has ever happened to me.

I thought *she* needed this.

But now *I* need her needing it.

She's still high on it. Her knees are splayed over my shoulders, and I feel the aftershocks in the little tremors of her legs, the way she flutters around nothing. I trail my mouth up her stomach and down again, the taste of her thick on my tongue.

I reach where she's dripping for me, tease her oversensitive pulse point just to hear that strangled little wail, like she's embarrassed to want it that much. Because she doesn't know how to stop herself anymore.

Good.

Neither do I.

'Charlie,' I murmur against her belly button, scraping my teeth over warm skin. 'You ready for me to fuck you, baby?'

'Yes... Brodie. Yes!'

She reaches for me and wriggles down my body, tries to grab me like she needs me inside her now, now, now.

And Christ, do I want to fill her up, let her feel just how far gone I am.

I'm so fucking hard I'm about to burst.

I reach for my wallet from my bag beside the bed, and fish out a condom. Last one. Haven't stocked up since I gave up on casual fucks.

I rip the foil open and slide it over my rock-hard length. 'You told me to "glove up". Here we go.'

A sharp inhale. And then she giggles, rolls onto her back and tugs me down with her, fisting my hair as she shoves her mouth against mine in a bruising, frenzied kiss. She's trying to devour me whole, to make me feel everything she's allowing herself to feel.

'Now, Charlie.' I murmur low against her chin. 'Open up for me.'

I pull her shorts and soaked thong down her legs, then off completely.

And fuck.

I take a moment to look at her.

She's sprawled out in front of me, hair a goddamn mess, pupils wide, skin shimmering in the dim glow of the street-light outside. Her legs are spread, inner thighs pink from my beard. She's got the prettiest fucking cunt I've ever seen. Plump, flushed, with a soft strip of caramel-blonde hair.

I have never, in my entire life, seen anything so damn beautiful.

I nudge my tip up and down her wet mess, notch it at her tight entrance, pressing enough to feel her quiver. She sinks her nails into my biceps, breath ragged, chest heaving, so fucking horny she can barely stand it.

'Please, Brodie. N-now… Please…'

'Told you that you'd beg for my cock.'

I push inside.

Jesus fucking Christ.

She's soft. Not too tight, just snug enough that I feel every tiny give and drag, every velvet inch as she stretches around me.

I go slow.

I don't want to.

I *have* to.

Because she's so wet, so fucking perfect, I already feel that tightening in my balls, that dangerous, burning pressure in my backbone, threatening to blow.

Her head lolls back, a broken gasp torn from her as she digs her heels into my arse, pushing me deeper.

'Fuck you, Brodie...' Her voice breaks. 'You feel too good. So hard. Big fucking dick. Too much. God... Oh god...'

My name on her lips when I'm buried inside her? Fucking lethal. My teeth snap together, and I push all the way in, watching her writhe beneath me.

'That's it, baby. Feel me. Take it.'

She clamps down around me, so hot, and I'm shivering now, barely holding on. Because it's her.

It's Charlie.

And I'm done pretending I don't need this. Don't need her.

So, I give her everything, grind my hips to make her feel it. The stretch. The weight. The friction.

'AH! I-I love the way you fuck me... I'll take it, I'll take all of it ... Please keep going... Please. Don't be gentle. Don't you fucking dare... Brodie... Brodie...'

I groan, and a slow, filthy roll of my hips makes her cry out. She's still sensitive from the way I ate her out, from how I made her grind on my tongue.

'So soft. So fucking soft.' I lean in, nose grazing hers, trembling with the effort it takes not to lose it right there, buried in the sweetest fucking grip I've ever felt.

'You feeling me, baby?'

She nods, feverish and sweaty, eyes rolling back, white flashing under heavy lids.

'God, you're fucking beautiful when you're taking me so deep.'

'Yes. M-more. I need it… I need you…'

Lord have mercy.

I kiss her again. Make her feel it in her spine.

This is it. What I've been dying to give her. One tit in my mouth, the other in my hand, fucking her slow. Long, dragging thrusts that make her shiver. I pull out, let her feel every inch of me slipping free – then slide back in, bottoming out with a splintered groan.

'I didn't know it could…feel like this. Didn't know *I* could feel like this. Fuck, yes. Yes!'

Her body is pulsing around me like she never wants me to leave. She writhes, thighs trembling, head rolling back against the pillow, a broken string of sounds spilling out of her.

'Faster… Please… Brodie. N-need you harder…'

The words shoot straight through my core, detonating what's left of my control.

She's the boss.

I rear up, take her thighs, pin her open, and fucking give it to her.

A sharp snap of my hips. A brutal thrust that knocks another cry from her. Back arching, hands scrabbling for something to hold on to – me, the sheets, anything – begging, taking every hard, hungry stroke like the champ she is.

I hit that perfect spot inside her, again and again, slap of skin-on-skin and the squeaking of the bed frame filling the room, drowning out every thought except *more*.

She clamps down hard, legs shaking, eyes dazed, mouth open on panting moans.

I lower my head. 'There?'

A frantic nod. A choked sob. 'Yes! Yes! AH! Don't stop—'

As if I could.

I'm a good boy, and I keep going in that rhythm she needs to crest.

Her channel tightens around me, squeezing me so tight my vision blurs, and I know – I know – she's right there. I bury myself in her, rough and fast, chasing her over the edge.

Her whole body locks up. Her mouth drops open, and a little scream breaks loose, hitting the air as if it hurts to hold it in. And she shatters, rhythmic pulses pulling me under with her. A roar rakes out of me as I thrust, my balls tightening, throbbing, and then – fuck – I'm coming so hard my arms give out and my heart explodes.

The world narrows to her. The feel of her. The smell of her. The way her body keeps clenching, like she's holding onto the last shreds of pleasure.

To me.

I drop my forehead to hers, fighting for air, completely undone.

She's shivering, arms looped tight around my shoulders. Her skin is damp, her hair is tangled, her breath is hot against my mouth. She's looking up, half-wrecked, half-stunned, like she doesn't believe it happened. Like she doesn't know how to handle the way I'm still inside her, still holding her like she might disappear.

Her cheeks are pink with heat, lips swollen from kissing me.

'Wow,' is all she whispers.

I look down and see this little mole on her left tit. Tiny, dark, heart-shaped. I trace it with my nose, taste it with my tongue.

Charlie closes her eyes, and her fingers ease off my back. I gave her everything. Still might not be enough.

I'm already burned alive just from being this close, just from being the one making her look like this. And I don't ever want to move.

But I can already tell she's going to make me.

Chapter 14

Charlie

It's too early. The kind of early where the world's still blue and nothing makes sense yet. My brain hasn't caught up to my body, and my body – fuck. It feels rearranged. Stretched, filled, and hollowed all at once.

And I'm not alone.

I'm cradling a furnace. A living furnace. His chest is solid under my head, heartbeat slow and steady, and it's thudding in my bones.

And god help me, I don't want him to move. I don't want any of this to move. I want to capture the moment, preserve it forever, keep it safe and warm and unbreakable.

He's still asleep. I can tell by the way his breath coasts over my forehead, a soft, even rhythm that doesn't match the shallow tempo of mine. He smells clean and musky – soap and skin and sex and Brodie – and I'm wrapped up in it, drinking it in like it's the only air I've got.

My thighs are sore. Bruised from how he took me apart last night. My hips ache from being gripped, my neck burns where he bit me, and there's this slow pulse between my legs that's more memory than pain.

And I should be freaking the fuck out.

Telling myself it was inappropriate, irresponsible.

Because it was.

But my whole body hums with satisfaction, as if it knows something my brain doesn't, basking in the fact that I'm still tucked against him, his arm under my head, hand holding my shoulder in his sleep like he plans to keep me pinned right here.

Brodie.

God, he's so warm. Weight and muscle and something I could lean into forever. And I didn't know… I didn't know it could feel like this. I'm whole and emptied. I gave something I didn't know I had. And now I don't know how to take it back.

It wasn't just the way he moved. But the way he *looked*. Like he wanted to learn me by heart. This raw, steady devotion that I didn't see coming.

It felt like being found.

Tears pool. Embarrassing shit. I'm not supposed to want this. He's my client. My career. My biggest fucking project.

I catch the first one with the heel of my hand and swipe it away as though it were never there.

Brodie shifts in his sleep, and every part of me stills. His thumb sweeps over my skin, a lazy, unthinking stroke, and a quiet sound catches on the edge of my breath before I can swallow it down.

His rhythm changes. He's waking up. His thumb drifts again, stroking.

His voice rumbles against my hair, gravelled with sleep. 'Hey.'

And it's that single word – that sleepy, unguarded murmur full of tenderness – that undoes me. It runs hot down my cheek. I bite my lip and swallow the ache.

I lay still. My head is pressed to his sternum, listening to his heartbeat. It's the only thing keeping me together.

He stirs, and his hand comes up to cradle my face. 'Hey, what's all that now? You crying, Champ?'

I go stiff, and he feels it. I know he does, brow furrowing as he looks at me.

'No,' I lie, too fast. 'Bit of grit in the eye.'

He cups my chin and keeps me right where he wants me. 'Charlie.'

'It's nothing. Probably allergies. Dust or something.'

He swipes gently beneath my eye, chasing another tear. 'Don't.'

I try to draw air past the tightness beneath my ribs, but it makes it worse. So, I force myself to tilt my chin up and meet his gaze. It's like staring straight into the sun.

'It's fine, Brodie. I'm fine.' My voice is way too small.

'You don't cry for no reason.'

I blow out a laugh that feels more like a wince. 'Maybe I'm just… I'm sore.'

His lips twitch, but his eyes don't soften. 'Sore's one thing. This is something else.'

I shove at his pecs, try to put some distance between us, but he doesn't let me go far. Just turns enough to look me in the eye, his thumb still brushing softly, as if he thinks stopping might tip me over.

'Talk to me.' His voice is rough but not harsh. 'Don't lock me out.'

'I'm not…' The lump in my throat's too big to swallow, but I try anyway. 'There's nothing to say. All good.'

'That's a load of shite.' Brodie lets out a low, frustrated sound.

He draws his hand back and fists the duvet instead, like he's fighting the urge to grab me and shake me until the truth comes out.

Loaded silence hangs between us.

Part of me wants to give in. To bury my face in his neck

and let him hold me until this hot mess inside me stops burning.

But not when I know the cost of wanting this. Of wanting him.

It's a disaster in the making.

I turn and pull myself up to sit against the pillows. Brodie watches me, eyes far too perceptive. He doesn't close the gap. He's waiting me out.

And I'm not sure what's worse. That he's giving me space or that I wish he wouldn't.

What the fuck is wrong with me?

He scrubs a hand down his face, holding back from pushing too hard.

It hits a place I don't let anyone touch.

I shove my hand through my hair, trying to comb out the tangles, but it's useless. Everything in me is knotted up and backwards. I glance at him, and he's still watching me. Reading me. Careful not to press too hard.

'You gonna keep staring at me like that?' I mutter, aiming for a smirk and missing miserably.

'I'm trying to work out what's going on in that pretty head of yours.'

I shrug and pull my knees to my chest, wrapping my arms around them. 'Nothing. Brain's still half asleep.'

He doesn't buy it. Not for a second.

'Last night was…' I start, but the words dry up.

'Aye,' he says softly. 'It was.'

A shiver rolls through me, and I lower my forehead to my knees, squeezing my eyes shut. 'But we shouldn't have done it.'

'You regret it?'

I whip my head up, and the expression on his face cuts through me. 'No. Fuck, no. That's not… I mean it wasn't…' I'm struggling for words. 'It wasn't a smart call.'

A slow exhale. 'Smart doesn't come into it, Charlie. You know that.'

My mouth twists. 'Doesn't change that it was reckless as hell.'

'Possibly. Doesn't mean it wasn't real. So, what's the problem?'

I dig my fingers into my shins. 'You know what the problem is. I have an agency to think about. You have a comeback to make. We can't afford distractions. If this goes wrong… This was—'

'Don't even start.'

'Brodie…'

'No. I'm not playing that game where you call it just sex. You were mine last night. You can't lie to me about that.'

My lungs seize. I can't lie, but I can't give him what he wants, either. I can't let him know how close he is to breaking my resolve. Because if I admit it, it'll unravel everything I've worked for. I've fought tooth and nail to get where I am. One mistake and it could all come crashing down.

I can't let him be that mistake.

Not him.

He shakes his head, eyes narrowing. 'It wasn't just sex, Charlie. You know that. You ever come like that before?'

I don't answer.

'Thought so,' he mutters.

A beat passes. 'Callum was…my first,' I blurt. And I hate that I need him to know this. 'And…my only.'

His expression goes dark. 'You're shitting me.'

I stare at the wall. 'We were together for almost two years, and—'

'And that prick didn't know what to do with you, did he?'

I try to play it off. 'It wasn't that bad. It was…okay.'

Brodie curses under his breath, working hard not to let it piss him off too much. 'Jesus, Charlie. Okay is not enough. Never enough. You deserved better than that. Still do.'

I look at him then, and his eyes are darker than usual, heat simmering under the surface. It makes my skin tingle, and I hate that I want him all over again.

'You don't need that much experience to understand last night was fucking phenomenal,' he says and almost sounds like he's arguing with himself. 'I've been around, Charlie. Coming together like that, first go? Can't fake that kind of connection. That's rare.'

His words hit low, right where I'm soft and aching. I don't know what to say to that, so I don't say anything at all. Just stare at my hands, fingers twisting together.

'You fucking melted on my cock, Champ.' He reaches out, brushes his knuckles under my eye. 'You deserve someone who makes you feel like that every single time.'

My eyes burn. 'I'm not looking for that. I'm not looking for anything.'

He scoffs. 'Right. Too focused on your agency to let someone take care of you.'

Anger flares up inside me. 'I have too much at stake. I can't afford to lose my head over you.'

'You wouldn't. You're way too stubborn for that.'

'I mean it.'

He rolls his eyes. 'Oh, I heard you. Doesn't make it any less bullshit.'

I exhale hard, tension winding through me, and he seems to sense it because he lets his hand drop, backing off without pushing. Only makes me want to throw myself at him more.

No.

No. No. No.

I've done enough damage already. To him, to myself, to my company.

I shove back the covers, swing my legs over the side of the bed, and stand up.

Distance. I need distance.

I go to the dresser, rummage through my suitcase, ignoring the burn of his stare on my back.

'You're not wrong,' he says calmly. 'You've got your career. I've got my game. We're both trying to prove something. But don't fucking stand there and act like last night was just a nice shag.'

I grip the dresser, glaring at the floor. 'It wasn't. But we can't—'

'You can walk away if you need to. I'll let you go. But look at me, Charlie. Look at me! I'm saying this only once, and I need to be sure you understand every fucking word.'

I turn around. He's a storm front, all dark edges and heat.

'All right. I'll give you your space. I'll respect your boundaries. Makes sense. I get it. Just know this…' He leans forward, gaze spearing straight through me. 'If this *ever* happens again – if you so much as fucking *look* at me like you want me – I'm not giving you up a second time. And you'll have to live with the consequences.'

My heart pounds so hard it hurts.

'I'm not a toy. You get me, Charlie?' His tone's quieter now, but still laced with that fierce, unshakable certainty. 'So, you better think really fucking carefully before you ever let this happen again. Because I've got boundaries too.'

That landed. Harder than I want to admit. I steady my voice enough to make it sound like a decision, not a retreat. 'Don't worry. It won't happen again.'

He's sitting on the edge of the bed now, elbows on his knees, chin propped on his hands, looking at me like he's trying to figure out what to do with me. His jaw is tight, shadows cutting hard lines across his face, and I still feel the weight of his words.

'All right,' he says. 'We'll focus on your agency and my game. Clean slate.'

I nod, not trusting myself to say anything, because I'm

pretty sure my voice will crack. He's doing what I asked – being reasonable, being rational.

I'm almost out the door when something flies at me. I catch it just before it can hit my head – a granola bar. I look up, and there's a hint of that wicked glint back in his eyes.

'Eat something, Harrington,' he says gruffly. 'God knows you earned it last night. And take off my Rebels shirt before I change my mind, bend you over that fucking dresser, and show you what it means when you wear it.'

Chapter 15

Brodie

It's louder than I expected. Not packed, not deafening. The new stand looms to my left. Five thousand seats, maybe half full. There's a hum in the stands. Low, electric. Still not nearly as loud as the racket in my skull. My pulse knocks behind my eyes like fists on a locked door.

First home game. The Caerwyn Chargers from Wales. Mid-level, but scrappy, hungry to prove themselves. We're raw, still figuring each other out, but we've got fight. And even more to prove.

End of September and Scotland's showing its teeth already, wind slicing through my shirt. Sky's a dull grey. Grass is damp under my studs, slick enough to make traction a gamble. I haul in a breath and flex my hands to keep them warm. Knuckles crack. Good. A reminder I'm still in one piece. Still holding it together.

Finn jogs up beside me. Scottie's right behind him, eyes steely, mouth set in a grim line. Jamie smacks Finn's shoulder, muttering something that pulls a crooked grin from him.

I glance up toward the stands. Can't help it. VIP section's raised just enough for a clear line across the pitch. A glass-fronted box, open to the weather.

There she is.

Charlie.

Handling the press, making connections, charming, schmoozing. Fierce, poised, magnetic. Her caramel hair's catching the wind, whipping around her face. And I mustn't look too long because it messes with my head.

I exhale, shake out my shoulders, and nod to the lads.

We huddle up. Close, focused, no noise but the wind and the buzz of the crowd. Eyes on me.

'First game. First shot to show who the fuck we are. Keep it smart. Keep it tight. Don't play for the media.' I jerk my chin toward the stands. 'Play for each other. Let's fucking go!'

The huddle breaks.

I clamp down on the lump rising behind my sternum, scan their faces, and know it's on me to set the tone. Heart's in my throat, gut in a vice. But it's time to move. Time to fight. Time to show what the Stirling Rebels can do and that Brodie MacRae is still worth a damn.

The game's a blur of impact and instinct. Sweat, breath, blood howling between my ears. I'm in it, but not fucking in it. I'm a microsecond behind every play, pushing past the edge to catch up.

Ball comes flying at me, and I snatch it mid-air, feet digging into the ground. Shoulder to ribs, my arm locked around the ball. Pass to Scottie – clean, quick, right through two massive bastards trying to smash me into the dirt. He bolts up the line, dodges a tackle, and gains another ten.

Good. But I'm still playing catch-up.

The next hit comes fast and brutal. The opposing flanker levels me just as I cut behind the scrum. His shoulder jams into my ribs, and I slam down with a crack that scrapes straight through my spine. Winded. Mud in my teeth, coating my palms as I push myself up. Jamie's there, hauling me upright, and I'm back in position before the Chargers can capitalise.

'Come on, MacRae!' Cameron Wallace barks from the sidelines. Our coach is pacing like a caged wolf, eyes blazing. He's been behind me from the start. Can't fucking let him down.

Focus. I need to fucking focus.

I take the next pass – perfect spiral, straight to me – and surge forward. Someone's on my right – Jamie, ready for the handoff – but I see an opening and go for it. Lower my shoulder, break through a gap, but there's too much fucking pressure. I'm caught, as three of them swarm me, dragging me down. I hit the ground hard, ball tucked tight, no backup. Before I can place it, they've snatched it clean.

I hear the ref's whistle, sharp and merciless, and it's done. Ball's theirs. Another fucking turnover.

Time's running out. We need one good play. Just one more.

But it never comes.

The whistle blasts, slicing through the noise. 14-16. Close loss. Closer than anyone thought we'd get in our first game.

Should feel like a victory. It doesn't. Not to me.

Because it's not the team that let it slip. It's me. I wasn't good enough. Wasn't sharp enough. Didn't read the pitch right. If I'd been faster, better, more tuned in, we'd have won.

The lads are on their knees, breathing rough, slapping each other's backs like they're proud of what we did. They should be. They fought like beasts.

But I didn't lead them the way I should've.

I hang back, shoulders tense, teeth set like I'm trying to keep the whole damn day from spilling out.

There's no pride in today. A loss is a loss.

My lungs are burning, sweat running down my back. My ribs ache, back's sore, and my thighs are cramping up. I scrub my hand across my skin, wiping sweat from my eyebrows. My forearms are streaked with dried mud.

They're waving me over to the improvised media tent by the touchline. I want to tell them to fuck off. Not happening. Captain's duty, can't dodge this one. I take a resigned breath and slog over. My legs are dead weight. Everything fucking hurts.

Coach is already there, leaning on the rail with that stoic look of his. Gives me a nod. He knows I'd rather be anywhere else. I wipe the sweat off again, roll both hands into fists to keep them from shaking, and step up to the mic.

I look for her. She's not here. Just cameras and nothing I give a shite about. Right. She's probably still up in VIP, doing her job. Keeping the journos onside, pushing the narrative. Makes sense.

Even if I don't see what the hell there is to spin after that performance.

I know I'm talented as fuck. I just need more focus. More bite.

The first reporter doesn't waste time. 'Respectable start for a new side, Brodie. How are you feeling about the result?'

I nod and keep my tone even. 'Aye, a score like that hurts. But in the end, the Chargers had the upper hand. The lads gave everything. It was a close contest. We had our moments. Plenty to build on. We'll keep pushing.'

Another voice jumps in, fast. 'Plenty of eyes on you today, Brodie. How does it feel stepping back onto the pitch with all that…controversy ?'

Honestly? Like getting punched in the nuts and told to smile. I knew it was coming. Knew someone would bring it up. And if Charlie hadn't made me sit through those extra media sessions – hours of pacing, reframing – I'd probably be throwing fists instead of sound bites.

I was pissed with her for it at the time. But that's the only reason that guy isn't picking up his teeth from the turf right now.

I square my stance, meet their eyes. 'Feels right. Feels like home. I'm here to play rugby. Nothing else.'

Someone else calls out, 'What's your take on the team's potential this season?'

I keep my expression neutral. 'We've got talent. Grit. You saw it. Still a few things to tidy up, but the effort's there. The belief's there. And we're only just getting started.'

Cameron steps in before the next question can land. 'That's all for now. Brodie's got recovery to do.'

I slap his hand low as I pass, shoulder past the reporters, and make for the tunnel.

It's calmer there. But that doesn't stop the thudding between my temples. The lads will be gassed up, riding the high of a decent debut. And aye, it could've been worse, over-all. And yet... It doesn't sit right with me. I could've done more. I should've done better.

The changing room's dead quiet. Steam clings to the air. I've half a mind to go find the physio and make him fix whatever the fuck's wrong with my back.

I'm clean, showered, and dressed, but I still feel filthy. Stale. The game's clinging to my skin. Chin tucked to my chest, I stare at the floor. My boots are shoved under the bench, mud caked around the cleats, and I'm too fucked to move.

The lads were riding the mood when they left, already on their way to the Sin & Tonic for the after party.

Not me.

Coach said it was a good start. But I was meant to carry us through the tough spots. Break the deadlock. Get us over the line.

Instead, I got put on my arse more times than I care to admit.

I've played worse games. Hell, I've lost by a lot more. But

that was before. Before I had to earn back every scrap of respect. Before I knew what it felt like to have it all stripped away and start over.

The door creaks open, and I can't even be arsed to look up. Just brush the grit off my jeans, even though there's nothing there, and mutter, 'Don't feel like talking.'

Charlie's voice cuts through the silence. 'Too bad. One more interview. They're waiting.'

My throat pulses, heat rising fast. I bite down so hard I feel it in my ears. 'I've given enough.'

'Apparently not. They want the man of the match.'

I shake my head. 'That can't be me.'

Her heels echo on the tiles, each step measured against the silence. I don't look, but I feel her watching. A current flickers along my cheek like static.

'If you weren't good enough, they wouldn't be waiting.' Charlie steps closer, voice low but fierce. 'You're not Atlas. You don't have to carry the whole game on your shoulders. Snap out of it, MacRae. You're leading a new team. This was never going to be perfect from the get-go. Ever heard of expectation management?'

She doesn't give me a choice. Crouches in front of me. Her hand's on my knee, small and warm, keeping me tethered. She grazes the fabric, and it's fucking nothing, but it feels like everything. She looks at me like I did something right. Like I held the team, held the line, held my own. She believes it. Feels it. Says it like it's fact. And for some fucked-up reason, that sinks in.

Because she doesn't hand out faith lightly.

And she's giving it to me.

Even now.

Even when I can't give it to myself.

She's close enough that I see every detail – the way her lashes dip low, that faint line between her brows, the slight quiver of her lower lip. I lift my hand, and my thumb moves without permission, tracing the curve of her cheekbone. She leans into it just a fraction, like she can't help herself, and it nearly kills me.

'I hate that you make so much sense.' Didn't mean to say it. Definitely didn't mean it to sound like that.

Her eyes don't drop. She hears it. All of it.

'I hate that too.' Her tone catches at the end.

'Aye?' I'm so close I taste her breath on my tongue, and my heart's pounding hard enough to crack my ribcage.

Her gaze darts to my mouth, and her grip firms on my thigh. I know she feels it too – this agonising fucking draw between us.

And I'm screwed. Because now I *know* how Charlie tastes. Feels. On my mouth. Around my cock.

I brush her nose with mine, and I'm two seconds away from saying '*fuck it*' and kissing her, taking what I want for once instead of holding back.

Her gaze softens, something fragile breaking through before she shutters it behind a breath. Locks it down and swallows the heat like it'll choke her otherwise.

'Brodie,' she whispers. 'You…did good. They want to hear from the captain. Go give them something good to print. You got this.'

'Awright.' I shake out my shoulders like I'm gearing up for another round. 'Let's get it over with, then.'

She squeezes my thigh once before letting go.

That was a damn close call.

But I want *her* to break first.

I want her to close the distance and show me she's just as fucking helpless as I am.

Because I might be a goner for Charlie Harrington and have fucked up our first shot at a win, but I'm also a proud and stubborn bastard. And I can wait. For the victory and the girl.

Chapter 16

Charlie

My heart's still racing from the phone call when I pull up outside Brodie's place. I had to tell him in person. Biggest sponsorship deal I've ever landed, and it's his. And, by extension, the Rebels'. I've been working on it since August, behind the scenes, and now it's sealed.

It's almost nine, but there's light upstairs. He's home and awake. Relief loosens something in my chest. I half expected him to still be at the gym, pushing himself like he has since the last games.

Their season started two weeks ago with one close-run loss. Then one massive loss – against Glasgow in Glasgow. And one *very* pissed off MacRae.

I jump out of the car, walk up, and rap on the door. If he doesn't answer soon, I might kick it in. I knock again, harder this time. Still nothing. I put my ear to the wood, straining for any sound.

I'm about to text him when he finally opens.

My grin dies.

He's hunched over like a question mark, one hand braced on the doorframe, the other pressed to his lower back. Sweat mats his hairline. His shoulders are rigid, breath shallow, and there's pain in his eyes that he can't hide.

'What happened to you?' I shove my way inside before he can stop me, careful not to touch him.

He tries to straighten. 'Training. Took a hit.'

'You're kidding me.' I scan him, catching every wince he thinks he's hiding. 'Your back?'

He nods, lips pressed into a line. 'Just pulled something. Probably QL spasm. Doc says it's not too terrible. I'll walk it off.'

'Walk it off?' I drop my purse and turn to face him. 'You can barely stand, MacRae.'

He doesn't meet my gaze, just swipes a hand over his face.

I step closer and soften my tone. 'Brodie. Talk to me.'

'It's fine. Just…need a day or two.'

I've never seen him like this. Crumpled, struggling to catch his breath. And that iron grip he's got on his pride is making it worse.

'You need to lie down, MacRae.'

'You need to chill, Harrington.'

'Now.' I cross my arms, feet planted. 'You're going to haul your surly arse upstairs and lie down. Don't argue; don't even think about it. Let's move.'

Getting him up the stairs is a bloody battle. But one glare from me shuts him up. I practically frogmarch him to his bedroom, ignoring his huffy complaints.

'Sit.' I give him a gentle nudge toward the bed.

'You and your orders.'

'I'm the boss, as you well know.'

He grunts, but doesn't argue, and sinks down gingerly on the edge, mouth set like a locked door against whatever pain is in his back.

That is worrying.

I point a finger at him. 'Stay put. I'm getting ice. The first forty-eight hours ice, then heat. You know the drill.'

He grumbles something unintelligible, but doesn't move an inch.

When I come back, he's still looking like he'd rather be anywhere else.

'Take these.' I drop the ibuprofen into his palm and hand him a glass of water. He swallows them down without a word.

I glance around the room, taking it in for the first time. It's not just a bedroom.

It's also a damn greenhouse.

Plants everywhere. Vines draping down from the shelves, a huge potted fern in the corner. I can barely see the walls.

I raise a brow. 'Are you secretly running a garden centre?'

'It's a hobby, keeps me grounded. Plants don't judge, they just grow. And they help me sleep. Calm me down.'

I snort, amused, endeared, and taking the piss. Just a little.

He shoots me a look. 'Shut up.'

I sit down beside him on the bed, shoving the ice pack under his shirt, pressing it right to the sore spot on his back. He hisses, but I don't ease up.

'You're such a bloody fool,' I say louder than I should. 'Pushing yourself like this. What good are you to anyone if you break yourself in half?'

He scowls at me with a side-glance 'I'm fine. Only a knock. Nothing I haven't handled before.'

'Doesn't impress me. You're not a machine, Brodie. Throwing yourself past the line doesn't make you a leader.'

'It's my job to push. To take hits. You think I can afford to half-arse it? Not when the lads are looking to me to set the bar.'

'Set the bar, not hurt your spine,' I fire back. 'You're the captain. Act like it. If you're out there throwing yourself into tackles like a maniac, they're gonna think that's the standard. You want your team to end up in A&E because you're too thick-headed to know your own limits?'

'Oh, I know my limits.'

'Clearly.' I shove the ice into place, no mercy. 'You can't lead or play from a hospital bed, MacRae.'

'You done lecturing me?'

'You done being a dick?' I don't back down. 'So, no. Not till you admit you're being an irresponsible arse.'

His shoulders drop, and some of the fight bleeds out of him. 'Fine. *Maybe* I overdid it a wee bit.'

'Maybe? A wee bit?'

He grunts, not conceding but not denying it either. And that's about as close to an admission as I'm going to get from him. Still, it's enough to take the edge off my own temper.

I ease up on the ice pack. 'Next time you throw yourself around like that, I'll kick your arse myself. Got it?'

He glances at me, a half-smile softening the line of his mouth. 'Like to see you try.'

'Oh, don't tempt me,' I mutter, but a smile pulls at my lips before I can stop it.

My eyes snag on something bright, pink, and sparkly on his dresser, overshadowed by an obscenely huge monstera.

I squint, tilting my head. 'What on god's green earth is that?'

His gaze flicks over, and he actually looks sheepish. 'It's for Hannah. On our promo tour, you mentioned she likes sparkles. Thought she could use a cowboy hat for that Beyoncé performance.'

And the world just…stops.

A burn starts behind my eyes. I stare at this brooding tank of a man. Buying pink cowboy hats with sequins for my sister's talent show.

He remembered.

It's not just the hat. It's the way he remembers everything I say. Like he's been saving it all up, waiting for a chance to get a smile out of me. That's how he cares. Quietly. Fiercely. Without ever needing credit.

I've spent my whole life bracing for the let-down. For someone to prove I was right not to trust them. And here's Brodie, the last man I ever thought would crash through my walls, showing me I've been wrong about everything.

About him. About me. About us.

I'm trying to keep my shit in check, but it's too late. I'm crumbling because he's the one thing I never saw coming. The man who makes me want more. Want better. And I don't have a script for that.

Shit.

I can't make myself breathe properly, and I don't know why it hits so hard. Just that it does. A cheap pink hat and suddenly my entire world implodes.

He notices, glancing at me with a frown. 'Charlie? Look, if it's weird—'

'It's not.'

The ice pack drops from my fingers. I can't speak. Can't do anything but stare at his back, his broad shoulders so tense.

A pink cowboy hat. For Hannah.

He remembered. The sparkles. Her.

The part of me that doesn't trust splinters open. The feeling is raw and unfamiliar and has me wanting to crawl out of my skin. I don't even realise I'm moving until I lay my hands flat against his back, palms sliding over the taut muscles as he stiffens under my touch.

'Charlie?' He says it carefully, as if he's not sure if I'm about to lose it or hug him.

My chest is so full, and my pulse is ticking at the back of my neck. I shake my head, holding back the words that want to spill out. Words I shouldn't say.

He shouldn't be like this. He shouldn't be kind and patient and thoughtful. He should be selfish. Like Callum. Like my dad. Like every man who's ever let me down.

But he's not.

He's...Brodie. Real and unbreakable, even when he's hurting. Even when he's doubting himself. He buys a pink cowboy hat for a girl he's never met, because he remembers me mentioning it in passing.

Because he fucking cares.

I feel it like a knife between my ribs, cutting out every doubt I've ever had.

I drop my head against his shoulder, and I draw his scent into my lungs. Clean, musky, familiar. I brush my lips against the warm stretch of skin on the nape of his neck. It's not enough. I want to climb inside him, burrow under his skin and never come out.

'Charlie. Don't touch me like that. Don't kiss me.' His voice is dark. 'You don't get to tease and run. One more move, and you're mine. You might own my arse professionally, but I'll make sure I own yours in every other way. That clear enough for you?'

A pause.

'Yes.'

'Not enough, Charlie. Spell it out. Say it like you mean it. You want this? You tell me. Loud and clear. Once and for all.'

I'm fucked. Because nothing's ever felt this right. Or this terrifying. I comb my fingers through his thick hair. It might stop me from tipping over. Behind my ears, everything rushes. Need claws through me so fast I forget how to stand.

The truth is out before I can stop it. 'I'm already yours.'

He lets out a pained sigh. 'Then get in front of me, baby. Let me see what's mine. Let me fucking *feel* it.'

I get up and move around him until I'm standing in the space right between his thighs. He reaches for me without thinking, but I shut him down with a look, then haul my jumper over my head. My bra comes off next – hook, slide, drop. His gaze flicks to my tits, and his whole face changes, reverence and hunger colliding. He's barely holding it together.

So am I. Every part of me is hot with it – want, need, whatever the hell this is. The way he looks at me – like I'm his fucking religion – hits so low I almost moan. My mouth parts. And for a second, I don't know if I want to cry or beg or climb him like a ladder.

All of it. The answer is all of it.

I shimmy out of my jeans and thong, kick them aside, and lean in, mouth to his ear. 'You've got me. So, what are you gonna do with me, captain?'

His breath punches out like I've knocked it from his lungs. Hands fly up to my hips, yanking me close.

He kisses my stomach. 'Charlie. Baby.'

The sound of his voice guts me, and I sway on my feet. One of his hands coasts up my side, thumb skimming under my breast like he's checking I'm real.

His gaze is pure wildfire. 'You don't even see it, do you? How beautiful you are. How fucking gone I am for you?'

He drops his hand and cups my bare mound like it's his. No patience or softness. Just calloused fingers dragging through the mess he's made of me.

'Christ, Charlie. So fucking soft and wet. You need me that bad again?'

The sound he lets out tears straight through my core. Like the only thing keeping him upright is how close he is to fucking me.

'Always,' I whisper – and something cracks wide open in his face, like I just gave him permission to hope.

He sinks two thick fingers into me, drags them in slow and deliberate, then does it again. Like he's testing how much I can take. How much he's allowed to give.

'Fuck. Clench around me like that again, and I'll come in my fucking pants.'

He shifts, working deeper. And I feel everything – his breath against my skin, his fingers slick with how soaked I am. He's carving space for himself inside me with the push of every knuckle.

He's still too careful. Too in control. And it's torture, because I feel the restraint shaking through him. He's holding back a storm.

But I want that storm.

His digits catch a spot that makes my thighs jerk.

He grips my hip, steadying me. 'You feel that? Baby, that's need. Don't think I don't feel it too. Every time you touch me, my body fucking forgets who it belongs to.'

He crooks his fingers inside me, hitting that spot again, and I whimper, clinging to his shoulders, desperate for something to hold me together.

But nothing makes sense. Nothing except him.

'Oh my... Fuck, Brodie. That... Jesus, that's so good. Where the hell did you—?'

I'm grinding down on his hand like it's the only thing holding me together, and all I can do is gasp. 'How are you this good with your fingers?'

'Fast hands, Champ.' He leans in, lips brushing my ear. 'Comes with the position.'

He pulls out, fingers glistening, and I'm already aching. I want to sob, want to grab his wrist and shove him back inside me like I'll fall apart without him there.

'No one's ever touched me like this.' My voice breaks over it. 'Like they know my body better than I do. Like they fucking care.' I grip his wrist, trying to hold myself steady. 'I don't want anyone else. I don't think I ever did. I want you. All of you. I want to feel what it does to me when I finally stop holding back.'

His eyes are black now. Hunger flaring, restraint snapping thread by thread.

'God. Charlie... Yes. We're doing this right. All in. But the only way I can fuck you tonight is flat on my back. So come ride me.'

He shifts carefully, one hand reaching back to tug the shirt over his head with a breath that slips through gritted teeth.

I plant my palms on his chest, pushing him back gently. His lips slant like he's trying to smother a grimace with something cocky. He lets me guide him down, easing onto the bed.

'Let me be in charge.' I trace my fingers over his pecs. 'You don't always have to carry the whole damn world. I promise to be gentle.' That last bit slips out on a smug grin.

'No.' His chest rumbles with a sound that's half challenge, half surrender. 'I want to watch you bounce on it, baby.'

He sinks fully back against the mattress, eyes locked on me, daring me to take the lead.

I reach for his waistband, working the button open, knuckles brushing the flat of his stomach. He lifts his hips with a wince, breath catching as I ease his jeans down. His briefs follow, and then he's bare – swollen, proud, and so fucking beautiful it makes me dizzy.

Good lord. That's a lot of cock.

And it's all mine.

I barely get his clothes to the floor before he grips my waist and pulls me over him.

'You've got me so fucking thick I can't think. My cock's aching, my heart's fucking worse, and I still want you closer.'

I shift, soaked with want, sliding over him slowly. I'm making him wet so he gets in easier. He jerks beneath me, impossibly hard. Like the rest of him. Built to break me open and make me thank him for it.

'Holy fuck! You gonna ride me? Or are you just trying to kill me?'

I can't help the giggle that slips out. 'You think I'm *that* cruel?'

He grabs my tits with both hands like he's staking a claim.

'Charlie…'

'Yeah?'

'We good? I mean…you clean? On anything?'

I nod. 'Implant. Got tested last month. All clear.'

His relief is almost palpable. 'Same. Never bare.' His gaze locks on mine, serious. 'Never wanted to. Till now.'

Something melts and rushes at that confession, all at once, and I'm gone. I hook my fingers under his jaw, tipping his face to mine, and kiss him. 'Don't hold back.'

'You want me to come inside you? Claim that pretty cunt?'

'Yeah.' I nip at his bottom lip. 'I want to feel you. Nothing in the way. Nothing between us.'

'Jesus suffering fuck.' His head drops back. 'You're gonna *destroy* me.'

'Possibly,' I whisper. 'Let's see who breaks first.'

He laughs out loud. I don't think I've ever heard him laugh like that, and it sets my heart on fire.

I sink down on him slowly. He's so big, so hard for me, and my body can't decide whether to give up or whine for more. We both gasp at the connection – one shared, ragged sound – as if our bodies are the only ones brave enough to admit what this is. I brace my hands on his chest, fingers digging into solid muscle as I take him all the way, until I'm flush on his lap, and he's deep enough to squeeze the breath from my lungs.

He's forcing himself to stay still, to let me set the pace. But his hands are rough on my tits, squeezing enough to bruise, and his muscles are flexing under me, eager to thrust up.

'Fuck, Charlie. You feel like…like I've been waiting my whole goddamn life to be inside you.'

I rock back and forth. The friction sends sparks fizzing through my veins. I roll my hips again, sharper this time, and he groans – a broken sound that bursts from inside him, like he's helpless to stop it.

'You look so fucking pretty riding my cock.'

'I always…look good…on top.'

His laugh melts into a growl as I fuck him faster, greedy for the full stroke of him, my calves cramping, and I can't care. I keep going just the way I need it.

'That's it, baby. Use me. Fuck yourself on me. Make a fucking mess.'

Oh god. This man.

I'm so close I can taste it, heat snaking up my spine. Pressure pulsing in my core.

'Please,' I gasp on a sob. 'Please, Brodie. Make me come… Make me…'

He drives the heel of his hand right where I'm throbbing for it, and I cry out.

'That what you need? Need me to rub that clit?'

'Yes – fuck – yes!' I claw at his chest. 'Please, Brodie. Need it so bad. Oh GOD!'

He circles me fast and relentlessly, and the pressure lights me up from the inside. I can't hold back… Can't stop how I'm shaking, thrusting down harder, using him the way he told me to.

And I crest with a scream.

Savage heat barrels through me. I writhe against his palm, soaking him, clutching around him. He keeps working his hand on me until I'm nothing but sobs and pleasure, begging for mercy I don't want.

A hoarse sound tears from his throat. Now both hands seize my hips, dragging me down, deeper, holding me there.

'AH! Yes. Yes! Fuck. Cha—' He chokes on my name, and I feel it.

His body jolts under mine, hips lifting enough to drive up. He groans, loud and ragged, as he comes. Hot, helpless, spilling in thick spurts. His breath fractures. His grip bruises. He goes still, letting it crash through him.

I feel his heart jumping against his ribs. He slides his hands up my sides and pulls me down, crushing me against him as he groans out the last of it.

One last pulse hits, snug inside me, and I feel every twitch.

'Oh god. Charlie. Can't…fuck…can't even breathe.'

There's something stunned in his expression, like I broke him and he doesn't know how to put himself back together.

I know the feeling.

He wraps his arms around me, holding me so tight it hurts. I lick my tongue over his neck, tasting sweat and salt and something achingly real. My body's still pulsing, and I'm caught between bliss and disbelief. I can't help it that my heart trips over itself at the way he's holding me, like he's never letting go.

Good. Cause I'm here to stay.

'You're mine,' he murmurs against my hair. 'But god help me, Charlie, I'm so fucking yours.'

Chapter 17

Brodie

If there's one thing better than my girl in my rugby shirt, it's my girl in my rugby shirt in my bed, eating my beans on toast after I fucked her six ways from Sunday.

She's perched cross-legged on the bed, hair wild and sticking up in places, my shirt drowning her. Bare legs peek out from underneath, and her cheeks are all pink. Sex suits her. Being worshipped suits her. The empty plate's balanced on her knees, and she's licking tomato sauce off her thumb with a little furrow between her brows.

It's a masterpiece, that sight. I could stare at her for hours. Would, if she didn't catch me and shoot me that look that says, *'stop being a creepy bastard'*.

I shift on the mattress, half-expecting my back to seize up, but it doesn't. Feels good, actually. Loose. Like she fucked the tension right out of me. Guess that's one way to sort out a muscle problem. Flat on my back while she rode me like a cowgirl. Better than physio, honestly.

She looks up, catches me staring again, and raises a brow. 'You good?'

'Better than good. You fixed me.' I stretch my arms, testing the movement. Barely a twinge. 'Might have to prescribe that treatment more often.'

Her lips twitch, and she scoops up the last bit of beans with her crust. 'Mm. I'll bill you for my services later.'

'I'm already paying you. And I'd say I added a generous tip last night.'

Her throaty chuckle makes me grin wider. 'Your ego is the size of Scotland, MacRae.'

I lean back, elbows wide, fingers clasped at my neck. 'Can you blame me? Fixed my back and got the girl. Feeling a bit invincible, to be honest.'

'Beans on toast,' she scoffs. 'I was hoping for your spaghetti and meatballs.'

Charlie's giving me this look like she's just dropped the mic. I feel it low in my gut, satisfaction settling there. I almost forgot about that cooking show.

'What, you think I'd waste gourmet on you when I know you'll eat me up either way?' I toss out, a little cocky, and aye, that earns me a squint.

'Gourmet? You made spaghetti with tinned tomatoes.'

'Fancy tinned tomatoes,' I correct. 'Organic.'

She rolls her eyes and sets the plate on the bedside cabinet. Then she leans back.

'Maybe I'll whip up some pasta for you later.' I inch closer until I'm right up in her space. 'If you're good.'

Her mouth forms a teasing slant. 'I'm always good.'

'Debatable.' I steal a slow kiss, tasting ketchup and that faint sweetness that's Charlie. 'But you have potential.'

She laughs, and it's like every knot in my chest unravels.

Christ, I'm done for.

I'd make her spaghetti every day for the rest of my life if it meant hearing that sound on repeat.

She pulls back to look me in the eye, and I see it coming before she even says it. That guarded look. I steel myself, try to hold on to the warmth of her laugh like it's enough to drown out whatever she's about to throw at me.

'Brodie…' She hesitates, biting her lip. 'I'm all in with you. I am. But we can't let this get out. Not yet. I'm not ready for anyone – Callum, my father, the public – to tear this apart.'

It lands like a sucker punch to the solar plexus. My first instinct is to throw it straight back and say, *Fuck that, I'd fight anyone for this.* But I swallow it down, let it settle under my ribs, where the ache of her words burrows in.

'Right.' I try to make it seem easy. 'Secret. Under the radar. Whatever you need.'

She watches me and searches my face like she's not sure if I mean it. I reach out, trace my fingers over her jaw, and tuck a stray strand of hair behind her ear.

'It's fine, Charlie. We'll keep it quiet for now.' I make it sound like it's okay. I want it to be. 'One day you'll be ready. You're worth waiting for.'

Her shoulders ease a little, and she leans into my touch. But it doesn't stop that hollow feeling from creeping in. I'm already bracing for the hit when she decides she's had enough of me.

Me? I'd shout it from the rooftops if I could. But if she needs space, needs time to adjust, I'll give her that. Even if it feels like ripping my own heart out. Even if it means playing pretend that this is casual when it's anything but.

Because I'd do anything to keep her.

I push off the bed, fighting the tightness in my chest, and go to mist the plants. Anything to give my hands something to do other than grab her, trying to slip under her skin. Charlie shifts behind me, probably watching my arse, and I can't help the grin that creeps up on me.

'What are you, a houseplant whisperer?'

'Can't leave them to fend for themselves. These beauties need attention.'

She clicks her tongue. 'Should I be jealous?'

I turn my head and lift a brow. 'They don't give me nearly as much attitude.'

She grins wider. 'I can't believe you've got an actual rain forest growing in your bedroom. Is this your secret life? Captain of the Rebels by day, Tarzan by night?'

My cheeks heat up. She's got no idea. But I should tell her. I should trust her.

I mean, it's no big deal.

It's just…

Nobody knows.

'They're good for stress.' I try to sound casual. 'And maybe I, erm…share some of them online.'

She sits up, and curiosity sparkles under her lashes. 'Wait, what? Like, you post about *your plants*?'

I shrug, forcing nonchalance. 'Aye. On Insta. Only a few pictures. Some leaves. People seem to like it.'

Her jaw drops, and she squints at me. 'Are you telling me you're a plant influencer?'

'It's not like that.'

She squints her eyes. 'What's your handle?'

I pull a face. 'Naw.'

'Come on, spill.' She pokes my arm. 'You can't drop a bombshell like that and not give me the goods.'

'Och, it's not that interesting,' I grumble.

Her eyebrows nearly hit her hairline. 'You're kidding, right? You just admitted to being a green-thumbed fairy king. I'm invested now.'

I still hesitate, knowing damn well what's coming. Then I let out a resigned sigh. 'It's @PlantDaddy.'

She blanks, as if she's buffering, and her mouth falls open. 'No way.'

Before I can stop her, she's lunging for her phone, typing furiously. It only takes a few seconds before she's staring at the screen, wide-eyed and slack-jawed.

'Oh my god,' she breathes. 'Twenty-one thousand followers? Brodie MacRae. You're a walking plant kink. A horticultural hazard.'

My ears burn. 'It's just green stuff.'

'No, it's not just green stuff. It's your forearms. Your veiny, muscly forearms and huge, capable hands cradling houseplants like you're some rugged botanical sex god. I'm...I've never been so turned on in my life just from looking at plants.'

Her laughter rings through the room, and the part of me that's always braced goes soft for good. I can't help it.

Because I've never been this turned on in my life just from making someone laugh.

Still feels like I handed her a loaded gun and hoped she wouldn't pull the trigger. Showing her that part of me – the quiet, careful side – it's risky. But fuck me if it doesn't feel good seeing her light up over it.

Charlie's wiping tears from her eyes. 'Unbelievable. I'm dating a hot plant influencer.'

'We're dating?' I ask.

'We aren't?'

'Up to you, Charlie.'

I would fucking marry her this afternoon. But I can't tell her that.

She deflects. 'Jesus, I'll have to rein myself in or you'll end up in GQ posing with nothing but a fig.'

I grunt and cut her a glare. 'You done?'

She just grins wider. God, I love that smile.

Charlie's still scrolling through my feed with this glint in her eyes, and I'm half-tempted to snatch the phone away before she gets any more ideas.

Then she suddenly freezes and her eyes widen as if she's been struck by lightning. 'Shit. Brodie. I completely forgot to tell you.'

I wipe the mist from my hands. 'Forgot to tell me what? That you signed me up for a prostate cancer campaign?'

She flaps a hand in my direction and rolls her eyes, but there's something serious there too. 'The sponsorship. I landed it. The biggest deal for Elite Edge yet. And it's all yours, Brodie.'

It takes a moment to sink in. 'What?'

'Yeah. You. A two-year contract with MacKenzie Sporting. Low Six-figure sum. I got the call last night right before I showed up and you…distracted me with your entire existence.'

My brain catches up with what she's saying, and a slow grin spreads across my face. 'You're taking the piss.'

She shakes her head. 'Nope. It's done. You've got it.'

I know how much this means to her. How proud she is. And so am I. She's not just mine. She's unstoppable.

'You're a miracle worker. Always knew you could do it.'

Her features soften, and it seems as though she's trying not to show it meant something. But it did. I can tell.

I turn back to the plants, but I sense her sneaking up behind me. She hooks her chin over my shoulder, slides her hands around my waist, and slips her fingers under my shirt, tracing the line where the hair below my navel starts to thicken.

'Should I call you Plant Daddy from now on?' She purrs, low and teasing. 'Do you want to *mist* me?'

'Don't push your luck, Champ.'

She stretches up on her toes and seals her mouth to my neck, grazing her teeth along my skin.

I turn and tilt her chin up, closing my lips over hers, kissing her slowly and deeply. I spent weeks fisting my cock to the thought of her. God knows I've earned the right to take my time. Her round arse fills my palm – fucking made for my hands. Soft, warm, so goddamn perfect. I give her a smack and she gasps into me.

I'm done pretending I'm not starving for her every second of the day.

So, I nudge her back, guiding her to the bed.

She sinks onto the edge, staring up at me like she's daring me to make good on every filthy promise I whispered in her ear last night.

'*You* had beans on toast,' I murmur, sliding my hands to the backs of her knees and easing her open, 'but *I've* still got an appetite.'

Her breath hitches. 'What? Brodie…'

'Don't be coy, Champ. You know what's coming.'

'Me?' She grins, wicked.

'Damn right you are.'

I drop to my knees, palms skating up the backs of her thighs. Her scent hits me – sweet, tangy, fucked-out – and my mouth waters. She's parted and swollen, lips flushed dark where I took her hard. Like her body hasn't stopped missing me since I pulled out. Knocks the breath clean out of me.

Time to show that brave little pussy some love.

'Don't bother being quiet.' I glance up, voice gone gravel. 'Let me hear every fucking sound. The plants don't mind your screams.'

She smirks down at me. 'Told you that you'd be thanking me on your knees for saving your career, MacRae.'

I laugh, settle in, and drag my tongue over that spot that makes her buck.

My horny, bossy girl.

She tilts her hips up, chasing the heat of my tongue. I swirl around her needy little bud until she's panting. That's everything.

'You're not getting up until you're dripping down my face,' I murmur, nipping at her skin.

She lets out a wobbly giggle that melts into a moan when I lick into her again. Her taste hits deep in my throat. I earned that, too.

Her phone rings.

She tenses, but I don't let up. Just grip her thighs tighter, and keep fucking her with my tongue.

'Shit,' she breathes, trying to wriggle free, but I don't let her go anywhere.

Her phone keeps buzzing.

'Answer it,' I growl. 'Wanna hear you try to keep quiet while I eat you alive.'

She glares down at me like I'm out of my mind, but her hips rock forward anyway. I grin and lick up the length of her pussy. She fumbles for her phone, glancing at the screen.

'I-it's Theo,' she whispers.

'So?' I mouth against her slick flesh. 'Pick up.'

She hesitates, and I give her a warning nip. That gets me the sweetest little yelp. Her hand flails for the phone like her brain's split in two.

Then she takes a deep breath and answers. 'H-hello, The-Theo.'

She has the cutest clit I've ever seen. Just peeking out from under its hood, pink and pulsing like it knows I'm coming for it. And I am. I suck it between my lips. Her mouth drops open in a silent gasp, and fuck, it's glorious.

'H-hey,' she says, trying to sound normal. But it tangles with the moan she tries to smother. She's all breathless, like she's run a marathon. Theo's voice crackles through the speaker, too muffled to make out.

God help me if she ever figures out what I'm doing to her boss while she's asking about schedules. Right now, I don't give a damn. All I care about is Charlie's gorgeous wet pussy in my face.

She reaches down with her free hand, tangles her fingers in my hair and pushes me closer. I get the hint and double down. Her legs clamp around my head, and I hear her stutter, 'I...erm...sorry, Theo. W-what was that?'

I hum against her, and she shudders. She tries to keep talking, but it's useless. Her words keep breaking, gasps slipping out when I trace tight laps over that tender peak and work it. I slip two fingers into her. I want to make her take it, make her understand how greedy her pussy is for me, and she tries to smother her wail with her fist. Almost doesn't work.

She mumbles some excuse to Theo and hangs up, dropping the phone like it's on fire.

'God, Oh god,' she chokes out. 'Brodie...keep doing that and I'm never letting you leave. Never. You're... Fuck! Fuck! AH!'

I don't stop, giving her my mouth where I know it counts and fingering her fast.

My girl likes it rough.

And that's it. Her body jerks, a gush of slick soaks my face, and she's screaming my name, thrashing so hard I have to pin her down to keep her in place. She's gone, lost in it, and the sight of her is enough to make my cock ache like I'm the one getting off.

I fucking did that to her. Made her lose it so completely she's all over my face. Savage pride claws at my chest, knowing I'm the one who gets to see her come undone like this.

What a privilege.

She's shaking, gasping out curses, her limbs squeezing me so tight around the ears that I start seeing static. Doesn't matter. I'd suffocate right here, face buried in her lovely cunt, and die a happy man.

When she sags back, I glance up at her. She's got that dazed, blissed-out look, hair sticking to her forehead, chest heaving.

I wipe my beard with the back of my hand. She's all over that now. 'Told you I had an appetite.'

She groans, hiding her face in her hands, but she's laughing, panting and trembling and so damn beautiful it hurts.

Yeah. I'll thank that woman on my knees all damn day.

I kiss my way up her body, over every inch of skin I can reach. When I finally get to her mouth, she pulls me down, kissing me hard and hungry, tasting herself on my tongue. I don't think I've ever been this fucking happy.

Chapter 18

Charlie

I t's been two weeks since I've stayed at my flat in Edinburgh. Two weeks of acting like it's convenient, practical, easier to sleep at Brodie's place. But that's bollocks. Truth is: I sleep better with his arm around me, and nothing makes sense anymore unless I'm curled up against him.

He's made me spaghetti with meatballs four times. I've obliterated him in Mario Kart every single night, and the smug look on my face has nearly got me kissed to death. We've made it through every Rocky film, arguing over which one's best. He likes his popcorn sweet. I like mine salty. We compromise by dumping both into the same bowl, and I act like it doesn't make my teeth ache.

He's fucked me on every surface in his house, and I fucked him right back.

I never thought I'd be happy like this. Nobody meddling or interfering, no expectations or photo ops. Just us, getting to know each other, figuring out how to exist together without the world pressing in.

Except for Theo, obviously.

She's the only one who knows, and that's mostly because I couldn't stop myself from telling her. One look at me after I sealed the sponsorship, and she sensed something was up. Plus, there was the little incident with the phone. After that, there wasn't much point in lying.

Theo's been her usual no-nonsense self about it. She doesn't push. Right now, she sweeps into my office, a coffee in each hand, and nudges the door shut with her hip. 'Ready for South Africa?'

The coffee smells like salvation. I take it with a grateful hum. 'As ready as I'll ever be. You'd think two weeks of prep would make this easier.'

Theo flips through her folder. 'Media schedule's locked, but we might have to squeeze in an extra interview with MacRae if the last game goes well. Sponsor's pushing for more face time.'

'He'll love that,' I say. 'Thrives under pressure.'

'He thrives under *you*.'

I choke on my coffee. 'Theo!'

She doesn't even look up. 'Please. You're glowing from all the sex. I've seen less obvious neon signs.'

I press the cup to my lips and hope it hides how my cheeks have caught fire. 'You know we're keeping it quiet. At least for now. If anyone catches wind, it'll—'

'Yeah, yeah. The professional fallout, the media shitstorm, yada yada.' She waves a hand like she's heard it all before. 'But you're happy, correct?'

I open my mouth to answer, but the truth sticks in the back of my throat. Happy doesn't quite cover it. It's terrifying and huge and makes me feel like I've been set on fire from the inside. I don't know how to put it into words without sounding like I've lost my mind. So, I just nod, and Theo narrows her eyes at me like she knows exactly what I'm not saying.

'Good,' she mutters, shoving the folder into her bag. 'Don't let him muck it up. Or I'll gut him like a fish.'

'I'll tell him you said that.'

'Do that. Maybe it'll keep him in line.'

And for a minute, I forget about the stress and the travel and the endless juggling act that is my life.

I'm so grateful for her friendship.

'Okay, I'll wrangle Brodie's training clips into something postable and schedule your client check-ins for next week. Someone needs to keep the show running while you're away,' she says and turns around.

Seven minutes later, Brodie saunters through the door. Suitcase in one hand and a tiny plant in the other. Two months since the first time he set foot in here. Instead of a suit, he's wearing joggers and a hoodie, cap pulled low, and I have to suppress an actual fan-girl squeal at how effortlessly, insanely hot he looks.

He holds a tiny succulent out to me. It has pink-tinged leaves, potted in a blue ceramic cup.

'Awww, you brought me one of your plant babies?'

'For your desk. Figured you could use something to keep you company while you boss everyone around and pretend to work.'

I snatch it from him. '*Pretend* to work? You do know I'm the reason we're flying business class to South Africa, right?'

He grunts, like he doesn't believe me. Then his eyes flick to my suitcases. 'You planning on moving to Cape Town?'

'I like being prepared,' I say and lift my chin.

Brodie drops his gaze to my mouth. Before I can throw out another smartarse comeback, he moves. He cradles my jaw, and I barely get a breath in before he kisses me, lips just a little chapped from the wind. He licks into me, deep and possessive, tasting faintly of mint and a whole lot of longing.

'Not here…'

Brodie cups my breast, rough palm hot through the silk. He squeezes hard enough to make the lace bite, the faint scratch sending heat straight to where I'm throbbing for his mouth. I gasp into the kiss, and he takes it like a promise, backing me into the desk. Then it's all him – urgent, unrelenting – as he grinds against my core.

He grins, cocky and pleased with himself. 'Damn, Charlie. You're so easy to wind up.'

I glare at him, or at least I try to. It's a bit difficult when his knuckles work my peaks through the fabric. 'Control yourself, MacRae.'

He trails his mouth down my neck, teeth grazing skin, and his voice drops to a low murmur. 'I don't want to. I want you squirming right here, trying not to make a noise. Let's see how quiet you can be, aye?'

I shove at his chest, but it's like attempting to move a mountain. He chuckles, pinches my nipple again, and I let out a moan.

'There's my girl. I remember her from this morning when she was riding my face before breakfast like a fucking rodeo star.' Then he draws back. 'When's she gonna let me take her out for a proper date?'

'Brodie.' My stomach tightens. 'You know why we can't.'

He grips my waist with both hands, staring me down. 'Why the fuck not? You think I'm losing sleep over what other people think?'

I shake my head, trying to break free of that magnetic gravity he has. 'It's too risky. The media, the team, your image and career, my agency, the sponsors—'

'Let them talk. I don't care.' His tone goes flat, eyes blazing. 'I'm done sneaking around like we're ashamed of each other.'

'Nobody is ashamed. But if anyone finds out we're together, it could screw things up. For you, the Rebels. Everything I'm building here. We've worked too damn much to fix your image, and I'm not letting it all unravel.'

He glowers at me, but I know he understands. He just hates it.

'We can't keep this a secret forever.'

'I know.' I trail my fingers through his hair. 'Let's wait till the season's over. Please.' I hate how small I sound.

'You're making it really fucking hard, Charlie Harrington. And I don't just mean my dick. Not sure how long I can play by your rules.'

My heart slams into my ribs. 'Yeah. I hear you.'

And I do. It's just …

Brodie swears under his breath, frustration rippling through him, but he softens when he sees my face.

He pulls me closer, resting his forehead against mine. 'Fine. Have it your way for now. But hear me out, woman.' His voice is merely a husky rasp. 'When it's over, I'm taking you out. A real date. Dinner. Dancing. Fucking karaoke again, if that's what it takes to get you to see I'm serious.'

He draws back to look me in the eye. His erection pushes against my stomach. 'And then I take you home, and when I'm fucking you so deep you can't breathe, I'll make sure you know it's not just your body I'm claiming. It's your smart mouth, your stubborn head, and your fucking heart. Got it?'

'You don't like being my sexy little secret?'

'I want the world to know I'm your sexy big boyfriend.' He says it low, serious now. 'I'm not giving you up, Charlie. Not when I've just started to get this right.'

I can't even process how that knocks me in the chest. It's everything I've denied myself to feel. To be wanted so fiercely it's inevitable.

To be loved like this.

To … love like this.

It almost makes me mad.

Because I'm aware that I'm the one holding back. I'm the one too scared to let the world see us. And see me as weak and irrational, irresponsible, and unprofessional. I couldn't even make it a full year without another rugby player in my bed. They'll think I've got no spine. That I roll onto my back for thick biceps, chunky thighs, and a bit of beard.

He lays it out there like we're the most natural thing. He's already decided, and I'm gonna have to get on board.

And god, I want to. I want to be that person who doesn't give a shit what people think or how it might blow back on me. I want to be brave, let him take me out and make me laugh and hold my hand without looking over my shoulder. Piggyback rides and public smooching and kissy brunch.

But that's not me. Never has been. I play it safe and keep things tidy. Professional. Managed. Contained.

Except with Brodie.

With him, I'm already becoming someone I don't recognise. Someone uninhibited, desperate to keep…whatever this is from slipping through my fingers.

Dammit. I have to figure this out. But not now. I need more time.

I can't speak, so I nod, lips parting on a shaky breath. 'Okay.'

'Good. Now grab your shite, Champ. We're gonna miss the flight.'

Chapter 19

Brodie

The plane's a different kind of playing field, and Charlie dominates it. I take her in from my aisle seat, trying hard as hell not to look as besotted as I feel.

She's perched in the window seat next to me, laptop balanced on her knees, explaining something to Finn about social media engagement. His pink hair looks neon under the overhead light as he leans over from across the aisle, actually paying attention for once in his life.

'So basically, you're saying I should post more thirst traps?' Finn waggles his eyebrows.

'I'm saying you should post content that aligns with your personal brand while maintaining professional standards.' Charlie doesn't miss a beat. 'Though given your…aesthetic, that probably *does* mean the odd thirst trap.'

'Personal brand?' Scottie says from the row behind us. 'Finn's brand is chaos incarnate.'

Finn turns around to flip him off. 'At least I have a brand. What's yours? Professional wallflower?'

'Boys, let's keep it civil at thirty thousand feet.' Charlie smiles but gives them both a pointed look over the rim of her computer.

Pride settles low in my gut watching her handle them. These lads gave me shite for weeks when we first pulled the team together, testing every boundary. But she's got them eating out of her palm.

Finn tips his chin at me. 'And when's MacRae getting his own cooking show, eh?'

Laughter ripples through the lads. I sink my teeth into my cheek.

Charlie doesn't lift her head. 'Careful, Lennox. Last bloke who took the piss ended up signing a three-series deal. You keen to be my next client?'

Finn's cackle dies mid-choke.

Scottie leans into the aisle. 'Naw, he's allergic to success.'

'Fuck you, Kerr.' Finn pegs a scrunched napkin at Scottie.

Charlie taps her pen against the screen. 'Finn, the only stats I've got on you are from your dating profile. And they're not impressive.'

A beat of silence. Then Jamie's dry chuckle. 'Brutal. I like it.'

Finn sprawls across the entire row like he chartered the flight. 'Who's the worst client you've ever had? Besides this grumpy bastard, obviously.' He jerks his thumb at me.

'Client confidentiality, Lennox. But I'll tell you this – MacRae's not even in my top five. Not for lack of trying, though.'

The lads howl with laughter. Even my lips break their stoic line.

Charlie's knee leans against mine, and I don't move. Just let her leg burn a hole through my joggers while she works on her laptop.

Jamie swaggers down the aisle, cool as ever in his designer tracksuit. 'Harrington. That sponsorship deal with MacKenzie for MacRae and us …'

'I know. Brilliant, wasn't it? I keep telling you guys I'm the best,' she says. 'Time to wise up and believe me.'

'Brilliant's underselling,' Jamie says. 'But the clause about social media—'

'Requires one post per month per player, with product placement that doesn't look staged. I've got a photographer who can help you nail the aesthetic.' She keeps typing, multitasking like a pro.

Jamie's eyebrows hike up. 'Sorted then?'

'Sure.'

Scottie lobs a peanut at Charlie's head from two rows down the aisle. She catches it mid-air and pops it between glossed lips. Cool as a cucumber.

'That all you got, Kerr?'

'Show-off,' he grins.

She throws one of her own nuts back. It bounces off his forehead, and he looks…bewildered.

Her dirty laugh hits raw, and everything under my skin answers. I want to bottle the sound, inject it straight into my veins. Want to drag her into the loo and lick her lipstick off. Want to drop to one fucking knee right here.

Christ. I'm going to marry her someday.

The thought hits me like a tackle to the chest. But it settles deep in my bones, certain as gravity.

Coach Wallace passes by, grizzled jaw working around a mint. He pauses at our row. 'Charlie. Got a minute? Want to make sure Brodie's press stuff isn't clashing with training or team commitments.'

'Of course.' She closes her laptop. 'Hold this, would you?'

Our fingers skim, and electricity zips up my arm.

Then she squeezes past me, and my face is inches away from her round arse. I remember the sting in my palm when I slapped it last night. The way she moaned like it was her favourite thing. And now I'm meant to sit still and play the role of her client, while every part of me is screaming to drag her back onto my lap and remind her how it felt?

Charlie holds her composure, professional mask firmly in place as she follows Wallace to the galley.

I fake reading, ears straining to catch their conversation. No chance. The cabin hums around us, engines a low growl. Then Wallace's rare laugh catches me by surprise. Took me ages to get more than a grunt out of Wallace, and she's got the old grump *laughing*.

I stare straight ahead, fighting to keep my expression neutral. But inside? I'm bursting with pride. That's my girl.

When she returns, sliding into the seat beside me, I keep my eyes on my book.

'What?' She nudges my knee with hers, making it look casual.

'Nothing.' I turn a page I haven't read. 'Merely observing you charm the trousers off my entire team.'

'Jealous, MacRae?'

'Naw, impressed.'

She shrugs, but I catch the pleased blush on her cheeks. 'Athletes are all the same. Speak their language and they fall in line.' Her voice is light, but there's a weight behind the words that I don't miss.

'Is that what you did with me? Made me fall in line?'

Her hazel eyes meet mine, that spark between us flaring hot and bright. 'You're still a work in progress, MacRae.'

Her fingers graze my wrist under the table, featherlight. And yet, my pulse roars louder than the plane.

Hours later, it's dark, the dim aisle lights glowing like a runway stretching into nowhere. Noise drones steady around us, underscored by twenty-odd rugby lads snoring into neck pillows. Most of the team is either passed out or in that twilight zone between awake and dreaming, headphones clamped on and sleep masks pulled down. Finn's is a unicorn, for fuck's sake.

My knee bounces, counting the seconds until Charlie shuts her laptop. Her profile is washed in that faint screen glow. I memorised the slope of her nose months ago, but it still drills straight into the place I don't let anyone near.

Finally, she settles back, and I put two scratchy airline blankets over us.

'Everybody's asleep.' I say. It lands more breath than voice. 'Let me hold your hand.'

She hesitates for a second. Wary. Looking around. Then she quickly slips her hand under the blankets and threads her slender fingers through mine, squeezing hard enough to crack bones.

It's fucking embarrassing how much that touch settles me. I've gone without for months before – no sex, no comfort, no one's hands on me, except the physio's – but now that I know what it's like to have Charlie touching me, I can't go back.

She half-turns and shifts closer a few inches, her hair tickling the side of my neck. She dips her other hand inside my joggers, and I go still.

'What do you think you're doing there, Champ?'

She hums and grazes my balls with her nails through the cotton. I bite my tongue. Of course, I'm hard as a rod for her, but that's not what I'm after right now. She slides her hand into my briefs and wraps her fingers carefully around the precious MacRae Crown Jewels.

Where her future babies live.

She just doesn't know it yet.

I've never let anyone do this before. Every other time, it's been eager tongues and greedy mouths, like they were trying to win points for enthusiasm. But this – her warm hand on me, still and steady – it's not about getting off.

It's about letting her in.

'That's right. Hold them. Just hold them.'

Her palm cups me, warm as sunrise, and her thumb strokes the sensitive seam infinitely gently. 'Like this?'

'Aye. That's it.'

My eyes roll back. Saints preserve me. I'm not sixteen, I'm twenty-six, and she's got me trembling over a handshake with my balls.

My heart's pounding so loud I'm sure someone's going to hear it. But no one stirs. Only the hum of the plane and the slow, soothing hold of her soft fingers.

My dick's raging, and every nerve in my body's lighting up like a fucking Christmas tree. But that's nothing compared to what's going on in my heart right now.

I press a kiss to her temple.

This is it.

I'm going to tell her that I love her. On Table Mountain. With the city lights and that daft cable car and a bottle of fizz.

Her breathing's changed, slower and heavier.

'Want me to touch you?' I whisper against the shell of her ear.

She nods – reluctantly, but she nods – and I work my hand inside her yoga leggings to find her warm and wet. She lets out a quiet gasp.

I trace her with two fingers, never pushing in.

'Still think you're the boss?' It's not about making her come. It's about reminding her who she belongs to. 'Still reckon you own me?'

'Y-yes.'

I cup her, thumb pressing down where I know she likes it. 'But who owns this pretty pussy?' I'm so hushed, it's barely audible.

Her stifled moan vibrates through my bones. She doesn't have to say it. By now, we both know.

'Can't fuck you here, baby. Barely fit into that loo by myself.' I tuck her hair behind a reddened ear. 'I'd split that sink in half. Just feel me for a minute. Just know I'm here.' I let my palm rest over her mound.

She smothers a giggle against my collarbone. 'Romantic.'

'Me? Naw. I would fuck you like a raging bull until you're too tender to take me.' I bury my nose in her hair. 'But we're in public, on a plane, so all we're gonna do is hold hands under the blanket while we fall asleep.'

I withdraw my hand from her sweet, swollen heat and pull hers out of my joggers, then I tangle our fingers together again, hidden underneath the blanket. 'Sleep, Champ. I'm here.'

I lean back and pull the blankets tighter around us. She drifts off first, breath evening out. Her head lolls onto my shoulder, and I count her lashes in the dim cabin light.

I love you. I love you. I love you.

The syllables in my head beat louder than the engines.

Finn farts in his sleep. Scottie groans. Charlie's hand stays tangled with mine under thin, scratchy polyester.

This must be what peace feels like.

Sunlight stabs through the oval window. I wake up to the sharp scent of airline coffee and a crick in my neck. Blinking the sleep out of my eyes, I try to shift, but something tugs at my hand.

Charlie's hand.

Still laced with mine, right out in the open. Bare skin on bare skin. The blanket is slipped down our laps, exposing our tangled fingers for the whole cabin to see.

Fuck.

I shift my gaze sideways. Jamie shifts, rolling his shoulder like he's scrumming in his dream. Across the aisle, Finn's drooling on his neck pillow. A few rows back, one of the lads cracks his neck, stretching before sinking back down.

Most of the team's still scattered in various states of semi-consciousness, either dead to the world or caught up in their headphone universes.

The toilet door clicks open behind us. Footsteps approach

from the back. I don't turn. Just track the movement as Scottie walks past and drops into his seat two rows ahead. He doesn't say a word. Doesn't look back.

But he definitely saw.

Someone coughs.

Charlie stirs against me, lids fluttering. When she catches sight of our hands, she stiffens like I've slapped her. Then pulls away fast and tucks her hands into her lap like they've been caught committing a felony.

'Relax,' I murmur, 'no one saw.' I'm not so sure, but I don't tell her. She's freaking out enough already.

Her shoulders don't drop. She scans the cabin with a calculating look. Then she meets my gaze, and, for the first time, I see it clearly. Fear. There's something else, too. Guilt bleeding through the cracks in her game face. She glances away too fast, like she knows I caught it.

Christ, I hate that she's looking at me like that. Like I'm the one making her life harder by being in it.

'It's fine,' I keep my tone low. 'They're all half-dead. Nobody's noticed.'

Her lips press into a line, but her breathing slows a bit. I reach out, touch her knee under the tray table, give it a squeeze. She pushes me away.

And it lands like a kick to the groin.

Touching me, holding my hand in public, is enough to send her into a full-blown panic.

'What the fuck are you so scared of?' I whisper.

She doesn't say a word, just stares down. The breath backs up in my lungs, like I swallowed a fist, thick with everything she won't say.

Is it me? Am I not enough for her to risk it? Or is she still somehow hung up on Callum, still dragging his shadow around like it's stitched to her heels? Or maybe afraid of what her dick of a dad might think?

I want to shake it out of her, make her see I'm nothing like either of them. But I shut my mouth and let it settle. Doesn't mean I'm not thinking it. Doesn't mean it doesn't hurt like fuck. Aye, I get it. But how long am I supposed to stand here with my arms open, pretending it doesn't sting every time she retreats?

She shakes her head, voice barely a breath. 'I'm just careful.'

Careful. That's what she calls it. Like it's professional caution.

I pull my hand back, rubbing the back of my neck. 'You're acting like being seen with me would torpedo your life.'

'No, but… This isn't a game, Brodie. One tabloid headline about us and everything I've built—'

'What?' I lean closer, inhaling the scent of her shampoo. 'You lose clients? Get called a tart chasing athletes? Daddy being mad at you? That it?'

'Don't be dense. I'm also trying to protect you.'

'From what? Being happy?'

Charlie twists away, fumbling with her buckle, that stubborn jaw set like steel. She's not protecting me. She's protecting herself. From the messiness. The risk.

Lads are waking up, stretching, muttering about jet lag. The plane lurches, slowly descending through clouds. My gut churns worse than any turbulence ever could. And the doubt creeps in, slow and insidious. Does she not feel what I feel? Am I making this bigger in my mind than it actually is?

Everything in my face pulls tight, but I force it loose. No point in getting worked up now.

I unbuckle, standing too fast. 'Need the loo.'

The cubicle's a fucking coffin. I brace against the sink, watching my reflection sneer. Bloody eejit. Maybe I've been kidding myself this whole time.

Knuckles rap the door.

'MacRae.' That's Finn's sleepy drawl. 'You birthing a rugby ball in there?'

'Piss off, Lennox.'

Half an hour and one podcast episode later, the plane dips and wobbles as it descends. I steal another look at Charlie. She's already pulled her game face back on, all business. But I can't unsee it now. How hard she works to keep me at arm's length.

I make myself smile and crack a joke about Finn snoring like a chainsaw, but the feeling doesn't leave.

The plane touches down with a thud, and I command myself to focus.

We stand to gather our bags, and Charlie's already two steps ahead. My eyes follow her, trying to ignore the hollow burn behind my breastbone.

It's nothing. I'm tired. Long flight.

But when she flicks a look over her shoulder and finds me tracking her, the smile she sends me slips at the edges.

Something's shifted.

And I'm not sure how to fucking fix it.

Chapter 20

Charlie

My hotel room's too quiet. Too big. Feels like a warehouse with a bed stuck in the middle. It's only half past nine, but I'm ready for bed – or I would be if I could sleep. I pace the space between the door and the window, trying to unhook the knot between my ribs.

The bed's too wide without Brodie. Absurd, because we're not even living together, and I've managed on my own just fine before. But now? Now it feels like if I fall asleep without his warmth next to mine, I'll wake up wrong. The pillow doesn't smell like him. The sheets don't feel right.

It's not just the bed that feels too wide. It's me. Hollowed out in the exact shape of him.

I flatten my palms over my eyes until colours pop behind my lids. I think about what he said. About how I'm acting like just being with him would destroy me.

And maybe that's what scares me most.

Because it might.

Because he *could* destroy me.

Not like Callum or Dad. Not like anyone else who tore bits off me until I didn't know who I was anymore. Brodie doesn't chip away at me. He builds me up. He makes me feel like I could be and have all the things I was too afraid to want before.

And that's what's dangerous.

It's scary. Because if I get used to that and lose it? If I lose Brodie? I don't know how to go back to being the woman who didn't have him.

I breathe through the ache in my centre.

He didn't deserve my fucking shitshow on the plane. He didn't deserve me pulling away like that.

Brodie's been nothing but good. Stopped gambling, did all the shit I forced him to do. Cooking show, library, media training, karaoke. Massaged my feet. And the rest of it, too. He's never done a single thing to make me feel less than adored. Appreciated.

I'm the one being an arsehole, and for what? The fear of people talking? The worry about losing a few clients who can't handle me having a fucking life? They didn't sign me because I was some pristine, corporate lapdog.

They signed me because Charlie Harrington... Gets. Shit. Done.

Because I'm ambitious and clever, and I know how to make them money.

The MacKenzie deal for Brodie and the Rebels? Exhibit bloody A.

I'm good enough at my job to keep doing it even if I'm dating a rugby star. They can deal. They have to if they want me working for them.

And they *will* want me working for them.

Callum? Inconsequential. He can sneer all he wants.

And my dad? It's not his life. I don't need his approval anymore. I'm a grown woman.

And I'm in all-encompassing love with Brodie MacRae.

Love him so much it's turning me inside out.

The truth lands so fast I forget to breathe. When did that

happen? How long have I known? Doesn't matter. I know it now. And that's not something to run from.

My breath shakes as I pick up my phone. I'm done hiding and letting fear pull me backwards. I yank on my joggers and a baggy jumper, shove my feet into my UGG slippers. With trembling fingers, I grab my key card and head out, not giving myself time to second-guess it.

I'm going to find him and tell him I love him. I have to. He deserves it. And so do I.

My furry slippers shuffle over the carpet as I scan the corridor for any sign of Brodie. Nothing but stale air and hush. I knock on his door. Hesitant, like I'm afraid he'll actually answer.

Nothing.

I frown and pull out my phone, shooting him a quick text.

(ME, 21:44): You in there, babe?

The message stays unread.

Weird.

My heart's doing that strange fluttery thing that it never used to do before him. I hate it. It's irrational, but the longer I stand here, the more my thoughts pile up like a landslide.

I call him, but he doesn't answer.

Even weirder.

He's a night owl, never goes anywhere without his phone.

A muffled shout echoes down the hall, followed by a faint burst of laughter. I squint at the far end, where light spills from underneath the last door on the left.

I make my way down. Voices blend into a bassy murk that

thickens as I get closer. I don't know why the hairs on the back of my neck stand up, but they do.

I have experience with athletes. I could find anything in there. Anyone.

The door's slightly ajar, and the lads are yelling, laughing, there's the clatter of something hitting the floor. I rap my knuckles against the wood, louder than intended.

The door swings open. Finn's standing there, shirtless, tattooed all over, grinning like a maniac and not at all fazed by my panda eyes and South Park hoodie.

'Charlie! Come to join the fun?' He makes a sweeping gesture, and I catch sight of the scene behind him.

The two single beds shoved to one side, leaving space for the room's small desk dragged into the centre. Four chairs crammed around it. Scottie, on one side, Jamie and Tommy on the other. I guess the empty chair's Finn's.

And there's Brodie.

Back against the headboard, legs stretched out, cap pulled low over his eyes.

Relief whooshes through me as I see him. For a moment, I almost laugh.

Then I spot the pile of cash.

The cards.

Poker?

Ice pours down my spine.

Brodie doesn't gamble. Not anymore.

He promised.

We agreed.

I step inside, and the noise crashes to a halt. Brodie glances up, and his half-grin slips, confusion lining his forehead.

'What the fuck are you doing?' I hear myself shout, and every head whips around.

Brodie uncrosses his arms, straightening up. 'Charlie—'

'No, Brodie. What the fucking fuck?'

'He's not allowed to hang out with the team?' Scottie cuts

in with a lopsided smirk, clearly too distracted to notice the tension. 'Didn't know your girl was the strict type, MacRae.'

I don't breathe. Everything goes still. Everyone's looking at me, at him. Scottie's grinning like he just cracked the joke of the century, completely oblivious.

His girl.

They know. They all fucking know.

Did he tell them?

My mouth's gone dry, and my hands tingle.

Brodie shoots Scottie a look like he's just drop-kicked a puppy, but Scottie shrugs. 'What? We saw the hand-holding. Not exactly covert ops.'

'Scottie, for fuck's sake!' Brodie blasts out.

He moves towards me, but I hold up a hand and shrink back. I can't help it. The betrayal is like acid burning through my chest.

'Don't.' The walls are pressing in, and the air is getting too thick. 'Don't touch me.'

He reels back, pain splintering across his face. 'Charlie, it's not what it looks like.'

'You're sitting here with a mountain of cash and a deck of cards, surrounded by your teammates, and you're telling me it's not what it looks like?' My voice cracks on the last word, and I hate how broken and angry I sound. 'You know when I heard that fucked-up sentence the last time?'

His face tells me he does. I have to say it, anyway. 'When I found my fiancé with his trousers round his ankles.'

I can't even feel my fingers.

Scottie's staring at us like he's watching the roof cave in. One of the younger lads mumbles something about getting out of here, but no one moves. The whole room's frozen, tension so dense you could drown in it. My hands shake, and I have to tuck them into my sleeves. I feel every eye on me, waiting to see what I'll do next, and I'm naked. Exposed. Like they're dissecting each word and gesture, like they're already thinking of how this'll play out when the press gets hold of it.

I shake my head, fighting back a flood of tears. 'I-I have to go.'

'Charlie!' He steps forward, and his hand touches mine for a second before I yank it back. 'Don't fucking walk away. Let me explain—'

If I let him talk, I'll cave. I'll crumble, and then I'll never claw my way back out of the mess I've made.

I don't give him the chance. I spin on my heel and storm out, ignoring the shock I leave in my wake. The world blurs as I shove my way out the door, running from it with teeth and claws. My feet barely touch the ground, slippers skidding over the hotel floor.

I don't stop moving until I'm back in my suite, door slamming shut like a full stop. My ribcage rattles with every panicked beat, my hands trembling so badly that I drop my key card twice before throwing it onto the bedside table.

It hurts. Hurts worse than anything has a right to hurt.

A knock.

'Charlie. Please.'

No. Not now. Probably tomorrow. I need a moment.

'Go away.'

Nothing. He stays.

'You really think I'm that fucking careless? You think I'd risk it like that? After everything?' He sounds muffled through the door, but he's mad and he's loud and I hear every word.

'How the hell am I supposed to know what you'd risk, Brodie? I thought I knew you. I thought I could trust you.'

The air itself is bracing for impact. Then a sharp thud. My body jerks. I recognise that sound. His flat palm on the wood. Not forceful enough to scare me, but enough to tell me he's on the edge.

His fucking temper.

'You're the one still too scared to call this real!' He's yelling now. But I hear how he's fighting it. Fighting the anger.

'That's not fair,' I say towards the door, suppressing the sob that's building in my throat.

'Isn't it? You keep me at arm's length and then get pissed off when I'm… hanging with my team. You don't want anyone to know, but you're furious when they figure it out on their own. I can't fucking win with you, Charlie!'

A dull sound. Like he's leaning his forehead against the door in defeat. I can almost see it, his hand braced against the frame, shoulders hunched, his whole body trying to cage in the frustration.

'Listen to me, woman. I did NOT play cards.'

'You shouldn't even have been in that room! If anyone took a photo—'

'They didn't. No one did. They're good lads.'

I don't know how to answer. All I can see is the headlines. The fallout.

'Charlie. For the last fucking time: I didn't gamble. I just sat there with them because they're bonding, and I'm supposed to be their captain, and—'

'And telling them about us? Is that bonding too?'

'I wouldn't do that to you. I didn't tell them, Charlie. You heard Scottie. They figured it out. I've given you everything. Every damn part of me. And you still think I'm going to break it.'

I say nothing. A lot of nothing. For too long.

Because…

'That's it, Charlie.' His voice is flat. 'I've had enough. I'm not a fucking plaything. It's over.'

Silence. Dense as fog, pushing in from all sides.

And I know he's gone.

Not just physically. But he's gone from me. I can feel his

absence. I want to scream. Punch something. Anything to drown out the roaring in my ears.

Instead, I curl up on the bed, dragging the covers over me like a shield. I jam my fist to my mouth to keep from making a sound. If I let it out now, I'll fall apart. And if I fall apart, I'm not sure I'll be able to collect the pieces.

Then I grab my phone and book the first flight back to Scotland.

Damage control. Fixing things. Regroup.

It's what I do.

Chapter 21

Brodie

Have I mentioned how much I hate Charlie Harrington?

Because now I know how it feels to love her. And it's over. And *I* told her it was.

I'm not the kind to stick around while she yanks me back and forth like a dog on a lead. She drove me too far.

I also acted like a dick with anger issues. So, there's that.

Aye, she gave me reasons. Not trusting me? Not talking to me? She crossed a line there.

I fucked up, but I didn't play. I sat there like a twat and still managed to lose her. And I let my temper get the best of me again. When I'm hurt, I lash out. A low, mean swing to cover the sting.

That was four weeks ago, and it still feels raw.

The boys are scattered around the changing room, getting patched up. Cuts, bruises, niggling injuries from a brutal first half. There's talk, low and grim, the stink of sweat hanging in the air.

Derek, our physio, presses his thumb deep into the muscle above my spine, and pain streaks through me. I suck in a breath between clenched teeth but don't let anyone see it on my face.

A memory hits me. Charlie, pressing an ice pack on my back, calling me a bloody masochist for battering myself like this.

I stopped looking for her in the grandstand three games ago. She's been avoiding me for a full month. After South Africa she handed me off to Mac like a boot caked in shite – someone else's mess to scrape off.

Probably for the best.

I've been avoiding thinking about her.

Because every time I do, it's barbed wire through my ribcage.

So, I train harder and push myself. Every session. Every drill. Nonstop. The lads joke about me being possessed, but they don't know half of it. Gotta be the best, or what's the fucking point? If I let up, even for a second, it all floods back.

Her nose with my spaghetti sauce on it.

How her eyes sparkle when she deepthroats me like the boss she is.

Her face, her voice, the way she looked at me right before I lost her because we're both too fucked up to make it work.

Derek mutters something about the tension in my back and asks if it's been worse lately. I grunt. Can't be arsed to have that conversation. Just want him to do his job and bugger off.

I'm still on the pitch every game, doing my job, dragging us to wins. But I'm playing angry. Coach knows it. The boys know it. Took off on a sniping run from our own twenty-two like I thought I was Superman. Cost us the game. Then I lost my head and smashed into a ruck like a fucking bulldozer, and Wallace tore me a new one. I just shrugged and walked it off.

What's the worst that can happen? They bench me? Make me rest?

I'd go down swinging. Throwing myself into the mess till my lungs give out is easier than sitting still and replaying the look on her face when she flinched from me.

Derek hits a spot that makes my vision blur, and I brace my hands on my knees. If the pain cuts sharp enough, it drowns out everything else. Beating my body past its limits, grinding through the ache like I'm punishing myself for feeling anything at all.

But that's how it's always been. Push harder. Be better. Outwork the pain.

Derek's done with me. The lads are rehydrating, wolfing down gels and bananas. Coach has just wrapped up his half-time speech, and the tension's still hanging like a nasty fart. No one's saying a word, but the side-eye glances are coming at me from every direction.

Jamie's the first to crack. Kicks a stray water bottle across the floor, making it clatter off the wall. 'What the actual fuck was that out there, MacRae? You trying to get yourself killed?'

I don't answer. What's the point?

Scottie barks out a bitter laugh. 'Aye, well, maybe that's it. Maybe he's too busy trying to knock his own brains out to think about the rest of us.'

'Fuck off,' I mutter.

'Naw, pal. You don't get to sit there like the wounded warrior.' Finn's perched on the bench, blood streaking down his shin, eyes blazing. 'What the fuck's your problem, man? Charging into rucks like a demented rhino – you're gonna snap your spine to prove your dick's still attached? You're not a forward, you absolute knob. You're meant to have a brain. Gonna break your neck one of these days, and we'll be scraping you off the pitch like roadkill.'

'And that chip kick?' Jamie cuts in. 'What were you think-ing? You had options, and you went for glory like a one-man army.'

'You're supposed to be better than that,' Scottie growls,

wiping sweat off his neck. 'You know it, we know it. So, what the hell are you doing out there? Trying to make some point nobody's asked you to prove?'

My jaw aches from grinding my teeth. 'I'm playing to win. You lot should try it sometime.'

'Fuck that,' Finn fires back. 'You're not playing to win, you're playing like you've got a death wish. Thought you had more brains than this.'

'You're a headless chicken, MacRae,' Jamie throws in, arms crossed tight over his chest. 'You think smashing through the line like a tank makes you tough? It doesn't. Just makes you reckless. Think.'

'I'm doing what needs to be done,' I grind out.

'No, you're acting like a twat,' Finn says. 'And we're the ones paying for it. You've been a miserable prick for weeks now, and I'm done tiptoeing around it. Get your shite together, big man.'

'You think we don't see it?' Scottie adds. 'You think we're blind to what's eating at you? We get it. Heart's fucked. Head's gone. But dragging all of us down with you? That's selfish.'

Heat crawls up my neck. 'You don't know shite about it.'

Jamie throws his towel at me. 'You think you're the only one who's been fucked over? Grow up. We've all been burned. Difference is, we're not trying to break every bone in our body over it. Pull your head out your arse.'

'You're not playing for the team,' Finn cuts in. 'You're playing for your own bloody pride. And it's costing us.'

My heart's thumping in my ears, drowning out reason. I know they're right. It's like being skinned alive, every word slicing through. But I can't swallow the rage rising up like bile.

'If you're gonna fall apart, do it on your own time,' Scottie mutters. 'We're busting our arses out there while you're too busy wrestling your demons. You're not the only one who's got stuff to deal with. We're all carrying something. You're the captain. Act like it.'

Silence swells. I can't lift my head, can't meet their eyes. Shame gnaws through the anger, twisting it into something ugly and bitter.

Finn wipes his bleeding shin with his shirt. 'A broken heart's no excuse to break your spine, mate. Or get us the wooden spoon.'

'Aye,' Scottie agrees. 'We're building something here. Don't piss it away. You've got two choices, MacRae. Keep tearing yourself apart, or take that energy and fight for her. Your call.'

I press my palms against my knees. The fury's burnt itself out fast, leaving nothing but nerves and a knot of guilt twisting in my ribs.

Jamie walks past, shoving my shoulder as he goes. 'Play smart, MacRae. Or don't play at all.'

He's right. They all are. Doesn't mean it stings any less.

Coach ducks back in. 'Let's move, lads. Second half. Two minutes. MacRae, a word.'

I've been getting my arse handed to me so often in the past month that I could draw it from memory.

'One more high tackle and I bench you. You're not just risking yourself, you're risking the whole team. You think I'm gonna let you trash your back *and* our season just because your head's fucked? Get it together!'

I nod, tight and quick.

Fine.

Coach gives me a long look, like he's weighing up whether to poke or let it lie. Then he lets out a rough exhale and walks off.

Smart move.

I swallow down the sting, forcing my shoulders back. I thought being unbreakable would mean something. They're sharing energy gels, cracking jokes. Jamie and Scottie huddled up, Finn smacking one of the new lads on the back. No one comes near me.

They don't see strength. They see a loose cannon.

Proving I'm not weak shouldn't feel this fucking hollow. I worked harder, played rougher. For what? Respect? Pride? Trying to prove I'm more than just some heartbroken loser who lost his edge?

The whistle shrieks, cutting through my thoughts.

I shove down the ache, shake out my hands, and force myself to move.

Chapter 22

Charlie

The succulent's dying. Brodie gave it to me before everything went to hell, and I've not managed to keep it alive, not even for over a month.

Cruel symbolism.

It doesn't even need much. Just enough light, a bit of water.

I hate how much I want to call him. How I wake up at three in the morning with my phone in my hand. Or how I've scrolled through his socials like a goddamn addict – yes, @PlantDaddy, too – desperate for any hint that he's as miserable as I am. But he's out there, clawing his way back to the top one game after the other.

I should throw that plant out. Let it die like the rest of whatever's left of me. But I kept watering it, as if keeping it alive meant I didn't mess everything up beyond repair.

Well, I fucked that up. And there's no one to blame but myself.

A memory slips through the cracks. Brodie in his kitchen, frying bacon at 3 a.m. because I couldn't sleep, wearing nothing but boxers and a lazy grin.

I keep telling myself it's better this way. Better for him to be free of me. And vice versa. We're too much alike. Too ambitious, too stubborn, too broken.

But he didn't deserve me tearing into him like that, blaming him for my own fear.

I fumble the mug, barely getting a grip. Coffee's gone cold, thick sludge at the bottom, but I swallow it anyway. Anything to distract from how my chest is caving in on itself.

I swallow, bitter heat rising behind my tongue.

God, I despise him for making me feel like this. For turning me into a wreck. For proving me right and wrong at the same time.

But he never should have been there in the first place. Shouldn't have put himself in that room, surrounded by cards and cash and temptation like it didn't matter. Like our deal didn't mean anything. I trusted him. Mostly. It was the recklessness that made me snap.

One photo, one story, one misstep potentially ruining everything.

My career. His reputation. Us.

And maybe I didn't trust him enough. Maybe that's the real truth. Maybe I never believed I deserved him to begin with. Always waiting for the other shoe to drop, for him to screw it up so I could say *See? I knew it.* Like proving I was right would make losing him hurt less.

It didn't. It doesn't.

I focus on the emails piling up on my screen. Meeting requests, sponsorship updates, contract revisions. Busy work to drown out the brutal, constant squeeze in the centre of my body.

The agency's doing twell, though.

Maybe because I've been throwing myself into it, taking on clients like a workaholic on a bender. Any distraction is good. Last week, I took the train to London to visit Mum and Hannah, hoping a change of scenery and some tough love would shake me out of it.

It didn't.

I came back lonelier. Emptier. As if I'd tried to outrun it and just dragged it along behind me.

Brodie's not one of my direct clients anymore. I handed him off to Mac because it's the professional thing to do. I've kept my head down, stayed away from games and events, haven't been near the Rebels in a month. Too much like picking at a wound that's never gonna close.

They're in Italy now, and the updates keep pinging my phone. Interviews. Brodie's back from the brink and playing the part. The media are lapping up the comeback story as if it were their idea. No bad press, not even a whisper about the poker game. Nothing leaked.

He's overzealous on the field, smashing into every tackle like he's got something to prove and nothing to lose. Playing with rage. Borderline illegal half the time.

But it's working. His redemption arc is in full swing. And it's good. For him, for the team, for my agency. His career's on an upward swing again.

I should be relieved, right? It's what I wanted — a success story.

But all I feel is this gaping void. I'm bleeding out slow and silent, nobody noticing because I'm too good at faking that I've got it together.

I'm not spiralling about Brodie. I'm surviving. That's the plan. Don't think about him. Don't wonder how Italy's going. Don't check the sports news. Don't replay the crack in his voice when I tore his heart out.

A soft knock at the door drags me out of the fog. Before I can answer, Theo strolls in, balancing a plate of shortbread and a glittery travel mug that's probably full of some over-priced chai.

'We don't have a meeting,' I point out, trying for brisk and efficient. I sound scratchy instead.

'We do now.' She shuts the door behind her, unfazed. 'And

I need you to listen.' She sets the shortbread in front of me like I'm some charity case she's trying to feed. 'You look like shite. Talk.'

I shove the plate back at her. 'Not hungry.'

Theo raises an eyebrow, picking up a biscuit and nibbling the edge. 'You haven't eaten properly today, have you? Or yesterday. Or the day before. This is me, remembering the takeaway boxes still sitting on your desk last time I was here. Jesus, Charlie.' She sighs, leaning back in the visitor's chair. 'You're telling me what happened, or do I have to force it out of you?'

My jaw sets, and I focus harder on my computer. 'There's nothing to tell.'

'Liar. Even your hair looks sad. And it's supposed to be the indestructible, always gorgeous kind.' She gives me a pointed once-over, like she's trying to figure out where all the bones went. 'Talk to me, Charlie. Please.'

I glance at the biscuits again, stomach queasy. 'He fucked up. And then I fucked up. And then he fucked up again and here we are.'

'Yeah, I got that much from the way you're rearranging your life like you're in witness protection. Care to elaborate?'

'He was in a poker room. I mean, a hotel room where poker was being played.'

She frowns, waiting for more. When I don't give it, she leans in. 'Okay, and? Did he gamble? Did he make some massive mistake I don't know about?'

'He says he didn't.'

Theo rolls her eyes. 'Charlie, that's not an answer. Did he or didn't he?'

'He didn't. Said he was just there to build rapport with the team, as their captain. But it doesn't matter. He was *in* that room, Theo. Cash everywhere. Cards. The whole fucking setup. It could have torched everything.'

She watches me carefully, quiet for once. 'Yeah... But it didn't.'

I drag my hands through my hair, squeezing the roots. 'It could have. One second of him appearing like he's back to his old ways. That's all it would've taken. Months of rebuilding his image – gone. And I—'

'And you panicked and freaked.'

'Yeah, I snapped.'

Theo's mouth pulls into a half-smile, soft around the edges. 'And you're mad at him for putting himself in that position.'

'Yes!' I throw my hands up, words spilling out too fast. 'Because he's not that naïve. He knew better. He knew the risks. We talked about it a hundred times. Stay clean. Stay out of trouble. One mistake and it's all over.'

She nods slowly. 'You're not wrong. But...was he trying to hurt you or ignore you or treat you like crap?'

I stare at her like she's grown a second head. 'What?'

'Was he trying to hurt you? Was he trying to blow his career up on purpose? Or was he just being a bit of a daftie because he wanted to be pals with his teammates and didn't think it through? Underneath that gruff routine and ruthless ambition, he's a wee people pleaser, in case you haven't noticed.'

My vocal cords cinch tight. I don't let the thought take shape. Rage is simpler. Rage keeps me standing.

Theo doesn't let up. 'What did he actually do to hurt you, Charlie? Not the risks, not the *potential* fallout.'

I want to argue. Want to say he broke my trust. Want to insist that he put everything on the line for a night of cards. But the words won't come. Because she's right. He didn't *actually* do anything. He made a mistake. A thoughtless mistake. Not one that deserves—

'You're comparing him to Callum,' Theo says gently, like it's obvious and I'm too dense to see it. 'But Callum lied.

Repeatedly. Callum hurt you intentionally. He knew what he was doing when he was shagging other women. He was proactively and consciously choosing to hurt you in a very personal way. What did Brodie do? Did he lie? Did he cheat? Did he manipulate you? Or did he just fuck up because he's a bit of an eejit?'

'I'm not comparing him to Callum,' I fire back, but it tastes like a lie.

'Aren't you? You're terrified of getting played. I get it. You're scared of looking like a fool. But Brodie's not Callum. Just sayin'.'

The urge to scream crowds every inch of my insides. I stare down harder at the emails again. They blur into nothing, shapes and lines that make no sense.

'Boss…' Theo leans forward 'You're in love with him.'

The words hit like a slap. I don't answer.

'You're hurting because you're in love with him, and you're afraid that makes you weak. But Charlie,' she says quieter, almost a whisper, 'it doesn't. It means you're human. And for humans, love can be a superpower.'

I shake my head, but I'm not sure who I'm denying – her or myself.

Theo picks up the mug and nudges it toward me. 'Drink. And stop acting like your heart isn't dragging you through hell. You might be able to fool everyone else, but not me. I'm next door if you need me. For hugs or biscuits or talks. Anything. I'm here, okay?'

She leaves me there, staring at the shortbread and the dying succulent, stomach in knots and hands trembling, because somewhere deep down, I've run out of excuses. I curl up in the chair, hands over my face, and let one broken sob tear out before I shove it back down.

Because I've already done the damage I can't come back from.

Chapter 23

Brodie

The Sin & Tonic reeks of pine needles and pretence. String lights flicker overhead, too bright and too close, like they're straining to hold the place together. Forest-green velvet panels mute some of the noise, but the bar along the far wall hums with a low buzz of boozy laughter and forced festivity. The back booths – half-lit, wood-panelled, and inti-mate – look like they were built for secrets.

It's the only bar in Duncraig. Why the hell are we having our Christmas party here instead of a fancy place in Stirling? Fucking beats me. It's not a shite bar, but it isn't class, either. Low key, local, bit lame to be honest.

Mum's perfume wafts through the air before I even see her. 'There you are.' She slots in next to me, Dad trailing with two whiskies. 'Smile, son. You're grimacing like a gargoyle. This is a professional event.'

I loosen the grip on my glass of water before it can crack. 'Having fun?'

'Your father's explaining rucks to the MacKenzie CEO's wife.' Mum's laugh grates. 'Go network. You're the star.'

'Not tonight.'

'Michael, tell your son to stop being a numpty.'

'You heard your mother,' Dad says, low and weighty.

A voice you don't argue with. Same tone he used when I'd whine about extra drills as a kid. Nine years old, shivering on a frostbitten pitch, him barking *Again!* until my passes stuck. I love the man, but Christ, he could make a drill sergeant weep for his maw.

I adore my parents, I do. But they can be a bit much sometimes. They encouraged all three of us to do organised sports to keep us busy, teach us resilience, make us excel. My dad is my constant rock and biggest pusher. If he senses I'm not giving a hundred per cent, he finds a way to push harder. My mum's equally tough. Half-Italian but double the amount of Scottish grit. *'Don't wait for handouts – earn it.'*

Her words, not mine.

My parents make the rounds. The party's buzzing. Laughter bouncing off the walls, drinks flowing, and I'm not even bothering to hide that I look like a haunted bastard.

Scottie's giving me shite from across the room, pointing at me like he's dissecting my misery for sport. Wanker. I give him the finger and turn back to my water, trying not to think about whether or not she'll show. Whether or not my heart can take it if she does. Or if it can take it if she doesn't. It's a rock and a hard place, and I'm trapped in the fucking middle.

This is a MacKenzie-sponsored event. She wouldn't miss it.

Every second she's not walking through that door is a knife to the ribs. But if she does…

The boys are scattered around the room, boisterous as ever. Coach Wallace is chatting with one of the MacKenzie guys. Big-shot sponsor pricks with deep wallets and loud opinions. Weirdly, our mysterious billionaire owner's not here for the glory lap. Though I suppose a reclusive Canadian with a yacht in Monaco doesn't fancy mingling with the plebs. Wouldn't want to get too close to the livestock.

I scan the room for the hundredth time and catch Jamie's

eye. He raises his glass, nods toward the door with a question in his eyes. I shake my head. No sign of her yet.

'Brodie!' A hand claps my arse. Of course, it's Finn. 'Fix your face and stop looking like someone's pissed in your porridge.'

'Are you telling me to smile more?'

'Would look good on you, darlin'!' He leans in with that signature smirk. 'Dry your eyes. Don't lose sleep over one fanny when the world's practically a buffet. Warm, wet, and eager to let you leave your boots on. Some even come as a double act. Chin up, Romeo.' He swans off to the bar, already chatting up someone.

Finn's a total knobhead, but I'm beginning to like that cheeky shite.

The MacKenzie CEO approaches, hand outstretched. 'MacRae! Hell of a season you're having.'

I slap on the PR grin. 'Appreciate the support.'

'That last match. Brutal stuff. Thought you'd crack your skull on that tackle.'

'Takes more than that to keep me down.'

His laugh booms. 'That's what we like to see! Fighting spirit.'

I nod, scanning the room again. My father catches my eye, nailing me with the patented 'don't fuck this up, son'-stare. I've been getting that same glare since I was in nappies.

The CEO drones on about quarterly projections and brand alignment. I keep nodding, grunting in the right moments, when the door swings open.

And there she is.

Charlie.

The world contracts, tight as a fist around my throat. Every sound dulls, every face fades, because she's the only thing in focus. She looks like she stepped out of my fucking dreams to wreck me all over again.

Green velvet, curves pouring out of that dress like it was

made just to drive me mad. Her hair's pinned up, but a few strands kiss her neck, teasing me as if they know how much I miss having my hands in it.

When she spots Coach, her face softens, and I hate it. Hate that he gets the smile that used to be mine. Then she laughs. It sounds jagged, too bright, too brittle.

I can't stop staring. Can't make myself move.

She looks breakable tonight. Like all that fire's wrapped in something fragile, and I'm the arsehole who smashed it to pieces.

She lets her gaze skid my way, and I see it. Hurt swimming under ice. A fault line splits straight through me. I'm battling the urge to shove past every arsehole between us and just grab her.

Apologise. Beg. Anything.

Acting like she doesn't sense me in this room like I sense her – that's like a fucking broadsword down the middle.

I'm still hers, I will always be hers, and it's killing me.

Coach Wallace's gravelly voice rises over the buzz. My parents wander over with him in tow, Mum's laugh slicing through the noise like a knife. Great. Now I'm boxed in on all sides. Parents, coach, sponsor.

Fuck my life.

My stomach twists, and I force down the instinct to leg it to the other side of the bar. Mum's in full charm mode, gesturing with her prosecco like she's narrating an epic tale. Dad's nodding along, giving her the stage like he always does. Coach looks like he's actually listening, which is a fucking feat in itself.

And then Charlie walks past, blazing a path through the room like a goddamn comet. Her eyes are fixed dead ahead, but Coach spots her and waves her over like she's just another one of the boys.

'Harrington!' he calls out, and Charlie hesitates just long

enough for him to notice. 'Come over here. Got some people you should meet.'

She doesn't have a choice. Can't exactly ignore the head coach in front of the MacKenzie brass. So, she squares her shoulders and walks over, looking composed as ever.

She isn't, though.

'This is Charlie Harrington,' Coach Wallace says to my parents, nodding like she's the MVP of the night. 'Made a right miracle out of MacRae's comeback here.'

My mum's eyes light up. 'Oh! You're Charlie!' She grabs Charlie's hand and gives it a firm shake. 'Sandra MacRae. Brodie's mum. This is his dad, Michael.'

Charlie's smile stays polite, but there's a glint of panic in her eyes. 'Nice to meet you. I've heard a lot about you.'

'All lies, I'm sure,' Dad says with a chuckle. 'Though if you've heard that being stubborn as a mule is a family trait, that one's true.'

'Oh, I figured that out on my own,' Charlie deadpans.

Mum laughs, delighted. 'I like you already. We owe you a drink for putting up with him. And for making him cook the family recipe on TV.'

'Oh, that's really not—'

'Nonsense,' Mum interrupts. 'God knows he needs someone to keep him in line. This one's been pushing back against everything since he was old enough to form an opinion.'

'Mum,' I mutter under my breath, but she's not listening.

Charlie glances my way for a split second before forcing her attention back to my mother. 'Sounds about right,' she says.

'Well, whatever you're doing, keep at it,' Dad says. 'He's looked sharper on the field lately. More focused.'

That digs under my skin. Because beating myself into the ground is the only way I've kept from suffocating in the fucking absence of her.

They don't know. They don't know I've spent the last month dragging myself through broken glass just to get through the day. Don't know I fucked it all up because I'm a bull-headed prick who pushed her away before she could do it first.

Charlie nods, forcing another smile. 'I'll do my best.'

Heat lances through my gut. It's like she's caught between wanting to run and wanting to listen, and I hate that I'm the reason she's stuck.

Coach glances at me, eyebrows raised. 'You alright, MacRae?'

I lie with a nod. 'Aye. All good.'

Charlie shifts on her heels, glancing at the exit like it's her last lifeline. Mum notices, naturally, and puts a hand on her shoulder. 'You look lovely, dear. I hope you're taking time to enjoy the party and not just running around after this lot.'

'Trying to.' Charlie looks down at her untouched drink. 'Not used to being…social recently.'

'Och, neither's Brodie,' Mum says, shooting me a glare. 'Got that from his father.'

Dad just shrugs. 'Introverts make the best rugby players. Tunnel vision. Nothing gets through.'

'Except bricks,' Coach grumbles.

Charlie laughs, and it's too fucking soft. Rips through me. She barely flicks her eyes in my direction again. Just says a polite goodbye and drifts off, looking like she's holding herself together with duct tape and spite underneath that velvet.

I love my parents.

My parents love Charlie.

It would've been so goddamn fucking perfect.

Takes everything I've got not to headbutt the nearest hard surface.

Mum watches her go, then turns to me, eyes sharp like

she's reading the subtext of my fucking soul. 'Your agent seems like a good sort.'

I let out an involuntary pained groan and make my way to the terrace.

The cold air smacks me in the face, scraping down my throat like razor blades. Stars overhead, sharp as needles, and my ribcage is too tight to breathe. I brace my hands on the terrace railing and focus on pulling oxygen into my lungs, forcing down the mess clawing up my insides. Love. Lust. Pain. Regret. Feels like I'm bleeding out from the inside.

A spark flickers at the edge of the terrace, and I spot Scottie leaning against the wall, fag glowing between his fingers. He doesn't look at me. Just lifts his chin in acknowledgement.

'Didn't know you smoked,' I grunt, grateful for the distraction.

He shrugs. 'One a year, in the run-up to Christmas. Bit of a ritual.'

Neither of us rushes to break the silence. I drop my shoulders like that'll trick my body into easing up. But it's no use. Still made of stone.

'Coach is thinking about having me sit out next week against the Dragons,' I say, just to fill the air. 'Says my back needs the rest if I'm gonna be fit for the Knights game at the end of the year.'

Scottie takes a drag and blows smoke toward the sky. His voice is nasal. 'Coach isn't wrong.'

'Aye, well. Not much else to do, is there?'

He doesn't answer. Just taps the ash off the end with his thumb. The quiet lingers, just shy of uncomfortable.

'You know, MacRae, for someone who hates being called an eejit, you sure act like one.'

My head whips around. 'What the fuck's that supposed to mean?'

Scottie takes another drag, eyes fixed on the horizon. 'You

still love her. It's written all over your ugly troll face. So, quit acting like a twat and do something about it.'

'That's not—' I cut myself off, throat burning. 'It's over. She doesn't want me.'

'Maybe. Can't say I blame her. You're about as easy to love as a pair of wet socks.'

A laugh gets stuck halfway up my throat. I curl my fingers tighter around the railing.

'You know I don't talk about this shite. But it's you, so… Don't make me regret it.'

Scottie's giving me that same patient look he gets before a scrum. Ready to take the hit if it means I'll finally cough up the truth. Don't know what it is about that bearded ginger gremlin, but he's got gravity. Calm. He's the buffer that keeps half the team from knocking each other out after a shite game. Makes you trust him with stuff you wouldn't tell your own shadow.

'What if I cocked it up so bad there's no coming back?' I say into the December night without looking at him. 'Destroyed the one good thing I ever had? She deserves better than me.'

Scottie flicks ash over the railing, giving me his calm, unimpressed signature look. 'Maybe you did. And maybe she does. But that's not for you to decide, is it?'

I let out a bitter laugh. 'Cheers, mate.'

'You're my captain. You're the one who always says to go after what you want, no matter how hard it is. Practice what you preach.'

I loathe how right he is.

Scottie stubs out his fag on the wall. 'You've got two options. Keep pretending you're fine, or swallow your pride and make it right. Your choice.'

He lets his hand rest on my shoulder for a few seconds before pushing past me and heading back inside. I watch his back as he goes, knowing I'll owe him for this one.

I stay rooted to the spot, staring at the sky, fighting to breathe through the ache. It's almost funny. I get my arse whooped by a bunch of massive raging bastards every week for a living and that doesn't scare me half as much as this. Handing Charlie every broken piece and knowing it might not be enough. Her seeing the truth and realising I was never what she deserved. Loving her with everything I've got and still getting it wrong.

But Scottie's right. I don't get to decide what she deserves. That's not my call. My call's whether I'm willing to fight for her.

I push off the railing, blood roaring in my ears. She's worth it. Every hit to the heart. Every breath. Every bruise to my soul.

Chapter 24

Charlie

The Langley House School auditorium is packed with restless noise. Parents crammed into squeaky seats, fanning themselves with crumpled programmes and checking their watches like this is some monumental sacrifice. Velvet curtains ripple at the sides of the stage, garlands dripping down from the balcony railings. A Christmas tree squats near the foyer doors, twinkling like it's making up for the rest of the grim mid-December drizzle in London.

It's a private school, posh as hell, with excellent SEN support and a performing arts program that could rival some of the city's fancy academies. I fought tooth and nail to get Hannah in here.

Worth it a hundred times over.

My sister wants to be a singer and an actress? My sister *will* be a singer and an actress.

I wrench a breath free, fighting the surge rising beneath my sternum. Hannah's bouncing beside me, her tulle skirt swishing with every move. She's always had a great, eclectic sense of style. Only one of the things I admire about her. I smooth a stray hair off her forehead, resisting the full-body pull to scoop her into a bear hug. God, she's buzzing like she's had five espressos.

'Charlie. Charlie! Miss Lorna says I'm third. Third! After the Year 13s do the boring carols. But what if my mic stops? Or I forget the words?'

'Batteries are fresh. You'll remember the words. There's a monitor as well. And if you don't, make up better ones and dazzle everyone with your moves.'

Her nose wrinkles. 'But you'll laugh.'

'I'll laugh either way. Because I'm happy, and you're brilliant.'

She grins, her cheeks dimpling like always. It's a little lopsided.

I shouldn't feel this raw. I should be laser-focused on her. But there's this gnawing in my stomach, this restless feeling like the ground's about to crumble under me.

A huddle of girls in elf costumes shuffle past, giggling over a TikTok.

Hannah's teaching assistant, Priya, shoots me a nod of encouragement. 'We've got this, Charlie.'

I know. But my shoulders stay knotted. Because Dad's somewhere in the crowd. I saw his shiny head glinting. I haven't seen or talked to him in months and would like it to stay that way.

But nothing could've kept me from watching my sister shine on stage. Not even him.

'Did you see my tights? They've got little stars on them!' Hannah lifts her skirt, just about to flash the whole room. I yank it back down, laughing.

'They're cute. And you're gonna knock 'em dead out there.' I lean down to kiss Hannah's cheek.

She giggles and hugs me. Then she bites her lip. 'Priya, I need to pee again. Guess I'm nervous!'

'Let's nip to the bathroom before we line up, just in case.' Priya gives me a reassuring look. 'We'll be right back.'

I watch until they're out of sight, a low charge running through me. Mum's somewhere near the back, probably in line for the canteen snacks or charming the ushers into better seats.

The crowd hums with chatter. I shove my hands into my coat pockets and breathe. The Christmas tree by the entrance twinkles far too cheerfully.

Last week, at the Christmas party, Brodie looked like a man sewn together by tension and heartache. Devastating in that suit, collar straining against his throat like it couldn't contain him. He stood rigid, one wrong move away from breaking. Eyes dark and hollow, every bit of pain he was holding back had carved itself into his face.

It messed me up.

Each nerve under my skin flared up and burned all at once. I felt I'd been kicked in the stomach and couldn't catch my breath. My body just wanted to close the distance and hold on to him until the hurt stopped.

Still does.

God, I need to keep it together. This is Hannah's moment, and I'm not letting my bleeding heart ruin it.

But I can smile through the tears. No problem.

The houselights dim. Someone clears their throat behind me. I stare at the stage, trying to swallow the ache.

Another throat clear. Closer this time, the air behind me tightens. Someone's crowding my space without warning. A looming presence, too big and far too close.

I whip around, already lashing out, 'Excuse me?'

My heart fucking stops.

My mind stumbles, trying to make sense of what my eyes see.

Brodie's standing there.

Brodie.

Here.

Coat half unzipped, hair a mess, stripped of all armour –

as though walking into this moment had cost him everything except resolve. He's holding the pink sparkly cowboy hat, and it's so absurdly out of place in his hands that I almost laugh. Except I can't breathe. Can't think. Just stand there. My brain's gone offline, and I'm waiting for a reboot.

He doesn't move and watches me with all his hesitation laid bare, as if he's terrified of doing this wrong.

'What are you doing here?' I sound almost steady. Almost.

He glances at the hat, then back at me. 'Brought something for Hannah. Figured she might need this.'

I'm fighting the tremor in my hands. 'You…came all the way from Scotland to London to give her that?'

'Wouldn't be right for her to go on stage without it.' His voice is low and unwavering. As if he's made peace with whatever this costs him.

My breath stalls mid-lung, and whatever's holding me together starts to fray. I can't look at him without coming apart. 'You should be playing today. It's the Dragons and—'

'Some things matter more. Wallace gave me leave. Said I should rest. My back. My…head. Whatever.'

The weight of that crashes into me, splintering through every rib.

He missed a game.

For Hannah.

For me.

The man who bleeds rugby put it on hold. To make sure my little sister has a sparkly hat and the confidence to wear it.

I hate him for doing this to me.

I love him for it, too.

It's unfair, and it's perfect, and I can't get any air in because it hurts so fucking much.

He holds the hat out to me, every inch of him braced. 'You can give it to her. Or…I can?'

I'm shaking, and I can't tell if I want to hit him or throw myself into his arms and never let go.

Bit of both?

'Why…' My voice breaks. 'Why did you—'

He squares his shoulders, but he doesn't back down. 'Because I couldn't…not. Couldn't let you go on believing I wouldn't show up when it mattered. And to say that I'm sorry.'

Before I can think of a single damn thing to say, a familiar voice threads through the noise.

'Charlie! Priya put glitter on my eyelids!'

I turn around, and there's Hannah, beaming like she won the lottery, her hair a little less tidy than when she left, a streak of glitter already smudged on her cheek. Priya's right behind her, giving me a thumbs-up.

'You are extremely glittery,' I croak out.

And then Hannah spots Brodie. Her features glitch mid-blink, and for a split second, I see her brain catch up to what she's seeing – a giant, ruffled rugby player holding the sparkliest pink cowboy hat known to man.

'Hannah, this is Brodie,' I manage to say. 'He's…a client and…a friend. He plays rugby.'

'Oh my God,' she half-says, half-gasps, staring at Brodie like he's some fairy tale prince. 'Is that…for me?'

Brodie's mouth tilts up in a soft smile. He leans down a bit, hat still in his grip. 'Aye. Thought you might need it for your show. Can't be a proper cowgirl superstar without a hat like this.'

Her hands cover her mouth. 'You brought it for me? Why?'

'Course I did. You're Charlie's sister – and you're on in a few minutes, right? Do you want to try it on?'

She nods, and he reaches out, gently placing the hat on her head and adjusting it so it doesn't mess up her hair.

'Perfect fit,' he says.

Hannah's dimples dent as she grins up at him, then at me.

'Charlie, your friend brought me a hat! That's really nice. Check it out!'

'I see that,' I say, barely making it come out normal.

Brodie watches her with a kind of awe that undoes me – like he's seeing her spark for what it is – and I can't stand how much that moves me.

'You know,' he says with a conspiratorial tone, 'I heard you're gonna sing something good tonight.'

Hannah's cheeks light up like traffic lights. 'I'm singing *Texas Hold 'Em*. I practised a lot. A lot!'

Brodie's jaw ticks. Then he nods. '*Texas Hold 'Em*, eh? Can't seem to get away from that one. Good tune, though. Bet Beyoncé herself would be jealous.'

I brace for something. Tension, bitterness. But it doesn't come. Only a faint smirk. Like he's daring the universe to throw more poker jokes at him.

And I didn't think I could be any prouder of him.

But I am.

Hannah suddenly lunges forward and hugs him, arms flung around his neck as if she's known him forever. Brodie goes still, only for a second, then he lifts his hands to hug her back, careful and gentle.

'You give very good hugs, Hannah.'

'I know!'

I'm not crying. I swear I'm not.

Hannah's never shy with people who feel safe. She turns to me and grins from ear to ear. 'You've got little love-hearts in your eyes, Charlie.'

My face goes up in flames. 'Jesus, Button! Boundaries.' I throw her a warning look, but she just lifts her chin, smug as hell.

She's a Harrington, all right.

Brodie's full-on grinning now, too, like he's won something without even trying.

Hannah pulls back, beaming like he granted her three wishes. 'Thank you. You're tall.'

'Aye. I know.' He chuckles.

'And scruffy,' Hannah declares. 'You should comb your hair.'

Brodie shrugs. 'That's accurate, too.'

Priya's watching the whole thing with a smile. She checks her watch. 'Oh, shoot. Time to get her backstage.'

I give her a quick smile. 'Alright, superstar. Let's go.'

Hannah grabs my hand. 'You're coming with me.'

'Of course, Button.' I glance at Brodie. 'You'll...find a seat?'

He nods, his gaze never leaving mine. 'Wouldn't miss it for the world.'

I make myself turn away, guiding Hannah through the bustle of kids and costumes, trying not to stumble under the tilt of it all. I risk a glance back once, one second, and he's still standing there. Looking.

I barely remember the performance. It's a blur of stage lights and harmonies. Hannah did it. She nailed most of the notes, remembered nearly every word, and owned that stage with her sparkling cowboy hat, radiating joy. She gave it everything, added a little shoulder shimmy during the chorus, pointed straight at the crowd. A little pop star in full command. She worked so hard for this. And the audience went mad. Cheering, clapping. I believe I heard Brodie's voice above the rest. But that might have been my imagination.

Now I'm waiting in the foyer, feet aching from standing, still thrumming with nerves and awe. Priya took Hannah to grab a snack from the canteen before they headed home and I back to my Airbnb – because I'm neither ready nor willing to sleep under the same roof as my father. So I'm left here with my thoughts.

And thoughts are a dangerous thing.

I keep replaying it in my head. Brodie showing up, his face when he handed Hannah the hat. He skipped a game and came to London. Not to win me back. Not to prove a point. Just… because he loves me.

He loves me.

Air staggers in slow and ragged. It's too much. But it's not shock anymore. It's something heavier. The start of a decision I'm not sure I'm ready to make.

I sense him before I see him. His presence fills the space and wraps around me. I turn, and there he is.

'Charlie. Can we talk?'

I don't know if I'm ready to hear this. But of course, I say, 'Okay.'

'This is…tough.'

'I know,' I whisper. 'It really is.'

'Listen, Charlie…' He drags a hand over his face, like he's trying to scrape the truth out of his own skin. 'I've spent my entire life thinking love was something you earned. It wasn't like that with you.' He lets out a dry laugh. 'I fucking hated you at first. Couldn't stand how you looked at me. Like all that shite about me was true. But that wasn't you. That was me. I looked at myself like that. You…you fought for me, regardless. You brought me back. Not because it was your job. You fucking *believed* in me.'

My heart's a frenzied mess, hurling itself against my breastbone.

His gaze stays pinned to mine. 'And I was too caught up in myself to see it. Thought I had to keep proving myself. Showing them I was more than a fuck-up. I was too proud to just…let you in. You deserved me fighting for you. And I didn't. I let you down. That's on me.'

My lungs are too tight, as if I'm drowning on dry land. I hate how much I want to believe him.

'I didn't gamble, Charlie. I swear on Nonna's grave, I

didn't. I thought you should believe me without question. Like I'd earned that. But you didn't owe me that trust. You've been hurt before. And I should've—'

'You didn't have to earn anything,' I say. 'I loved you because you were worth it. Because you made me feel safe and happy. But when I saw you in that room… I just—' The words wobble out. 'I panicked. I thought I'd been foolish to trust again. Like it was my fault for hoping too much. And then you…let me go.'

His face crumbles. '*Loved*, Charlie?'

I try to say something, but he barrels on.

'*Loved*? Fuck that. Cause I'm not done loving you. I'll never be done loving you for as long as I live. Do you fucking understand that?'

He's in pain. So much pain.

I am, too.

'You're my girl. You'll always be my girl. Even if you end up on a couch next to some other lucky bastard at seventy, in your heart, you'll know it. You're mine. You don't walk away from a love like that, Charlie. Even if you leave it behind, it stays with you until the day you die.'

My legs nearly give out, and I'm crying. I believe he's crying, too. But I can't see straight, so I don't know for sure.

'You don't only own my arse, Harrington. You own my heart. Think long and hard about what you're gonna do with it.'

His chest heaves, every word torn straight out of him. I'm about to speak, about to say something, anything. But then—

'Charlotte.' My father's voice cuts through the air like a blade.

Seriously? Now?

'Dad.' I haven't seen him in nine months. Have I been avoiding him harder than Brodie? Yes. Do I have good reasons for it? Also yes. Does it make me feel like crap? Hell, yes.

Brodie stiffens, each muscle ready to pounce.

'Glad you could make it,' my father says nonchalantly, as if he hadn't let me down cold when I needed him most. 'Hannah's been excited for tonight.'

'I know. I speak to her every day. Do you?'

He bristles, then deflects. His usual M.O.

'Brodie MacRae, didn't know you were interested in Christmas talent shows. Not unless there's poker involved.' My dad lets out a sonorous laugh at the sentence. It sounds straight-up mean.

Can't believe we share fifty per cent of our genes.

Brodie's coiled up like he's about to detonate.

And I'm right in the middle.

Oh God.

Brodie's face darkens. 'So you're the posh dick who treats his daughters like crap.'

'I beg your pardon?' My father seems consternated.

My father *never* seems consternated.

Something like joy sprouts up in a dark corner of my soul.

Brodie leans in, enough to make his presence loom. 'You've got two daughters and don't deserve either of them. You act like Hannah's a problem to solve. She's her own person.'

Dad's face goes pale, then red.

But Brodie doesn't stop. 'And when that cheating cunt broke Charlie's heart, you didn't have her back. Told her to suck it up and stay with him. And you kept working with him like nothing happened. You didn't only let her down. You made her feel like she wasn't worth anything. That's fucking *unforgivable.*'

I don't know what's happening. I've never seen anyone speak to him like that.

Brodie steels himself, eyes burning. 'But you know what? In spite of all that, you being such a disgusting cunt is the best thing that ever happened to me. Because it means I got to meet Charlie. And I'll be eternally grateful for that.'

His whole face softens, reverent and open. There's nothing defensive in him now. Just love. He takes my hand and squeezes it gently. 'Ball's on your side of the pitch, Harrington.'

Then he turns around and leaves.

Chapter 25

Brodie

One week since I flew to London like a lovesick martyr to hand over a sparkly hat.

Hannah's awesome. Full of energy and ambition, bouncing with nerves and sass all at once. And she's got pipes. Just like her big sister.

Who, as it turns out, is the love of my life.

I haven't heard from her since. Haven't called either. I made my point – couldn't have been any clearer if I'd painted it on the side of a double-decker. It's her move now. Space is what she needs, and I'm giving it to her.

It's torture.

I shove the thoughts down and tape up my ankles. Tight enough to hold, not enough to turn my feet blue. Then I wind the tape around my head. I love rugby, but I'm too pretty for cauliflower ears.

Focus on the game.

Second half's about to start, and it's a big one. Glasgow.

My old team. The team that kicked me out based on lies and rumours.

Callum Fraser.

That fuck-ugly piece of shite's on the pitch right now,

lording it up like he's Scotland's gift to rugby. Smashing his skull in is a real temptation, more so than ever. Now I've got a real reason to do it. The thought gnaws just behind my teeth, wanting out. But I can't give in to that.

Can't risk the sin bin today.

We're just behind – only by a few points. Nobody would've expected it, least of all me. On paper, Glasgow should've stomped us by now. But we've kept up, clawing back every time they pull ahead. That first half was savage. Scrums like battering rams, line-outs nasty enough to draw blood. And we're holding our own.

Finn's been a beast at the breakdown, Scottie's cut through their defence like a fucking laser, and Jamie's been robust as ever – relentless, boshing any poor sod who so much as breathes in his direction.

We're still not always consistent, still finding our feet. But today, the boys are working like a well-oiled machine. It's a sight to see. Days like these, I remember why I love this game. Why I put up with the bruises, the broken bones, the endless pressure.

But none of it fills the gaping hole where Charlie's meant to be. Not when I can still hear her ordering me to sit still while she rubs arnica into my back, claiming it's for recovery and not an excuse to touch me.

I told myself if she didn't show today, I'd find a way to let her go. I'd have to. Even if I'll be carrying the echo of her for the rest of my life.

Coach Wallace shouts a line about keeping composure and sticking to our game plan, but it's all a blur. I know what he's saying, know what's expected.

Keep your head, MacRae. You're the captain. Lead by example.

And I do.

I breathe in through my nose, force the air to fill my lungs. One half to go. We can take this. Glasgow's good, but they're not unbeatable. Not when we're playing like this.

And I'm not losing to Callum fucking Fraser.

He was giving me that smug grin all through the first half. I know he's waiting for me to crack, to boil over and throw a punch so he can gloat while I get sent off and then whine in the press. I'm not giving him the satisfaction. Not giving anyone a reason to write us off. We're in this fight. I didn't come this far to fuck it up.

I let out a slow breath and knock my knuckles against Jamie's.

He grins. 'Game to shut these arseholes up?'

'Born ready. Let's fucking maul 'em to death.'

We jog back onto the pitch. The cold hits harder than the crowd noise, but there's more of it tonight. Muffled cheers, claps, a low thrum of energy building in the stands. End of December and freezing, but folk still showed up.

Aye, we're getting somewhere with the Stirling Rebels. Bit of respect in the air now.

I lock eyes with Callum for just a second. He sneers, but I don't take the bait. He's nothing. Dust under my feet.

The noise dips. A lull between the chants and shouts, the kind of break that feels like the stadium's holding its breath. I'm wired, blood fizzing with adrenaline, prepared to show the world we're not just here to make up the numbers.

We're here to win.

Finn ruffles my hair, muttering about smashing those dickheads into next week. I nod, shoulders braced. Need to keep my concentration, keep from throwing Callum to the ground and grinding his face into the turf.

Then, in the hush before the whistle, a voice slices through the stillness. Bright. Clear. Unmistakable.

'Goooo Brodiiie!'

I whip my head up, searching. My brain's a second behind my body. Because my heart stops for half a beat, then slams back to life so hard it rattles my ribs and plunges straight to my gut.

Charlie?

Yes.

Standing in the grandstand, next to Theo, both of them grinning like they've just pulled off the heist of the century.

She's wearing my Rebels shirt – my fucking shirt – like a damn proclamation.

My number.

My name.

Everything goes quiet.

The breath rips out of me like I've taken a hit. For one perfect moment, it's only her. Standing there, making the universe brighter. The banner is a pink monstrosity with glitter bleeding off the edges. *'Go Brodie!'* sprawled in loopy letters, and the ten smack in the middle of a glittery heart. It's garish and loud and entirely too much – and it's perfect. I suspect Hannah had a hand in the design.

Charlie's here.

For me.

In public.

I don't know if I want to laugh or scream or collapse. Boots welded to the turf. The world shifts on its axis, and all I can hear is her voice.

My girl. My fucking girl.

Scottie elbows me, and I barely notice it. 'Looks like you took my advice, mate.'

I blink at him, brain too scrambled to make sense of anything, but he only grins like a madman and points at the grandstand.

There's a burn in my throat, as if someone's crammed a balloon behind my ribs and it's trying to pop. I glance back up and catch her gaze. She's lit up, so bright it's like the sun's shining right out of her, and she throws her head back and laughs at something Theo says.

The sight of her here... Fuck. It slams into my chest with the weight of a vow, rewrites my DNA.

This is what my eyes were made for.

To see her.

She's sporting my number, holding a pink glittery sign like some love-struck teenager, and I've never been prouder or happier or more humbled about anything in my goddamn life.

And then I clock Fraser's face. It's a fucking gift. That scrunched-up look. Sour and twisted, like he's swallowed a wasp. He knows. He knows this phenomenal powerhouse of a woman is here for me, and there's not a fucking thing he can do about it. He's glaring at me like he wants me dead.

Let him try.

Right now, I'm invincible.

Hell, part of me wants to thank him for screwing it up and bringing her into my life.

Charlie waves, and it's the smallest, simplest thing, but it rocks me. I don't even think about it – I blow her a kiss. Right there, in front of the entire stadium, the lads, the cameras – everyone.

I want them all to know. She's the best thing that's ever happened to me.

Scottie laughs and claps me on the back. 'Christ, MacRae. You soft bastard.'

I don't care. I don't give a damn if the press writes about it for weeks. That's my girl up there, and I'm never letting her go. Nothing else matters. Just her. Just this game. Just showing them all that I'm back, and in love, and fucking unstoppable.

The whistle blows. The lads bunch up. My pulse's still racing, but it's not from the game anymore.

I exhale slowly, like it hurts to let it go, and square up. Focus. Finish this. Win it for her, for the team, for everything I've dragged back from the edge with bloody knuckles and a heart that refused to quit.

I roll my shoulders back and straighten my spine, scan the pitch, and yell at the boys to form up.

And I look back one last time. She's still watching me, eyes shining with that fire, smile unshakeable. She made her move. Now it's my turn to show her what she's choosing.

I nod to her. Three words carved into my heart, caught in my throat. Too huge to speak, so I mouth them in her direction.

I love you.

And then I charge into the second half.

Epilogue

Charlie

'I still can't believe you killed a cactus,' Brodie mumbles, glancing over his shoulder from the stove. 'Who *does* that?'

He's wearing my shirt like it was made for him.

Which, to be fair, it was.

It's black and gold, 'Harrington' in bold letters across the back with the number one below. Of course, it's a cheeky, silly joke. But I thought it was a cute Christmas gift. Brodie thought so, too. It's unfair how good he looks in it. Enough that I almost forget he's roasting me.

I lean against the counter and make a face. 'It died alone in my office. I didn't kill it. It…gave up.'

'Because you neglected it. You don't get a plant and leave it to fend for itself.'

'That's what plants do! They sit there and survive. I didn't know it needed emotional support.'

He shakes his head and keeps stirring the sauce.

'Oh, don't give me that 'tude,' I zing, arching a brow. 'People follow you on Instagram because of your sexy fore-arms, not your horticultural expertise, *Plant Daddy*.'

He lets out a laugh that rocks his shoulders, then turns

around and tips the pan to let me see the meatballs simmering in sauce. 'Aye, well. The plants don't know that, do they? They like being admired.'

'Same, honestly.' I throw him a wicked look when he rolls his eyes. I stretch out my legs, toes grazing the floor. The kitchen smells like garlic and tomatoes, warm and comforting.

Like home.

Which reminds me... There's something I've been meaning to ask him.

It's Hogmanay, but instead of partying it out at the Sin & Tonic with the rest of the team in town, we're holed up in his place, cooking and planning to obliterate each other at Mario Kart. I did consider letting him win. Only once on the last day of this year.

But then I remembered I'm not a charity.

I haven't been apart from Brodie for a single day since the Rebels played the Knights, and I don't think I want to be ever again.

He catches me staring and winks. 'What're you plotting?'

'Nothing,' I lie. Not too convincingly, because he narrows his eyes and points the spoon at me. A splatter of sauce lands on the counter.

'You're thinking about beating me at something,' he guesses.

'Maybe,' I say. 'Or maybe I'm thinking about ravishing you right here on this counter. Haven't decided yet.'

His expression shifts, cocky and wild. 'Do both. I can take it.'

A little flutter goes through me – damn him – but I play it off. 'Big talk for someone who's about to get annihilated on Rainbow Road.'

'You're all bark, Harrington.'

I flip him off, and he laughs, loud and real. Best sound ever.

Outside, the first few fireworks crackle in the sky, but we don't need them. The air between us already sparks enough to light the whole place up.

I set the table, lining up the cutlery while Brodie plates up the spaghetti. The meatballs look like something out of an Italian food blog. Glistening, perfectly round, covered in rich, tomato sauce.

It's my new favourite dish.

Things are settling, mostly. The Rebels' ticket sales could still be better, but January kicks off the second half of the season, and I'm hopeful. We've got momentum. We've got Brodie. Who's somehow become Stirling's unofficial mascot. He reads to kids at the library every other week now. The toddlers lose their minds. So do their mums. I sit in the back and pretend I'm not swooning. Which I am. Hard.

'God, that smells amazing, MacRae.'

'Aye, well. I am amazing,' he tosses back while loading my plate.

He sets his plate down and wipes his hands on a tea towel before joining me.

It's a bit insane how right this all feels.

'Agreed.' I sprinkle enough parmesan to let it snow and take a bite – not ashamed to moan a little at how good it tastes.

I'm not ashamed of anything with Brodie.

That kiss he blew me and me in his shirt? Went viral. There wasn't any of the fallout I've been afraid of. Clients didn't bat an eyelid. Even the media wasn't all that vicious. Half of them wrote he's some kind of reformed hero now. As if finding balance means he's a new man.

Yeah, he is.

Mine.

Two weeks ago, I didn't think I'd ever sit in his kitchen again, let alone make sassy comments while he struts around in a shirt with my name on it.

But it's the only place in the world I want to be.

I swirl spaghetti around my fork. 'Still nothing from Finn?'

'Naw. Last I heard was before Christmas.'

'Just took him on as a client. Not the best start, him vanishing into the wilderness or wherever he goes to blow off steam.'

Brodie shrugs. 'He'll come back. Probably needs space to lick his wounds.'

That lets me relax a bit. For now, at least.

'Theo is looking for him,' I say. 'If anyone can find him, it's her.'

I pick at my food, suddenly restless. He watches me with that quiet patience, waiting me out like he knows I've got something on my mind, too.

Might as well say it.

'I was…thinking…' Deep breath. 'About…moving in. Here. With you.'

His fork stills mid-air. For a second, he just stares. It feels like my ribs are trying to contain a small, panicked animal, and I can't look at him properly.

'I mean,' I rush to say, 'I'm basically here all the time anyway. I thought… It might make sense. Unless that's – I don't know – too much?'

His lips part, like he wants to speak, but the words won't come. Then he puts his fork down, gets up, and pulls me out of my chair without a word. Just wraps me up in his big, strong arms and tucks his face into the curve of my neck.

'Move in, Champ,' he murmurs, almost rough with it. 'Kill all my fucking plants. I don't care. Just be here with me.'

I laugh, but it breaks halfway through. I pull him closer. 'You're sure? I don't want to crowd you.'

'Crowd me?' He eases back until our foreheads part and his gaze finds mine, his beautiful brown eyes warm and earnest. 'You're the only person who's ever made this place feel like home. Fucking move in yesterday, Charlie.'

His voice catches on my name, and that does it. I surge up to kiss him, threading my fingers into his hair. He tastes like tomatoes and wine and home, and I never want to stop.

'You're such a sap,' I say against his lips.

'Shut up,' he rasps, but he's grinning. 'You love it.'

'Yeah.' I kiss him again. 'I really do.'

Brodie's lips move on mine with the kind of urgency that says he's still making up for lost time. Like every second I'm not in his arms is a mistake he has to fix. He grips my hips and lifts me onto the kitchen table with shocking ease. Plates rattle, forks clatter to the floor. His eyes burn, that hungry look that turns my bones liquid.

'Now be a good girl and lose these fucking leggings before I rip them clean off.'

'That a threat, MacRae?'

'Naw.' He grins, feral and so fucking beautiful I ache. 'It's more of a promise.'

My hands fly to my waistband, but he bats them away as if I'm too slow. He peels the fabric down and tosses it without looking. Before I can catch my breath, his hands are under my arse, pulling me to the edge of the table, shoving my legs apart.

'Fuck. I'm not gonna last. That pretty little cunt of yours is going to be the death of me. Want me to use my tongue on that pussy?'

'Yes. God, yes… Please, I need your mouth on me. I just asked to move in with you, Brodie. Say yes with your tongue.'

His mouth crashes into the inside of my thigh like he's starving, hot and greedy. I'm sure he's gonna devour me right here. One tug and my thong is out of the way.

Hallelujah.

'Look at you,' he mutters. 'So horny for me you're leaking onto the table.'

One long lick just to tease me, and then his entire face is on me. He's messy with it, he doesn't care if he's loud or desperate. Heat surges in my belly. His tongue plunges into me, hot and wet, flicking slick and fast through every swollen inch.

I cry out, and my thighs tremble. He doesn't stop, he hums into me and the vibration shoots straight up my spine and down my limbs. His hands hold my thighs open like I might escape – as if I'd ever want to.

It's not foreplay, it's worship.

He makes me believe I deserve it.

I drag him up and smash my mouth against his, tasting myself on his lips. He groans into the kiss, hips rocking against me, rigid and thick through his shorts. With one rough shove, he frees his hard length, grips himself, and runs his tip through the mess he made of me.

'You ready for me?' His voice is hoarse with need, and he's watching me like he's never seen anything like me before.

'Y-yes. Brodie… Please, please. Now, n—' I don't get the words out before he thrusts into me, one long, slow stroke that makes me gasp.

He stills, buried to the hilt, panting, forehead against mine. 'Oh Jesus fuck. You feel good. Too good. Always too good.'

I'm hurting a bit from the sheer size of him, and I love that feeling.

It's the best.

He's the best.

And he's wearing my shirt.

'D-don't stop…' My voice is half-sob, half-snarl. 'Want to feel you for days.'

He pushes so deep and slow, as if he's trying to fuck the shape of himself into me. I dig my fingers into his shoulders, back arching, teeth catching on a moan, because there's no holding on when he possesses me like this. No breathing. No thinking. Just need. Just Brodie.

He keeps his gaze anchored to mine, watching every move

and shiver, and it's almost too much. Too intimate. Too fucking perfect.

He's holding back, like he doesn't want to rush this. But I need him to. I want him off the leash. That's where I love him most.

'Holy shit, yes! Big-dick my pussy. Yes! Harder. N-need you rough!'

'Jesus fuck Charlie. I never fucked anyone the way I fuck you.' He growls, biting at my neck, and his strokes get rougher, slamming me against the table with enough power to make it creak. I'm too far gone to care. I'm clinging to him, legs locked around his waist. I'm close, close, close, the tension corkscrewing through my belly, begging to burst.

'Oh, oh fuck. Brodie...Brodie, I'm coming... Oh god. Fuck, fuck, fuck.'

'That's it. Soak my cock. Make me a happy man.'

He slips one hand between us to press against my clit, and that's it – I scream his name, head thrown back, and he doesn't let up, working me through every last shudder. His hand never stops moving, dragging out the orgasm until I'm whimpering.

'You're so beautiful when you lose it for me. Can't get enough of you. Never fucking will.'

One hand fists in my hair, tugging my head back enough to give him better access to my neck, and he sinks his teeth into the curve where my shoulder meets my throat.

I gasp, hips bucking against him, and he groans like he's about to lose it right here. His gaze drops, and he watches himself sink in again and again, teeth gritted like he's fighting off a full-body breakdown.

'Dammit, Charlie. You feel that? How deep I am?'

I can't form words. Just cling to him, arching into his hands. His rhythm stutters. He's right on the edge.

I reach up and cup his jaw. 'Eyes on me, Brodie.'

God, he's stunning like this. Sweat-damp curls sticking to his forehead, eyes blazing with love.

I clench around him on purpose. He hisses.

'That's it, Brodie. You feel so good like this. Let go for me. Come in me. Need to feel it. To feel…you.'

His face crumples, open and vulnerable, and I'm delirious with pride and lust and love. This man reduced to shivering for me, rough hands digging into my tits like he needs to anchor himself.

He crashes into my neck, breath scorching my skin as his body jerks against mine. I feel every thick, aching pulse, his roar primal as he falls apart in my arms. Nothing held back. Nothing between us.

'Christ, Charlie. Fuck!' He pants as he rolls his hips to make me feel the last throbs.

I'm not letting him pull away, and I stroke his hair. We stay tangled together, panting, sweat-slick and raw, neither of us willing to let go. More Hogmanay fireworks are going off outside, but they're nothing compared to the million explosions in my heart.

I bury my face in his shoulder, breathing him in. He wraps his strong, battle-worn arms around me, cradling me like I'm breakable, and my ribs tighten with a love so fierce and bright it hurts.

He lays the softest kiss across my lips. 'I love you, Champ. To the moon and back.'

That's what Hannah and I say to each other. And that's perfect. Because that's what Brodie has become: my family.

'I love you, too.' Tears sting my eyes as he presses his mouth to mine.

'This is the best Hogmanay I've ever had.' He traces gentle circles on my hip.

Then he pulls out slowly, reluctantly. And I can't help the way I wince, feeling empty and incomplete without him.

With a gentleness no one would ever expect from a rugby

machine like this, he leans down and kisses my chin. 'Stay there, Champ.'

He snatches a paper towel from the counter, folds it neatly, and comes back to me. His touch is reverent as he cleans between my thighs, taking his time like it's some sacred ritual. I smile at the contrast between his huge, calloused hands and the soft, careful way he treats me.

Once he's done, he presses a kiss to my knee and straightens up, turning back to the kitchen drawer.

For a professional human wrecking ball, he's astonishingly tender.

I watch him move around, still wearing my shirt, looking unfairly gorgeous and completely unbothered by his own half-nakedness.

'If you're hunting for a victory snack, Brodie, the answer's yes. You earned it. But I want one too.'

My curiosity piques as he rummages around, muttering under his breath. I lift up onto my elbows. When he turns back around, his hand is closed into a fist, eyes glinting with that familiar mischief.

He leans over me, caging me in, and kisses the mole on my chest. 'Did you *really* believe you were the first to think about moving in together?'

Brodie opens his hand, and there it is – a shiny set of keys with a golden 'C' charm dangling from the ring.

He gives me that soft, crooked smile, the one that makes my insides go all gooey. 'No fucking chance. I beat you to it, Harrington.'

And this time, I'm more than happy to let him win.

– THE END –

∾

Want to read how Brodie takes Charlie on their first proper date? Get the FREE short story here: beatricebradshaw.com/ tackled

Don't miss out on part 2 of the series – Theo and Finn's story. **Get *Rucked Up Ruse!***

Interested in more spicy and cosy Scottish romance? Check out my 'Escape to Scotland' series of standalone books:

Book 1: *Love in the Scottish Winter Highlands*
Book 2: *Love on the Scottish Spring Isle*
Book 3: *Love on the Scottish Summer Coast*
Book 4: *Love in the Scottish Fall Forest*
Book 5: *Love in the Scottish Christmas Village*

Thank you so, so much for reading. If you liked Brodie and Charlie's story, please take a minute to leave a review on Amazon or Goodreads. Love! <3

Author's Note

Dearest Reader,

I wrote *Tackled by Trouble* because I wanted to write a sports romance. Simple as that.

And it had to be set in Scotland – like all my books – because, well, I live here and I absolutely love it!

But…which sport?

Oh, I have to disclose: I spent a significant chunk of my formative years in the general vicinity of American football in Germany. Yes, I was a cheerleader. No, the players weren't particularly interesting to us. Game days were more of a contractual obligation. We had our own competitions, cups, and medals to worry about, work for, and win.

There is American football in Scotland… Probably. I assume. I haven't personally witnessed it, but I'm sure it exists somewhere, quietly doing its thing. Too small for my purposes and not Scottish enough. It's called *American* Football, after all, not Scots Fitbaw.

There might be a bit of ice hockey somewhere, but I didn't go looking. Unfortunately, I'm also not exactly passionate about *football* football (what our friends across the pond call soccer), tennis bores me senseless, golf makes me vaguely angry, and tragically, nobody seems to care enough about curling. And while I briefly flirted with the idea of making my hero an axe-thrower or a tree-tosser, I diverged.

I enjoy watching basketball, but again – Scotland's not exactly known for its slam dunks.

You know what it is known for, though?

Rugby.

And thank God. Because – and this may shock no one – I do admire a chunky thigh and a bit of a brawl. So rugby it was!

Then one day, while mindlessly watching Netflix and definitely not avoiding deadlines, I stumbled across *The Last Dance*. It's about the Chicago Bulls, specifically the legendary '90s team with Michael Jordan, Scottie Pippen, and Dennis Rodman. I was hooked. These three brilliant, volatile, extraordinary athletes weren't just icons. They embodied the kind of larger-than-life energy that suits sports romance perfectly.

To be absolutely clear: Brodie, Finn, Scottie, and Jamie are entirely fictional. They are not based on any real people, living or dead. But watching those athletes – their energy, their intensity, their presence – simply sparked something that helped me imagine characters with their own personalities and stories.

For various reasons, I couldn't use a team that already existed, so I had to come up with a fictional one. Which meant I first had to figure out how professional rugby actually works behind the scenes – and then find a location. Edinburgh already has a team, so does Glasgow. That only left Stirling, more or less in the middle. So I created a fictional Canadian billionaire (because honestly, who likes American billionaires anymore?) and made him start his very own brand-new rugby team: the Stirling Rebels.

As a historian, I obviously wanted to call the team the Stirling Knights. You know – Bannockburn, Arbroath, and all that. But of course, I was not the first person to have that idea. So I had to pivot. That's how the team became the Stirling Rebels.

Because Brodie is very competitive, I gave him an equally fierce and ambitious counterpart to butt heads with: Charlie. Now I had the setting, the sport, the team, and ideas. The rest unravelled from there. Hannah just showed up, as did Theo, as fully formed characters. Hannah happens to have an extra chromosome. That she sings *Texas Hold 'Em* – and the fact that this is actually poker-related (!) – only revealed itself to me at the end, during her show.

In short: what you're holding now is a book that practically wrote itself. Brodie and Charlie demanded their story and, honestly, I just tried to keep up while writing it down.

I hope you fall for them the way I did – unexpectedly and completely. And if you're curious what's next: Finn and Theo are up soon. Aye, it's going to be WILD.

With love – and a healthy appreciation for men with serious thighs,

About the Author

Beatrice Bradshaw crafts spicy contemporary romances set across Scotland – whisking readers away to glens and windswept coastlines without the need for a plane ticket!

Photo: Kristy Ashton

By day, she's a German journalist, translator, and Scottish historian; by night, she transforms into a purveyor of page-turning passion and fun.

Beatrice Bradshaw is the pen name/ pseudonym of Jessica Beatrice Wagener – chosen so as not to have German narrative non-fiction confused with her (English) romance books.

And after trading Berlin for Scotland in 2018, Beatrice has been smitten with her adopted homeland and not once looked back.

With her knowledge of Scottish history and literature acquired at the University of Glasgow, she sprinkles authentic Scottish experiences through stories that venture well beyond predictable clichés. Her heroines are fierce, funny, and delightfully flawed. The kind of women who trip over their own witty comebacks but land on their feet with style. Her books deliver wit, heat, and men who are actually worth the emotional investment: charming, filthy, and capable of both finding the G-spot and the grocery store without assistance.

When not hunched over her laptop in her Glasgow flat (fuelled by industrial amounts of coffee and pastries), you'll find her hunting for inspiration in crumbling castles, exploring Scottish landscapes, or striking up conversations with the residents of ancient cemeteries. Her future grave-stone will immortalise the time she convinced David Hassel-hoff to sing, a tale best shared over whisky. And while she throws herself into ceilidhs with the same enthusiasm as karaoke nights, her dancing has been described as 'enthusias-tically hazardous'.

Connect with Beatrice here:
instagram.com/beatricebradshawauthor
facebook.com/beatricebradshawauthor
www.beatricebradshaw.com

Tackled by Trouble
By Beatrice Bradshaw

First published in the UK by Jessica B. Wagener under the pen name Beatrice Bradshaw 2025.

Copyright © Jessica B. Wagener as Beatrice Bradshaw, 2025

Suite 624
Claymore House
145-149 Kilmarnock Road
Glasgow, G41 3JA

Jessica B. Wagener as Beatrice Bradshaw has asserted her right to be identified as the author of this work.

Cover design: Jessica Wagener

Illustration: Richard Jackson

Proof reading: Micki McNie

Print ISBN: 978-1-0685768-8-1
Ebook Edition © May 2025
ISBN: 978-1-0685768-7-4
Version: 2025-05-04